BALLAD BEAUTY

ALEXA ASTON

OLIVER
HEBER
BOOKS
GNARLY WOOL PUBLISHING
EST. 2011

Published by Oliver-Heber Books

0 9 8 7 6 5 4 3 2 1

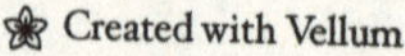 Created with Vellum

PROLOGUE

TEXAS—1875

F*lattery would get him killed. Why in hell hadn't he stayed with the Frontier Battalion?*

Noah Daniel Webster figured it was too late to second-guess himself at this point. Especially as Mc-Nelly's company crossed the Rio Grande illegally, under cover of the dark November night.

Captain McNelly himself had sweet-talked him, convinced that Noah was the crack-shot he needed to shoot thieving Mexicans along the border. Noah had served as a Texas Ranger four years now, mostly defending settlers from the rambunctious Comanche that roamed in menacing bands across the state. He figured a change of scenery couldn't hurt.

He'd only reported to Special Forces that morning when the message came from McNelly. Company D rode the sixty dusty miles to the border in less than five hours. Now Noah's horse was winded but good, he was dead-dog tired, and here he was following the captain on what even that gentleman termed *"a dubious project, from both a legal and tactical view."*

Thank God they were in the south of Texas. Even at that, the water was cold as it lapped against his long, muscular legs. He stroked Star's mane, as much to reassure the horse as himself.

McNelly was known for his bold actions and his men would crawl through hellfire for him—but Noah wasn't too sure about this endeavor. The army boys had chosen to remain behind on the U.S. side of the river. Hell, they didn't want to start another war with a piss-poor place like Mexico. Why should McNelly and his Rangers?

Of course, the man did stand on principle. Every Ranger that served under McNelly idolized him, despite the captain's short stature and poor health. The commanding officer had guts. And dreams. Noah admired him for that. At least he was one man who was as good as his word.

Unlike Noah's father.

They reached the Mexican side of the river and quietly dismounted, ready for their instructions. Fifty men gathered in the pale moonlight around McNelly. As always, the captain was soft-spoken. Noah leaned closer to catch the commander's words.

"Las Cuevas is known for harboring cattle rustlers. There's about two hundred fifty, up to three hundred, at the ranch."

McNelly coughed, the spasms racking his small frame. He cleared his throat and continued. "Our only hope is to take possession of the first house and hold it until the federal troops come to our assistance. I told them this before we crossed the Rio Grande. And," his eyes glittered as he finished, "I told them not one of us would get back alive without their aid."

McNelly signaled his scout, Casoose Sandoval, who stepped forward. Noah had no reason not to trust the guide but he'd never liked the man.

Sandoval held up a hand and flicked his wrist twice before he turned and mounted his horse.

"Fellow of few words," snickered someone behind Noah.

The men quickly slipped onto their horses and rode toward Las Cuevas. His stomach began churning, flip-flopping faster than his pulse. His gut screamed to turn Star around. But orders were orders. As he rode, the tiny hairs on the back of his neck stood at attention.

Something was off.

The Rangers moved closer to their target. He could see a few outlying buildings outlined in the moonlight. The main ranch house lay beyond them. A handful of lanterns lit on its porch cast a small circle of dim light. No guards were in sight.

A squawking chicken ran loose as it crossed the path of the Texans. Sweat broke out across Noah's forehead, despite the night chill. His fingers tingled as he drew his Colt from its holster. The men reached the patio when the whoop went up. Within moments, the clear night air filled with the smell of smoking guns.

Noah swung from Star, gun cocked, and raced toward the doorway. Mexicans spilled out into the night, their own guns in hand. He fired twice and saw a man go down. The moans of the dying quickly filled the air. He fired again and a second man fell. Suddenly, McNelly waved them away. Confused, he jumped on Star's back and followed his commander away from the ranch. The dust of their horses' hooves billowed clouds behind them.

Mistake.

It was the first word he caught. He realized Sandoval must have led them to the wrong ranch as they fell back into a thicket. He heard the rumble of horses in the distance and saw at least two hundred riders stream across the open land before them. He instinctively knew these men traveled from the real Las Cuevas.

Then who lay dead a mile back? Had he killed innocent men? He swallowed hard as the bile rose in his throat, threatening to erupt in a thick stream. He shook his head hard to gain control.

The first wave of men came over the rise in the moonlight, led by Juan Flores, owner of Las Cuevas. Even at this distance, Noah recognized the *alcalde*, then watched as he fell from his saddle.

The air soon stank with the tinny smell of blood. No matter how many times he inhaled it, he never quite hardened himself. He could look at blood as it poured from a man's wounds. He could even feel it as he turned over a body to insure a felon was dead. But he'd never become accustomed to the smell.

Especially the blood of the blameless. It weighed heavily on his soul that a mile back lay men brought down by his hand, men that would never see another sunrise or kiss their babies and women—thanks to him. He vowed in that moment to quit Rangering and find something else to do with his life. As long as it was different from his daddy's chosen path.

Noah took aim and fired his Winchester. It looked like it was going to be a long night.

CHAPTER 1
BOSTON

Jenny McShanahan tried to still her trembling fingers. She placed the letter in her lap and folded her hands tightly together, willing them to quit shaking. She had become an expert at controlling her feelings. She had to be. One didn't allow bullies to see how their words stung. No matter what raged inside her, she learned at an early age to place a placid look on her face and blankly stare at those who wished to hurt her.

She resorted to those lessons now.

Finally, her emotions under control, she lifted the letter with a now-steady hand and re-read its contents. Her heart raced as she scanned the words her father had penned.

DEAREST JENNY –

I hope this letter finds you well. I have at last come into some money through a recent venture and I would like nothing more than for you to join me here in Texas. I have sent a bit of money with this missive for I suspect you'll need to get a few clothes and some sturdy boots. The streets of Boston are nothing like those here in the dusty Southwest. Texas is a rough country, still fighting against being tamed, but I think you'll grow to love it as I have.

I also send to you something for safekeeping, which I will explain when I next see you. Please guard it closely. I will send you a telegram as to what transportation you'll need to take and wire you the money to pay for your tickets.

Thank dear Miss Thompson, too, for allowing you to stay on these past two years. I know you must have enjoyed teaching the young ladies, even if it was only for room and board. But Jenny, work is now a thing of your past. You'll never have to do without again.

I love you, my darling girl. I always have, just as I love your dear mother to this day. Say a prayer for me each night and perhaps we'll be together by the New Year, singing a chorus of The Irish Rover together.

Your loving Papa,
Samuel McShanahan

JENNY BRUSHED AWAY A FALLING TEAR. FINALLY. She'd waited ten years for this one letter. At first, Pap told her she'd be in school only for a little while, as he handled all the arrangements for her mother and settled his own affairs. Then it had been postponed for a year while he tried a few new business opportunities.

Eventually, his excuses numbered so high she no longer bothered to count them. They'd been as numerous as fleas on a dog. Yet she never gave up hope, certain he would one day send for her. She'd been only ten when she last saw him. Another ten years had now passed. Would he recognize her? Did he really still want her? Could they truly be a family once more?

She'd been incomplete for years. She lost the precious love of her mother with Suzannah's untimely death and then her father all but abandoned her for the last decade. She'd lain awake far into the night, wondering if she wasn't good enough or smart enough or pretty enough for him to want her.

The girls at The Thompson School teased her unmercifully. They always looked at a new student as fresh bait for their deadly hooks. They taunted her endlessly in the months after her arrival when she'd been so alone and resentful.

Gradually, Jenny developed a hard shell. She proved to be an excellent student and lost herself in her studies. Only holidays hurt because every girl had somewhere to go. Except her. Her father paid extra for her to remain at the school year-round.

Thank goodness for Dr. Randolph. The school's physician struck up an unlikely friendship with her, even allowing her to assist him in the infirmary and later the free clinic he ran. She gained both practical knowledge and self-esteem in the many hours they spent together. He was also kind enough to invite her to his home during long vacations for a meal or a few days' visit. He had four children of his own, all younger than she, and Jenny lived for the times she spent in their rambling, boisterous home. For a short while, she became part of a real family.

Guilt ate at her when she found herself wishing Dr. Randolph could be her father. His amiable, gentle manner, his trusting eyes, his words of wisdom—they all helped mold her character and provided her with love. His guidance gave her the courage for what she was about to do.

Jenny set her father's note on the desk before her and without hesitation jotted a few sentences in her neat hand. She stared out the window as the ink dried, barely taking in the falling snowflakes that drifted through the late afternoon air as she hummed *The Irish Rover* softly to herself.

She rose and changed into a fresh gown. She had come from Dr. Randolph's clinic, where she had assisted him with the birth of a child. She tidied her hair, as well, wanting to look polished and serene, despite the frantic beating of her heart.

Taking the letter she'd written, she ventured downstairs. Before her courage failed, she knocked firmly on Miss Thompson's door.

"Enter," called the familiar voice.

Jenny pushed open the massive oak door and closed it behind her. Miss Thompson looked up from her stack of correspondence, her glasses perched on the edge of her nose.

"Yes?" The headmistress's voice held the impatient tone that Jenny had come to know. The woman was all business, without a nurturing bone in her body. Instead of kindness and encouragement for her students and teachers, Miss Thompson only thought about how to turn a greater profit.

The older woman glanced at the timepiece pinned to her gown and frowned. "You realize it is not my usual hour to receive anyone. If you would be so kind as to leave?"

Instead, Jenny crossed the room under Miss Thompson's unwavering gaze and handed her the page.

"I've come to give you my letter of resignation."

❧

Bone weary, Noah Webster rode up to headquarters with his patrol, feeling much older than his twenty-five years. He rubbed a hand over his mouth and stubbled cheeks, a week's worth of beard coating his tanned face. His clothes remained wrinkled and stained from sweat and blood, courtesy of the stand-off at Las Cuevas last night. He had three things on his mind—a bath, a fresh set of clothes, and a long night with a soft woman.

Not necessarily in that order.

He waved a greeting to those he knew, nodded politely in passing to those he didn't recognize, and made his way toward his tent. The Rangers almost always were on the move. Pitching tents in a central location was a huge concession by those in command. Noah figured they had to have a base of operations and this patch of barren, dusty land was as good as the next. At least it gave him a place to stash what few personal possessions he owned.

He saw the tent flap raised when he got there. He lowered his tall frame into the opening. Patch Manning was stretched out on his cot, his long feet dangling off the bottom.

"Yer looking might pretty, boy."

Noah grinned. "Good enough for us to head into town?"

Patch snorted. "Gawd, boy, you might be a fine specimen of manhood and the Rangers'd always be proud to claim you—but you ain't that good." He shifted on the cot.

Noah pushed aside a stack of books and sat on the trunk at the end of his own cot. "Guess I could use a bit of sprucing up before I go to Miss Sally's."

Patch shook his head. "Rose and Lizzy done been missing you bad, boy. They nearly had a cat-fight talking 'bout which one of them would get to service you first when you returned."

Noah beamed at his friend. "There's plenty enough of me to go around. I'll service whichever gal needs it, I reckon."

The older Ranger chuckled. "Or read 'em some of your fancy-pants poetry."

Noah picked up a book of sonnets from the pile next to him. He stroked it lovingly. "You'd be amazed how successful reading a few of Mr. Shakespeare's poems can be."

Patch whooped with delight. "Then get all fixed up,

sonny, 'cause we're gonna have us a good one tonight." Patch slapped his knee and then turned away, trying to hide a frown.

Instantly, Noah was on the alert. He knew that look. "What's up?"

His friend hesitated before he spoke. "Got some news for you. Thought I could take yer sweet mind off work for a while but the guilt would probly eat me up."

"Give it up, Patch."

The Ranger whistled low. "Yer always trying to glean tidbits about Famous Sam and Pistol Pete."

His gut tightened. "You got some news?"

"Yep." Patch stared into Noah's eyes. "They done pulled a doozy of a bank robbery, nigh on two days ago. Up in Deep Creek. Looked like the jackpot of their careers. But," he added, his voice dropping low, "Pistol Pete done took a bullet in the getaway. He's deader 'n dead. Sam and another fella escaped. Vanished without a trace."

The news stunned Noah. From the time he'd been able to walk, Pete seemed invincible to him. He sadly realized that even his father was mortal—like all the rest of the gunslinging outlaws that peppered the west.

And Pete was dead, courtesy of that no-good charmer.

When his uncle Johnny, Pete's longtime partner, passed from a sudden heart attack, Pete immediately brought home a new partner. Sam McShan. The quick-witted Irishman was full of fun and mischief, everything that appealed to a boy of fourteen.

It didn't take long for Noah to realize that his father's new friend was *Famous Sam*, the west's version of a modern-day Robin Hood.

Sam captured the public's eye with his daring robberies. What captivated them more was how he gave most of it away. Widows, orphans, the aged and infirm

—many made it by just a bit longer thanks to the generosity of Famous Sam McShan.

Sam encouraged the young Noah to participate in their escapades—larks, according to Sam. Noah's mama, Sarah, had hit the roof. He could still remember her eyes wild as she reached over and drew Sam's own gun on him.

"There won't be anyone taking my son and bringing a life of crime upon him, Sam McShan. I don't care how amusing your adventures seem. It's wrong. No son of mine will ever follow his father into a sordid life of crime."

Of course, being young, it was exactly the kind of thing Noah wanted to do. He'd always been a good boy. Listened to his mama. Went to church regularly. Even faintly disdained his father's lifestyle. But now he was ready to see if there was more to life than hanging onto his mama's apron strings and getting educated. A whole new world waited out there for him. He knew he was almost a man. He was ready to take on life.

It was an unmitigated disaster.

Noah shifted from one foot to the other. He was nervous but would never have admitted it. Sam had talked Pete into letting Noah come on this lark. At the time, it seemed like a terrific idea. Now, he wasn't so sure.

He stood next to the horses, which were hitched to the railing in front of Shaw's General Store. Directly across the street stood the First National Bank. Actually, the only bank in town. He glanced at the clock above the structure. He was to give them two more minutes before he unhitched the horses—in order to make a speedy getaway.

But the girl sure was distracting him. He'd watched her go into Shaw's with her mama. She came out again, lingering in the doorway, casting sideways glances at him.

He decided there was no harm in speaking to her. "Hey, there."

"Hey."

She smiled shyly at him, blushing furiously. He knew it was because of his good looks. Mama always told him how handsome he was, with his dark hair and sky blue eyes. She warned him never to trade on those looks and never to break a young lady's heart. It was left unsaid how her own heart had been broken by her husband. Noah promised her he'd never be unkind to anyone, least of all a woman.

"Are you waiting on your mama?" He nodded at the store. "I saw you go in together."

She looked over her shoulder and then back at him. "Mama's getting some thread. She's making me a new dress for the barn dance. You from around here?" She grinned at him. "You look like you'd be a good dancer."

Suddenly, a loud boom sounded. Sam and Pete raced from the bank in his direction. Noah stood dumbfounded as the men came his way.

They jumped on their horses and turned to speed off, only their reins were still wrapped around the post.

"Boy!" Sam shouted at him. "You done been flirting and not manning your post." He struck Noah hard with the pistol still in his hand.

Stunned, he fell to the ground as Sam and Pete quickly untied the reins. Without a backward glance, both men rode off.

He stumbled to his feet, wiping at the blood that dripped from the lump at the top of his forehead. He couldn't believe they left him behind.

"Papa!"

He turned, as if under water, and saw the pretty girl lift her skirts and dash across the street. He watched a tall, thin man wearing a silver sheriff's badge and holding his bleeding gut slowly fall to the street. The crying girl dropped to her knees and cradled his head in her lap.

People ran out from the few storefronts and as he fumbled to untie the reins and leap onto his horse, he heard the piercing scream of the girl's mother. He quickly rode past the commotion. But as he went by, his eyes met the girl's.

Her look of anguish still haunted his dreams.

He'd never known such fear as when he hightailed it out of the sleepy town. He managed to reach Sam and Pete before a posse could form and track down the three of them for robbery. And murder. He was reasonably sure that Pete had never shot anyone before. He might be a thief but he was an honorable one. He'd supposed Sam was of the same caliber. Now, he wasn't sure about anything. The only thing he did know was that he'd never do wrong again. He'd stay on the right side of the law—even past the right side—but he never wanted to be on the lam. He would never become a man like Famous Sam McShan or Pistol Pete Webber.

He now looked at Sam with new eyes as they rode hard, hundreds of miles to Prairie Dell, to lie low for a few weeks. Sam's sister, Moira, lived there and he guaranteed she would take them in.

Most people would have been afraid of Moira, due to her having only one eye, but Noah took to her like a duck to water. He never bothered asking her how she lost her eye—though he did beg to try on her patch.

Moira had a few long talks with him during the time they stayed with her in Prairie Dell. She realized how shocked he'd been by the events surrounding the robbery. She encouraged him to continue to grow straight and strong. She promised him he would grow into a better man than his father. And Sam.

Noah fingered Moira's last letter that sat in his pocket. She'd made a habit of writing to him a few times a year for the last ten years. His friendship with her was the one good thing that came from his association with the outlaw Famous Sam McShan.

It almost surprised him how little he felt at hearing that Pete was dead but the hate for Sam that coursed through his veins didn't surprise him at all.

He pulled himself together and asked Patch, "Who drew the assignment?"

"Not quite sure, sonny boy. I just heard the news not ten minutes 'fore you waltzed in."

He looked the older Ranger square in the eye. "I'm taking it, Patch. And no one's going to stop me."

Noah thought again of the young girl from long ago. How she'd been raised without her daddy. How the sheriff hadn't been there to walk her down the aisle on her wedding day or squeeze his own wife's hand as their grandchild was baptized in the local church.

He thought of all the people who'd done nothing wrong yet they'd suffered the loss of their life savings in bank robberies too numerous to count. Maybe they'd gone bankrupt. Had to pull up stakes and move elsewhere. Maybe they gave up on what little dreams they had. But now he could finally do something about their devastation.

He'd toyed with the idea of his days as a Ranger being over after the disaster at Las Cuevas but he only fooled himself. He loved the work too much and was proud he was a part of a group of men who cherished honor and the law. He also knew he could never settle down. Rangering suited him just fine.

He squared his shoulders as he moved from the tent and made his way to HQ. He would be the one to bring in Pistol Pete's sorry partner, the infamous Sam Mc-Shan. Maybe there was some justice in the world, after all.

CHAPTER 2

Riley Withers leaned against the building as the raw December wind whipped about him.

Damn. Wasn't the girl ever going to come out?

He glanced up and down the quiet street as he rubbed his hands together for warmth. He hated winter. That's why he left New York in the first place. And yet here he was in Boston, of all places, slowly freezing to death. He longed for a hot cup of black coffee. He could imagine the smell as it wafted up to his nostrils before he took that first, welcomed sip. The liquid would scald like fire going down, warming a trail to his belly.

He shivered again. His head ached from the cold. The cook said the girl would leave today. He'd spent enough time sidling up to the woman to know everything that happened at The Thompson School. He'd even kissed the homely creature more than once, all to get the information he needed. Sometimes, he amazed himself at the lengths he would go to but his mind had been set. A fortune hung in the balance.

And Jenny McShanahan was the key.

A cab pulled up and a man in his late forties stepped from it. He gingerly picked his way up the icy walkway and entered the school. Moments later he emerged, a valise in one hand and a young woman that Riley assumed was Jenny McShanahan on his arm. They climbed into the cab and signaled the driver to leave.

He didn't panic. The train station was but a few blocks. He'd checked the departure schedule. He could walk to the depot and still be there in plenty of time to purchase his ticket and begin his task.

Riley could taste the money. And Jenny McShanahan would lead him to it.

৩৫৬

"THANK YOU SO MUCH, DR. RANDOLPH. I DO appreciate you escorting me to the train station."

Jenny tugged on her hat, which the winter wind tilted slightly. She reached into her reticule for her ticket.

"No problem, my dear." He smiled at her, his eyes twinkling. "I only wish I were going with you."

"You? In the west?" She stared at him incredulously. "I can't imagine someone being a less likely candidate." She eyed Dr. Randolph's immaculate white shirt and gray suit, the buffed nails and fresh haircut, and sighed. "You are far too well bred to consider it."

"Now, Jenny, you aren't the only one who longs to see the west. I have often thought that once the children are grown, Mrs. Randolph and I might travel there. If we like it, who knows? I can't name a place on earth which couldn't use a good doctor." He grinned mischievously. "Especially with all those outlaws shooting innocent people. And each other."

She laughed. "You get enough trouble in Boston, I'm afraid. I've learned so much helping you at the clinic."

"And I have enjoyed your capable assistance, child." He looked at her fondly. "Although you aren't a child anymore, my dear."

She gave him a nervous glance. "A part of me is

afraid Papa won't even recognize me. I've missed him so much, Dr. Randolph. I don't know how we're going to adjust being together after so many years apart."

He squeezed her elbow affectionately. "You'll get on admirably. I fear the only problem will be his regret in how long you've been separated."

She swallowed hard. "It has been a long time." She straightened her shoulders. "But there's new country to see and a decade to catch up on. I know we'll be fine."

Jenny saw the shadow that crossed the physician's pleasant features. She knew how upset he was with her father for practically abandoning her all these years. Dr. Randolph had warned her once he read Papa's letter how she must temper her expectations.

"You're a romantic, Jenny. Practical? Yes. Full of control. But you've built your father into something no man could live up to. You've got to take it slowly."

"It's almost time to board," she said aloud, putting aside his warning.

He led her to the track and handed the valise to a porter. "Please telegraph me once you've arrived." He enveloped her in his arms for a brief moment and brushed a fatherly kiss upon her brow. "We'll miss you. And remember," he said almost wistfully, "if things don't work out, you'll always have a place with us here in Boston."

Quick tears sprang to her eyes. "Thank you."

She stepped up carefully into the railcar, the porter guiding her gently. She turned and waved once and then entered the narrow hallway. As they had arranged, Dr. Randolph would now leave. She didn't think she could stand the thought of seeing him fade to a small dot as the train pulled out from the station and picked up speed.

Her emotions were a conflicting bundle at this point. More than anything, she was ready to unite with her father, yet Dr. Randolph had been like a father to her these past few years. Guilt tore at her for leaving him—and at her conscience for the small part of her that wanted to stay in Boston.

The porter assisted her in finding a seat, placing her case above her.

"Let me know if you need anything, miss." He smiled kindly at her.

She placed her sewing basket next to her and sat back in her seat, her reticule clutched tightly in her lap. She closed her eyes.

Jenny was scared to death.

❧

RILEY LET HER RIDE A DAY. HE SAT IN THE SAME CAR as she did but didn't speak to her. Once or twice, she must have sensed him studying her because she turned slightly in his direction. He made sure he was looking out the window or at the newspaper in his lap. He didn't want to tip his hand or frighten her in any way.

She was a pretty little thing. Or he supposed little wasn't the exact word he had in mind since she was taller than a lot of men, maybe five-eight, five-nine. She hunched a lot, her shoulders rolled forward as if she were self-conscious of her height. She had a trim figure and thick, blond hair. She kept to herself, not starting any conversations, but politely answering when addressed.

A family of five had been seated around her, the three children climbing everywhere—even over her—but she didn't seem to mind. He watched her mouth go soft when the mother asked her to hold the little baby for a moment. She cooed to it, rocking it gently, lost in the moment. He filed it away. He was used to looking for information and that included any weaknesses. He needed to know everything he could about Jenny Mc-Shanahan.

Riley shifted in his seat, tossing the paper aside. The family and their brats had disembarked at the last stop. He was glad. He hated kids. Couldn't stand their non-stop prattle. He stood, stretched, and then moved down the aisle. As he neared Jenny, he paused and looked out the window.

"Mighty pretty," he said softly.

"I beg your pardon?" Jenny looked up at the stranger hovering over her.

"Is this seat taken?"

She looked nervously about but no one came to her aid. One just didn't begin conversations with strangers on a train. Especially with a woman traveling alone. It simply wasn't done. Before she replied, the tall man seated himself across from her. He sighed, rubbed his eyes, and then stared out the window. She hoped he wouldn't address her again.

As he focused on some object outside the moving car, she fiddled with the needlework in her lap as she took surreptitious glances at him. He was what Mr. Johnson, The Thompson School's janitor, would term *slick as spit*. She'd heard him use the expression a thousand times over the years but the living example now sat in close proximity to her.

The stranger was tall, very muscular, and probably in his mid-thirties. His dark hair was thinning, his mouth cruel, and his nose had been broken more than once. Of that she was certain. If not for the hard mouth and crooked beak, he would have been termed a handsome man.

But he made her nervous.

His easy motions and smooth tones seemed to hide something. What, she didn't know. All she knew was that she was leery of him. He reminded her of Simon Legree from Mrs. Stowe's novel, *Uncle Tom's Cabin*. For all his comfortable airs, this man seemed out of place in his fancy suit. She recognized a slight drawl when he spoke to her but she refused to ask him about it.

"Where are you headed? Out west?" he asked suddenly, startling her into pricking her finger with her needle. She lifted the needlepoint away from her so as not to spill any blood on it.

Then the man boldly reached over and took her hand. He wrapped a handkerchief around it and pressed the injured finger tightly. Her skin crawled at his clammy touch. She tried to pull away but he held her firmly.

"Just a prick, ma'am. It'll be fine in a minute."

She very impolitely yanked her hand this time, which broke the contact between them. He smiled at her as she flushed, as if he knew how uncomfortable she was with her hand held intimately by a stranger.

She unwrapped the cloth. The bleeding had already stopped. She handed him the soiled handkerchief.

"Thank you, sir."

He flashed her a smile. "Happy to be of service. Withers is the name. Riley Withers."

"Then I thank you, Mr. Withers."

"And your name?"

She sensed herself turning pink at his question. Surely, he didn't expect a young lady traveling alone to divulge her name?

"Miss McShanahan, is it?"

She followed his eyes to her sewing box, where a tag prominently displayed her name. She blushed again.

"Don't mind, Miss McShanahan. If you are headed to the west, things are a bit more informal there."

She was on a train headed away from the east coast and could admit that much.

"Yes, I am."

"Well, then, I hope you're going to Texas. It's the place to be. God's country—that's what we call it." He smiled at her again.

A cold shiver swam through her. "If you'll excuse me, Mr. Withers, I would like to catch up on my reading." She'd been polite enough. She was ready to end this unwanted conversation.

At first, she struggled as she tried to read Mr. Dickens, her eyes simply glazing over the page. She turned them at periodic intervals. This man made her more than nervous.

Instead, she picked up *Milton Mulholland's Guidebook to the American West*. Just the feel of it in her hands gave her confidence. She opened to a random page in the well-worn book and began reading—

Western woman are more outspoken than their counterparts in the East. Though polite, a Western woman knows her mind and isn't afraid to speak it.

She smiled at the passage. She'd underlined it as a personal favorite. At the beginning of her time at The Thompson School, she had been in constant trouble. Miss Thompson, in particular, accused Jenny of being impudent toward her elders. Her parents raised her to be frank. She'd always spoken her mind, which delighted Papa.

The Thompson School's staff had been less enamored with her ways. She found herself punished severely until she'd learned to curb her tongue, as should befit a child of ten. She may have learned to exercise caution when speaking in public but her candor still simmered just below the surface. As far as she was concerned, she was about to become a western woman. She might as well start practicing now. The rude stranger before her would be the first recipient of her new manners.

She didn't wait long. The next time he tried to draw her into conversation, Jenny stared at him intently. No dropping of her eyes, no simpering or apologizing, as an eastern woman would do.

"Excuse me, sir. I do not know you, nor do I have any intentions of making your acquaintance. If you would be so kind as to leave me to my peace, I would be much obliged."

She tacked on the last phrase so as to perhaps soften her tone but she continued to look him boldly in the face.

Mr. Withers stood. "Forgive me for intruding on your privacy, ma'am." He tipped his hat, a snarl on his face, and exited the car.

She leaned her head against the window, a triumphant smile playing along her lips. She'd done it! Without mincing words, she'd graciously, yet firmly, let the gentleman know how she felt. She couldn't wait to reach Texas. Maybe she'd been a westerner in spirit all along. She knew that she would fit right in.

Jenny settled back, Mulholland's guidebook in hand, and reopened it to continue reading the now-familiar pages.

Mr. Withers continued to be her shadow for the next few days. He poked and prodded for tidbits of information, even eavesdropping when she asked the conductor questions, but she had been firm. She sensed his frustration but had no sympathy for him. She was proud to have put distance between them. Conversing with him without an introduction wasn't proper.

And even if it were, something in his manner warned her not to do so.

They both disembarked at the same stop—along with three other passengers—and he tried to assist her with her luggage. She put him off so completely that he abandoned further attempts to speak with her.

Now she was tired, dusty, and irritable. A stagecoach had to be the most uncomfortable place ever invented. Her bottom was sore after two solid days of bumpy trails in Texas. Thank goodness the driver asked Mr. Withers to ride on top so an expectant mother could ride inside in his stead.

Although why anyone would want to be inside the

compartment was beyond her. The windows were kept open, despite the cold weather, and dust poured inside the stagecoach. She constantly kept her handkerchief over her mouth, trading one hand for the other when her arm became too weary to hold up the cloth. The driver provided his passengers with dusters, which wrapped around them as a kind of protection over their clothing. Still, she seemed dirtier than a little boy who'd jumped headfirst into his first mud puddle. At least he could claim to be wet. She found it hard to swallow because she was so parched.

They began slowing. Jenny looked out the open window and saw a few scattered buildings. She spied a general store, a blacksmith, and a hotel as the stagecoach came to a halt.

"Apple Blossom!" called out the driver.

Jenny's heart jumped. Apple Blossom was her destination. She stood with the others, throwing off the messy duster, clutching her reticule and sewing basket. Although her gloves were filthy, she was glad she wore them. Her palms were damp. She was horrified because ladies did not perspire.

Her sweating palms told her, as if she didn't already know, just how nervous she was. Without realizing it, she began to hum *Lanigan's Ball* under her breath.

The driver helped her down. Unsteady on her feet after being cramped in the stagecoach, she gripped a wheel with one hand as she motioned which valise was hers. She turned as the driver went to fetch it. Her eyes skimmed over the few gathered around, greeting those as they left the confines of the stagecoach.

Slowly, one by one, the crowd melted away. Jenny found herself standing alone. The song died in her throat.

He wasn't coming.

Somehow she'd known it all along. Despite his letter, the telegram, the money for tickets, the directions on which trains to take and where to transfer to the stage, she'd understood her father wouldn't meet her. Not that she blamed him. Who wanted to be saddled with a daughter he wouldn't even recognize?

No, that was too harsh. Papa had simply been delayed. He wouldn't have gone to such trouble to get her to Texas if he didn't really want them to be together. And he always had run late. She remembered the times her mother was fit to be tied because he'd been tardy. He claimed it was part of his Irish nature and he'd usually been able to cajole her mother out of her foul mood with his charm and sunny smile.

What should she do? She thought of where she could wait for him. Or perhaps he'd left a message for her. Anything was possible with Samuel McShanahan.

Jenny glanced around the town of Apple Blossom. It didn't seem like much of a town to her. Lying southwest of Fort Worth, it was flat, dusty, and she could swear it had never seen an apple blossom since before Noah's Flood. If then.

The most likely place to wait seemed to be the hotel. She squared her shoulders, held her head high, and began walking up the street.

CHAPTER 3

Noah watched Jenny McShanahan turn and move up the street toward him, a determined look set on her lovely features. He'd been slumped against a hitching post for an hour, waiting for the two o'clock stage to arrive. He'd been wary, too, sure that Sam McShan would meet his only daughter when she arrived in Apple Blossom.

Thank God for his connections at the telegraph company. It had been his most solid lead. Everything else sure dried up.

Just then she passed him, still walking down the middle of the street. He wondered where she was going. He also wondered if she realized she'd left her case.

Noah tipped his hat and called out to her. "Ma'am?"

She turned, a puzzled look on her face.

"You left your valise." He pointed to the lone satchel sitting in the middle of the road.

It surprised him when the corners of her mouth turned up slightly. "So I did." She looked him up and down and he almost blushed. "Thank you, sir. Perhaps I'll retrieve it . . . and what's left of my brain, as well."

She started in the direction of the case. He moved quickly and stepped in front of her. "I'll get it, ma'am."

He ambled along and picked it up and returned it to her.

"If you'll tell me where you're headed, I'll make sure you and your bag get there."

He watched her think this over and then she nodded. "Thank you, sir. I'm headed to the local hotel."

She took off in long strides despite her tight skirt. He studied her carefully from the back as he followed her to her destination. She was tall and thin, with the tiniest waist he'd ever seen. He was sure his hands could easily span it with room to spare. Her hat was slightly askew, revealing thick, honey blond hair twisted up in some womanly way.

But Noah longed for a glimpse from the front again. She had the most enticing eyes he'd ever seen on a woman, a striking moss green, with long, thick lashes surrounding them. A man could get lost in those eyes. Or her mouth. Her lips were a soft rose and looked good enough to lick.

Where had that come from?

He smiled to himself and shook his head. She sure didn't favor Sam in the least, except for being tall. Must take after her mama. He remembered Sam going on for hours about his dearest Suzannah from County Kerry. Even though she was dead, Sam talked about his wife as if she were alive. He seemed to have loved her a great deal.

Noah wondered how much this daughter resembled her dead mama. Why had it taken Sam so many years to send for such a looker? And why now? Of course, it had to be the big score he'd pulled off. The thought of it left a sour taste in his mouth. Although he had no lost love for Pete, he was still angry at both Sam and Pete for getting Pete killed. You think the two of them would've known better by now. After all, they had enough experience between them.

"Thank you again, sir."

He looked up, confused for a moment. He'd been so lost in his thoughts that they'd arrived at the hotel without his realizing it.

"Any time, ma'am." He gave her a sheepish smile and took her valise to the desk, ringing the bell. When a portly attendant appeared, he said, "This lady needs to speak with you."

Tipping his hat to her, Noah strode away. Not too far, though. He needed to hear what Jenny McShanahan had to say.

⁂

Jenny calmed herself, not wanting to appear flustered. She'd already been foolish enough to leave her belongings in the middle of Apple Blossom's main thoroughfare. She took a deep breath and expelled it slowly.

"Good afternoon, sir. I am Miss McShanahan and I've just arrived—"

"Oh, yes, ma'am, on the two o'clock stage, that's for sure. He said you'd be on it." The desk clerk beamed at her through yellowed teeth.

Her heart skipped a beat. "You would be referring to my—"

"Your daddy, pure and simple. He left a letter for you a few days ago. Paid for you to have a room, too, that he did."

She had been right. Obviously, Papa's plans changed but he had taken the time to prepare for her arrival. Maybe she was to stay here the night and then they would travel to the ranch he always mentioned. It was possible he'd even purchased it by now and that was what caused his delay.

The clerk reached under the counter and pulled out a letter. Jenny saw her name scrawled across the front of the envelope. "Mr. McShanahan left this for you. Said to open it immediately upon your arrival."

She hesitated a moment.

"Go on, now. You wouldn't want to disappoint your daddy." The rotund clerk smiled encouragingly.

She tore open the envelope and removed a single sheaf of paper.

My dearest Jenny —

My plans have changed somewhat unexpectedly and I have had to alter our arrangements. I have left Texas for a small town called Prairie Dell. It is in the state of Nevada, near the southern part. I fear it's quite a ways for you to travel but I so look forward to you joining me soon. My sister lives there and she longs to meet you.

You can't reach it by stage—it's simply too small—and the train that way is unreliable and truly comes nowhere near the Dell. I've hired a guide, Slim Patterson, to take you there. I know this seems odd but you'll understand everything once we've had a chance to visit in person.

There's money in the bank down the street to pay your escort. If you leave tomorrow, it will take about two and half weeks on horseback. Please hurry, sweetest Jenny. We have so much to catch up on, especially our goodnight songs.

Your loving Papa,
Samuel McShanahan

❦

Noah watched different expressions flit across her face in rapid succession. He saw joy, surprise, anger, and bewilderment come and go as quickly as mosquito bites. He also wondered about the man that followed them to the hotel. Noah spotted him atop the stage that brought Jenny McShanahan to Apple Blossom. He knew the gentleman hadn't gotten off at the same time as the other passengers who had disembarked.

So, why was he here now? And were they both interested in the same lady for the same reason?

"Would you be so kind as to send my things up to my room?"

He turned his attention back to the desk.

"Yes, ma'am. Consider it done."

Jenny thanked the clerk. "And one more thing. Do you know how I would go about locating a Mr. Slim Patterson?"

The desk clerk visibly blanched. "Mr. Patterson, you say?"

She smiled sweetly. "Yes. My father would like me to get in touch with Mr. Patterson. He is to escort me to Nevada."

The man laughed uncomfortably, his giggle high and girlish for one so rotund. "I'm sorry, Miss McShanahan. It won't be possible for you to speak with Slim." He paused and swallowed hard. "You see, Slim Patterson died in a knife fight last night. Something about debts he owed was the story I heard from the barkeep."

Noah watched Jenny grow still, her green eyes dominating her face, which drained of color. She gripped the counter a long moment in order to steady herself. She seemed to come to some decision as she focused on the clerk.

"Would you recommend taking the train to Nevada, sir?"

Laughter filled the small lobby. "From Apple Blossom?" The clerk wiped his eyes with the back of his hand. "You could probably walk faster from here to there. No," he shook his head, "overland route's the only way to get there 'fore Jesus returns."

Jenny walked away, an odd look on her face. She moved toward the exit. Just before she reached the doorway, she looked over her shoulder.

Noah nearly dropped his teeth when she asked the clerk, "Would you please direct me to the nearest saloon?"

Jenny walked quickly to the town's lone saloon. She'd missed seeing it as the stagecoach entered Apple Blossom since it was beyond the point where she disembarked. She moved quickly before she lost her courage. She figured a saloon would be the best place to start in trying to find a new guide to see her to Prairie Dell. Wherever that was.

She wondered what Miss Thompson would say about a former pupil and teacher entering the confines of a saloon. That brought a low chuckle and she relaxed some. She wished for a moment that Miss Thompson *could* see her. It would probably bring on an immediate heart attack, allowing that sweet Miss Vines to take over running The Thompson School in the correct manner.

Oh, she must be tired and irritable for wishing such ill upon people, even if that included the likes of the horrible Miss Thompson. Jenny was almost glad this Prairie Dell couldn't be reached by stage. Anything had to be better on her bottom than what she'd suffered through the last two days.

As she reached the entrance to the saloon, she looked around. Not that she knew anyone in Apple Blossom, but she was a respectable young lady. She hated for anyone, even the residents of this pitiful excuse for a town, to receive the wrong impression of her —despite the fact she was now a forthright western woman.

Mustering her courage, she pushed open the door and entered. At once, her vision went dark. No, that was just the inside of the saloon. What a contrast to the bright day outside.

She glanced around as the room fell eerily silent. It was full of nothing but men—men smoking, men drinking, even men with girls sitting on their laps.

She stifled the noise that threatened to escape from her lips. These weren't just any girls. They were like the ones that visited Dr. Randolph's free clinic, which he operated on the weekends. She remembered the hardened, painted faces of some of the women that came to him for help. Her heart went out to them. To find it necessary to lower oneself to such a task was beyond her comprehension.

The hush continued. Those present began to shift uncomfortably. Jenny walked toward the startled piano player. His hands hovered above the keyboard.

"You may continue to play, sir. I'm sorry to have interrupted you. I won't be but a minute."

He flashed her a toothy grin. "Then I won't be playing for the next minute, ma'am. If I start banging away on the ivories and these boys miss why you've come in, I might as well go and beat myself black and blue."

Her eyes widened. "Oh. I see. Well, then, thank you." She made her way to the bar where a beefy man in a stained apron leaned an elbow on the counter.

"What'll it be, ma'am?"

She realized he thought she wanted to purchase a drink. "Oh, no, I'm sorry, sir. I don't wish to partake of any alcohol. I simply have need of some information. I'm told a barkeep is the best informed man in town."

The bartender sized her up. "Who told you that?"

Her face flamed. "You see, well . . ." She paused and then blurted out, "I read it in my dime novels."

Hearty laughter erupted throughout the room. She wished she could sink into the floor. Instead, she lifted her head and put on her best schoolmistress face as she gazed at the bar's patrons. The laughter subsided immediately.

"Now as to why I'm here, sir, I am in need of a guide." She looked across the room. "Does anyone here have experience in acting as a trail guide? I need to reach Nevada as quickly as possible."

No one dared laugh again although she saw many of the men wanted to do so. Slowly, the majority turned back to their drinks, their cards, and their cigars. Jenny had no takers.

Except one.

A scrawny man in bad need of a haircut approached her. He smelled awful. She supposed by his gait that he was semi-inebriated.

"Snake Burton. At your service, ma'am." He doffed a worn-out hat to her.

Jenny took in his pitiful appearance. She wasn't sure if he could make it back across the room to his seat, much less escort her clear to Nevada.

"I know I look poorly, but I've jes' fallen on some hard times is all. This little trip could hep me get back on my feet." He looked at her pleadingly. "I'd work real cheap."

She'd always had a soft heart. Her first, poor impression of Mr. Burton melted away. No one else offered her any assistance. If she were to reach Prairie Dell before the twentieth century began, it looked as if she'd have to take her chances with Snake Burton.

"Very well, Mr. Burton. You're hired." She tried to quell her doubts as to his suitability for their venture, but since no one present had stepped up to accommodate her, she would make the best of the situation. "I would like to leave early tomorrow unless you have any previous commitments."

Snake shook his head. "I'm looser 'n a goose, ma'am. We can leave tomorry . . . 'bout nine o'clock."

"Then it's settled. I will go to the general store and see about supplies for our foray, sir. Do you have a horse?"

He looked appalled that she would even ask such a question. "'Course I do. It's Texas, ain't it?" He narrowed his eyes and studied her a moment. "What I could use is a little stake afore we set out."

She understood at once. Mr. Burton possibly had a few financial matters to settle before undertaking such a long trip. She mentioned a figure to him for acting as her guide. His face lit up with pleasure. She then reached into her reticule and handed him five dollars in advance. She hoped he might consider a haircut and bath before they began their journey.

"Then we are to meet tomorrow morning at nine in front of the hotel, sir?"

Snake nodded. "We'll get to Nevada come hell or high water. Begin' your pardon, ma'am."

She held out her gloved hand to Snake Burton. As he shook it, Jenny noticed the tall cowboy who'd helped her with her luggage earlier. Had he followed her from the hotel?

❧

JENNY McSHANAHAN FASCINATED NOAH. HIS FIRST impression of her had been false. She wasn't an empty-headed woman who traipsed off without her valise in a strange town. She was simply bats in the belfry crazy. Nothing else could account for her behavior during the last ten minutes. What decent woman entered a saloon, much less tried to employ a guide from its rough crew of customers? If even one man in the bar thought she was actually serious about him taking her to Nevada, she would have had a line out the door clear to the next county.

As it was, old Snake Burton had already rooked her out of good money, five dollars from the looks of it. That was hard cash that Miss McShanahan would never see again. Probably Snake wouldn't, either. He'd have it spent in a New York minute and Noah suspected exactly where it would wind up.

Jenny left the saloon. He noticed every man's eye in the place followed her. His included. She had a certain sway in her walk that was mighty appealing. Too bad she was a good girl. He would have liked to get to know her better but he was never going to get married. That's what all the nice ladies wanted—a ring on their finger—and Noah wasn't about to place one there. Not on Jenny McShanahan's hand or any other woman's.

He'd watched the sham of his parents' marriage for too many years. He saw the heartbreak Pete brought into his wife's life. Sarah Webster had to work harder than she should have and she'd aged well before her time. She'd fallen in love with a man who was a thief, right there in the lobby of a St. Louis theater, as Pete cased the patrons in attendance and the jewels they wore.

Their whirlwind courtship and elopement, as well as her own daddy's disowning her, might be the stuff fairy tales were made of, but their love died pretty much before it ever had a chance to grow—all thanks to Pete's life of crime. Now his mama was a bitter woman. Of course, she'd given Noah all the love in the world and taught him right from wrong. She'd raised him, Mark, and Elizabeth the best she could. Her children gave her a way to make amends for the tragic mistake of marrying Pistol Pete Webster.

But she never let any of them forget her opinion of

marriage. Knowing how down she was on the institution, Noah had sworn to her that he'd never marry. He didn't want to disappoint a woman like his daddy had his mama. He was always worried that his own bad blood would surface. He refused to make anyone, least of all a wife, miserable. So he'd chosen never to marry. He didn't feel he was good enough—at least for a nice, decent woman.

Now, loving was another matter. He did like his loving, sweet and slow, but it was always with a soiled dove or even a widow woman now and then. And just as his mama taught him, he was impeccably polite—even to a soiled dove. He made sure he pleasured them as much as they did him. Between that and Rangering, his life had been all right. He was proud he'd made a different life than his daddy. A Ranger's reputation preceded him wherever he went. That meant everything to him.

Yet Rangering was about to be a thing of the past if he didn't catch up with Miss Jenny McShanahan. Noah had been bull-headed and gone out on a limb with the chief commander at HQ, insisting he go after Famous Sam McShan alone. This young woman was his only lead.

Sliding from his seat, he left the bar, determined to bring Sam to justice. It would prove that Pete's bad blood didn't taint Noah. Besides, if he didn't find Sam, he might as well turn in his resignation. He'd promised to bring in both Sam and the loot. A Ranger always kept his promise.

He walked along the wide street, the wind kicking swirls of dust around him. He knew Jenny headed over to the general store. Lord, she'd announced everything to anyone listening. Thank goodness no one but him had any notion of following her.

He moseyed into the store and watched from a distance as she did her business, asking this and that about what she'd need out on the trail. She explained her funds were across the street, deposited at the bank, and the store owner was only too willing to accommodate her request for supplies.

For being a tenderfoot, she made some wise selections. She didn't pinch pennies but she proved frugal, nonetheless. She examined each item carefully before making her decision. Maybe it was all those dime novels she claimed to read but she did seem to know a fair amount about what she was doing.

A shadow crossed on the opposite side of the store. He caught a quick glance of the stranger from the stage. If this fellow didn't back off soon, he and Noah Daniel Webster would dance in a dark alley real soon.

Noah turned sideways to let Jenny pass as she left the general store. "Ma'am," he said and tipped his hat to her.

God, he loved those green eyes.

❧

JENNY WALKED RAPIDLY FROM THE BANK, BOTHERED by the fact that the blue-eyed stranger crossed her path yet again. She chose to dismiss him from her mind as she conducted her short business and then made her way to the far end of the street. She needed a horse if she were to reach Prairie Dell and the bank manager had instructed her to see Whitey.

She recognized him the minute her eyes fell on him. He had the whitest-blond hair of anyone she'd ever seen. He scurried over to her.

"Good day, sir."

"Good day to you, ma'am. What can I do for you?"

Jenny explained that she would need a horse for a long journey across the open country.

Whitey frowned at her, his head cocked to one side. "And how much riding experience do you have, if I might be so bold as to ask?"

She hoped her blush wouldn't give her away. "More than most," she said succinctly.

Actually, she'd never been on a horse at all but she'd probably read every book ever written contained in the Boston Public Library. She had been eager to learn all she could about the west so she would be prepared when her father sent for her. She devoured volume after volume on the land, the people, the Indian dangers, the gunfighters, the railroads, and even the horses. She probably knew more about horses than anyone except a horse breeder. Year after year, she'd added to her knowledge. By this point, she was a walking encyclopedia of all things familiar in the west.

And more importantly, she had inhaled every word in *Milton Mulholland's Guidebook to the American West*. She knew exactly what Mr. Mulholland would recommend in this particular situation.

"I'd like one with a tough mouth and a gentle nature," she added. "And I'll need a saddle, as well. Western. Not English."

Whitey nodded, seemingly satisfied by her confident answers. He took her to his pen and pointed out the attributes of a few likely candidates.

"This one'll have the stamina for a trip like you're talking about. Pretty even-tempered. That sorrel over there has a tendency to nip you, but it's more like love bites, if'n you know what I mean."

"Hmm," she said without wanting to commit, having no idea what he meant. Then a lonely horse in the far corner caught her eye. "What about that one?" She pointed to the thin black horse with white socks.

"You mean the black?" Whitey snorted. "You don't want that one. Comet's nothing but trouble."

She looked at the horse again, curiosity burning. "Why do you say that?"

The horse seller shrugged. "He don't much like people. Was mistreated 'fore I took him in. Probably shouldn't have but I wouldn't have seen a dime of what Stanton owed me otherwise. He's also way too skinny. He'd never make a long trip like you're planning."

She didn't care about Whitey's opinion. This horse had a look in his eye that had already won her over. She knew Nevada was a good distance from Texas. She decided she would go as far as this horse would carry her and purchase another one if necessary.

"I'll take him."

"But–"

"I said, I'll take him. How much?"

He named his price, which she thought rather low, but she withdrew the cash from her reticule. "Thank you, sir. I'd like to come get him before nine tomorrow morning, please."

Whitey looked at her as if she'd been declared legally insane. "You're welcome to come any time for him, ma'am."

Jenny called out Comet's name and was surprised when the horse trotted over to her. She'd always fostered a love for animals.

"I can't believe you're mine," she whispered to him as she stroked his velvet nose. The horse nickered softly in return.

"I do believe we'll get along fine, Comet. I'm a fast learner. I've always had to be and you'll help me along." She leaned over and kissed him.

Jenny decided she better eat and get in the one last luxury she'd missed ever since she left Boston—a hot, steaming bath. Who knew when the next one might be?

Returning to her lodgings, she dined with the hotel owner and his wife. Obviously, not a lot of paying guests came through Apple Blossom from what they indicated. She expressed her wishes about the bath and after it was ready, she stripped off her clothes for a nice soak. She laid her head back to rest on the edge of the tub and let her thoughts float.

Jenny wondered what this trip to Prairie Dell would bring. She was nervous about going such a long way, especially with a dubious guide, but she knew her father must have extremely good reasons to ask her to journey to such an out-of-the-way place.

The slight noise in the total quiet caused her head to pop up. It had been a soft, scraping sound. Her eyes quickly roamed the room, noting the door was locked as before and the window sealed tightly from the cold wind. Then she spotted a single sheet of paper lying near the door. What could it be?

She quickly scrubbed until her body was pink and shining, her long hair hanging wet down her back. She grabbed the toweling and wrapped it around her as she went to pick up the sheet.

Watch the man following you.

The single line leaped at her from the page. A sudden image of the tall stranger with sky blue eyes appeared. So he *had* been following her.

But why?

She thought of what her father had sent to her in his original letter and hurried to her reticule. She dumped its contents out onto the bed.

It was there. Safe.

Jenny replaced everything in its usual order and calmed her shaking hands. She perched on the edge of the bed and took a deep breath.

Who was the tall, handsome cowboy with the strong build? Better yet, who warned her about him?

CHAPTER 5

Snake Burton wasn't coming. Jenny sighed again, for the seventh time in twenty minutes. She gazed about at the crowd that gathered around her. Or at least what would pass for a crowd in Apple Blossom, Texas.

The day had started beautifully. It was clear, no wind to speak of, and only moderately cold. She'd held such high hopes. Despite the ominous note she had received the previous evening, she slept soundly and awakened rested, eager to begin the last leg of her journey to Papa.

And then Mr. Burton didn't even bother to show up —drunk or sober.

At the very least, he could have sent her a message. Why would any gentleman let a lady wait at the appointed place, horse and supplies in hand, only to be humiliated in front of most of the population of Apple Blossom?

She knew the answer. Snake Burton was no gentleman.

Jenny looked up and down the street. Again. No Mr. Burton in sight. Well, if he weren't coming to see her, she would go to him—if only to tell him what deplorable manners he had.

"You." She pointed to a young man barely old enough to shave. She remembered him from the saloon yesterday and had been upset to see one so wet behind the ears in such a disreputable place. In her best school-marm voice, she commanded, "Come here."

"Me?"

He looked ready to jump out of his skin and leave it behind in one piece. Jenny didn't dare break eye contact with him. She had learned that lesson from teaching after only two days in the classroom and was surprised it took her that long to figure it out.

"I want to have a word with you."

He slowly came her way. Those gathered on both sides of the street did the same. If words were to be spoken, the citizens of Apple Blossom didn't want to miss them.

She stared at the young cowpoke, grateful for once that her height left them eye to eye. "Do you know a Mr. Snake Burton?" she asked crisply.

"Oh, I reckon 'bout everyone between here and Fort Worth knows Snake," he said affably and the crowd chuckled along with him.

"Then could you tell me where I might find Mr. Burton at this hour of the morning?"

He started to answer then thought better of it. Her gaze never wavered. Finally, he broke.

"I s'pose he's up at Miss Lulu's still."

"And where might I find Miss Lulu?"

"Oh, you don't want to go finding Miss Lulu, ma'am. She's six feet under or better and has been nigh on five, maybe six years now." He looked over to another man in the crowd. "Tom, how long do you think Miss Lulu's been gone?"

"Christmas, the year of that bad storm. I believe that would be '69, Ed."

Ed grinned. "You're right, Tom. That was when—"

Jenny interrupted their exchange. "I am sorry to

press you but is Mr. Burton at this Miss Lulu's house? Seeing that she's dead?"

Ed scratched his head but gave her a wide smile. "I reckon you could say that, ma'am."

"Then show me the way."

The crowd murmured its disapproval and Jenny wondered what she had said wrong.

"I'll show you where Miss Lulu's is."

The throng parted and her heart caught in her throat. It was the dark-haired stranger with the sky blue eyes. She almost took a step back as he approached then thought better of it. Treat him like Lucinda Smith, the ringleader of the bullies that picked on her in those early days when she first arrived at The Thompson School.

Jenny drew herself up to her full height and raised her chin a notch for good measure. He came toward her slowly, an easy confidence in his gait.

He must be an even six feet, she judged. Muscle hardened his otherwise lean frame. His jet-black hair had a slight wave to it. His complexion was dark, as if he spent most of his time outdoors in the bright Texas sun. Chiseled cheeks and a strong jaw accompanied a sensuous mouth.

But what she focused on now was the small scar. Funny, she hadn't noticed it before. It ran just above his chin, white against his tanned face. She thought it might be from a knife, based on her experience at the free clinic. She wondered how he'd gotten sliced in such a tender spot.

He paused as he reached her, his hat in his hand. "I can show you. But I don't think you'll want to go inside."

Her eyes flashed. "And why not?" she asked in a haughty tone.

"Because Miss Lulu's is a house of ill repute."

Jenny bit her bottom lip hard. *Hold on, hold on, don't*

panic. She met his level gaze. "If you'll give me a moment to hitch my horse, I'll go pay a call on Mr. Burton."

Audible gasps filled the air. She looked around and saw the shocked look on some of the ladies present. What did she care? She would never see these people again.

Ed came to her aid. "I'll hitch up the black, ma'am, if 'n I can get close enough." He started toward the horse but Comet snorted loudly. Ed backed off. "Maybe you better do it after all."

She led her horse to the rail and stroked his nose with affection. "Be good, little love. I'll be back shortly."

She fell into step beside the man that brought strange emotions to her surface. On one hand, she was frightened by him. He looked dangerous, like an outlaw in a dime novel, dressed all in black—hat, shirt, vest, and pants. His steady gaze seemed almost deadly. Yet another part of her found him to be terribly attractive.

Jenny wasn't certain which scared her more.

"It's not too far. Everything in Apple Blossom is just a stone's throw away."

They walked a minute or two in silence. She didn't have to look over her shoulder to know that most of the town's population traveled hot on their heels. The citizens must be hard up if she happened to be the biggest entertainment draw in town.

When they reached a large, two-storied house, he stopped. "This is it."

She stared at the white paint and neat, yellow trim. The yard held planted flowers and several shrubs, immaculately trimmed, lined up just below the front porch.

"Surprised?"

She nodded. This was certainly not her idea of what a brothel looked like—not that she had ever tried to picture one in her mind. If she had, though, she definitely would not have envisioned this neat, attractive place.

"Thank you," she managed.

Jenny walked up the stairs, lifting her skirts daintily. As she knocked, she took a deep breath and wondered what would happen next.

So did Noah. He watched with an amused look on his face. This girl was unpredictable, indeed. He kind of liked that about her. In a way, she reminded him of Moira. That shouldn't have surprised him. This was Moira's niece, albeit one his friend had never seen before. Jenny McShanahan had an air about her, though, that made her fun to watch. He didn't know what she'd pull next.

He never imagined her going this far. When the clerk said the guide Sam hired was dead, he expected her to fold up like a flower which had gotten too much sun. Much to his surprise, she'd had the guts to enter a saloon and try to find one on her own. He admired her gumption, both then and now.

He watched the door swing open. Jenny spoke with someone a moment before being admitted. Noah raced up the stairs just before the door closed. No way he was going to let Jenny McShanahan out of his sight now. Who knew what kind of trouble she would get into?

A pockmarked girl holding the door allowed him inside. He gestured for her to close it behind him. No need for the good people of Apple Blossom to see everything firsthand. Better to give them something to speculate on. Gossip was no fun any other way.

Jenny marched straight up the stairs, no hesitation in her step. Oh, he loved watching this girl from the rear. Walking behind her was a real treat. Her behind twitched and swayed as she climbed the stairs. It was a sight for sore eyes. It momentarily stunned him that

she had such an effect on him. He had to fight to concentrate on the issue at hand.

Noah followed her up the stairs, keeping a safe distance. He didn't want to interfere in whatever happened next.

He almost wished he could sell tickets.

৩২৩

EACH TIME JENNY CAME TO A DOOR, SHE KNOCKED
hard and marched right in. Her heart danced wildly in
her chest, not knowing what she would find. She had
seen the results of carnal knowledge at the clinic, the
unwanted pregnancies and diseases that even Dr. Randolph spoke of in hushed tones, but she only had a
vague idea of what actually went on behind closed
doors to cause such things. Thank goodness she had so
far seen nothing that had added to her limited knowledge. Yet.

She hit pay dirt on the fourth try. She pounded the
door with three heavy raps of her knuckles and threw
open the door. She heard Snake Burton before she saw
him, his noisy snores filling the dark, shabby room. A
girl lay next to him, her hair disheveled, the bedclothes
tangled around her as she opened sleepy eyes.

Jenny tried to hide her surprise as the girl, years
younger than she was, rose and padded naked across the
room as she pushed the hair from her face. The girl
slipped on her tattered wrapper and brushed by Jenny, a
saucy smile on her lips.

"He's all yours, sister. Too drunk to get it up,
though." The girl left her alone with Snake.

Looking about, she walked to a table that held a ce-
ramic pitcher and basin. She filled the basin to the brim
and took it to the bed. Fortunately, the girl had thrown
the sheets across Snake when she left the bed and he
was sufficiently covered. She took a deep breath and

tossed the water into his face. He barely stirred, which angered her even more.

"You no-good, dead-drunk, skunk of a man!"

Jenny shook his shoulder a good half-minute and then raised her hand and gave him a powerful slap.

That woke him. Snake Burton gazed up at her, a dazed look on his unshaven face. She didn't think it possible but he smelled even worse than before.

She shook her finger at him. "I gave you money in good faith. I thought you would get a haircut and a shave, maybe eat a decent meal." She wrinkled her nose in disgust. "And God forbid that you would think to take a bath!"

In reply, he smiled up lazily at her. "I did enjoy spending the money, ma'am. I haven't had a woman in . . . dang, I can't recall. Ain't that a fact," he mused.

"You, Mr. Burton, are despicable." She turned to go but whirled around to face him again. "And you . . . are . . . fired!"

Jenny stormed from the room. She flew down the stairs and flung open the door to her waiting audience, never breaking stride until she reached the saloon.

It was empty, all except for the same bartender from her previous visit. Did the man never sleep?

"Where is everyone?" she demanded.

"It's only ten in the morning, ma'am. My regulars ain't even out of bed yet. What'd you expect?"

"More than I'm getting from this sorry excuse for a town!" she cried angrily and stormed back outside.

As she anticipated, the group had followed her and hovered at close range. Exasperated, she called out, "I have paraded down this street and back again. I am looking for a guide to take me to Nevada. Are there any takers?"

There were none.

Eventually, in ones and twos, those gathered faded

away, knowing they had to get back to their tasks at hand.

All except her shadow.

He approached her cautiously. "I'll take you to Nevada. But it'll cost you," he added.

Jenny thought it over. She didn't know who the steel-eyed stranger was. She wasn't sure why she was so wary of him. She wondered how seriously she should take the anonymous warning she received about him under her door.

But he'd have to do. She was in a desperate situation that called for immediate action. She had to get to her papa. She wanted what she'd missed out on all these years—his love and companionship, a home together for the two of them—no matter what the cost. And for some inexplicable reason, she knew time was of the essence.

Miss Thompson would have an apoplexy if she knew Jenny were ready to cross the desert with a complete stranger. She smiled to herself, knowing that alone made her decision final.

"I must reach my papa in Nevada, sir. It's against my better judgment but I am willing to strike a bargain with you to act as my trail guide." She named a price and thrust out her gloved hand. "Do we have a deal?"

He took her hand in his. "Noah Daniel Webster, ma'am, at your service. And you would be?"

A giggle escaped her lips. She brought her free hand to cover her mouth. She composed herself before she blurted out, "What kind of name is that?" and then erupted into peals of laughter.

CHAPTER 6

Noah's pride prickled up. He dropped her hand. All his life he had defended the name he'd been saddled with. He'd been called out because of it more times than a soul could imagine. His mama explained why she honored him with this particular name but he'd finally reached the end of his proverbial rope.

"Who are you to question a fine name such as mine?" he shot back, his eyes narrowing as he tried to intimidate her.

Jenny McShanahan had the decency to look taken aback. "I'm sorry, Mr. Webster. I just hadn't heard that particular combination before. I don't wish to upset you."

"I'm not upset," he fired off, then amended his tone. "I've just taken teasing about it my entire life."

She smiled at him wistfully. "Well, sir, you carry the moniker of two very fine men. Why, Mr. Noah Webster and I have been friends since I was about ten and I began my first journal." She chuckled. "We weren't always friends, you know. Miss Wheadle caught me throwing Mr. Webster's dictionary across the room early in our relationship. I think it had something to do with blends. Or was it diphthongs? At any rate, I became a first-class speller, thanks to his marvelous compilation."

He was amused. "And do you have a personal relationship with Mr. Daniel Webster, as well?"

One corner of her mouth turned up. "I'm afraid not. Mr. Daniel Webster's speeches were not considered proper language to study for young ladies at The Thompson School in Boston." She paused. "However, my good friend, Dr. Randolph, indulged me upon occasion. I have read a few of Mr. Daniel Webster's orations in my time. I particularly enjoyed his defense of the Compromise of 1850. He saved our country from war for a time."

He whistled low. "You don't appear to be a typical young lady, ma'am."

"I don't? Perhaps not. My upbringing has been a tad unconventional." She presented him her hand again. "I am Jenny McShanahan, Mr. Webster. I am pleased to make your acquaintance."

Instead of shaking the proffered hand, Noah impulsively brought it to his lips and brushed them against her glove. He quickly lowered and squeezed her hand before she could protest. "Welcome to Texas, Miss McShanahan. Shall we get down to business?"

She froze for a moment before she flushed a pretty shade of pink. "If I have anything to say in the matter, Mr. Webster, we won't be in Texas for long."

"Yes," he drawled. "I hear tell you want to leave God's country and head up Nevada way. But you sure aren't going to do it in that dress."

She quickly glanced down at what she wore. "Why, this is a perfect dress for traveling, sir," she said indignantly as she stroked the skirt. "It is a dark, serviceable color, made of a sturdy material, perhaps not completely up to date in a fashion sense, but I doubt my horse will care."

He set his hat on his head, nudging it back from his

forehead with a slight push. "Oh, you look prettier than pansies in a vase, Miss McShanahan." He gave her a long look. "Have you ever ridden a horse before?"

"No," she answered. "But I've always been a fast learner." She grimaced. "It simply must be better than riding in a stagecoach. I was churned more on that stage in two days than butter that's been whipped for a week."

Noah laughed. "I'm not questioning your non-existent riding skills, Miss McShanahan. I'm questioning your wisdom in trying to mount a horse in a skirt that tight."

She looked down at her attire. "You're right, Mr. Webster. I'm afraid I didn't think this through properly. In fact, I'd taken a wee bit of pride that it had a small bustle which wouldn't be in the way. But thanks to your observations, I can see the way my dress is constructed will not even allow me to pull up a knee without straining the fabric."

She grew red in the face. He knew she was mad. Mad at him for pointing it out—and mad at herself for not realizing such a huge mistake. He figured that all her dresses were similarly constructed.

"Do you see those women leaving the general store? Their skirts are full and loose. Most women in the west dress in a similar manner. Forgive my being forward, but they usually wear a single petticoat or chose to ignore that undergarment for practicality."

She thought a moment. "Would it be acceptable to leave tomorrow, Mr. Webster? I seem to have my work cut out for me."

He grinned. "Tomorrow would be fine, Miss McShanahan. Say six in the morning?"

She opened her mouth to complain about such an early start but he saw she thought better of it. "Six o'clock will be perfectly fine."

"Would you do me the pleasure of dining with me

tonight, Miss McShanahan? Sort of a last farewell to civilization meal?"

"No, thank you," Jenny said curtly and began to cross the street.

"No?" he called out to her. "That's all you've got to say?"

She stopped and faced him. "No, thank you, Mr. Webster. I'm going to be too busy to dine with you. I do appreciate your kind offer, though. I'll take you up on it tomorrow night. On the road."

⚜

Jenny sighed and stretched her arms high over her head. Her back ached and her vision was beginning to blur. She had been sewing continuously all day, determined to come up with the correct clothes to wear for the long trip to Prairie Dell.

A quick stop at the general store satisfied her wish list of supplies. She was a natural seamstress, rarely needing a pattern to sew by. She had just put the final touches on her third outfit. Each gown had been simple to cut, once she studied a few pictures the clerk had. It had taken her all day. Her fingers had grown numb from all the stitches she'd taken. Of course, the dresses weren't the least bit stylish but she knew from her readings that the trail would be rough.

She placed the gown on the narrow bed and stood. Her right hand cramped painfully. As she shook it out, a light tap sounded on her door. She figured it was Mrs. Swenson, who had visited once earlier when Jenny failed to come down for dinner. Jenny explained to her that she had a tremendous amount of sewing to do before she left on her trip the next day. The sweet woman promised to bring Jenny supper on a tray when it grew dark.

She went to answer the door but the cramp seized her again. She called out, "Come in."

Turning her back to the door, Jenny shook her hand again. A sharp intake of breath escaped her lips as she placed her left hand over her right and rubbed it.

"What's wrong?"

The deep, low voice startled her. She whipped around to see Noah Webster standing in her room, an overflowing tray of food in his hands. Before she could order him to leave, another spasm hit. She bit her lip to keep from crying out as she presented him with her back.

She heard him set down the tray. He gently took her shoulders and turned her around. Jenny saw the concern in those clear pools of blue.

"Give it to me."

"What?"

He didn't ask a second time. He simply took her hand and began kneading it in long, deep strokes. She closed her eyes for a moment. It felt so good. She could smell his nearness. She caught a whiff of . . . well, she didn't know what to call it. It was clean and fresh and . . . she supposed . . . manly.

She had a very limited experience when it came to men but even she knew as good as this felt, he had to stop. Her stomach fluttered in the worst way. It bothered her more than her cramping hand. "You must leave at once!"

He went from concentrating on her hand to staring into her eyes. The butterflies in her belly roared into a flying frenzy. This wasn't any improvement at all.

"Is your hand better?"

"It's not quite one hundred percent—"

"Then I'm not leaving."

She exhaled the breath she'd been holding. "You must leave now, Mr. Webster. You're in my *room*!" she hissed in a whisper. "It isn't proper."

He continued to massage her hand. "Some folks would say it isn't proper to set out on the trail together, either."

She drew a sharp breath. "That's different."

"How so?" He looked at her with slightly raised brows, a trace of a smile hovering about his sensual lips.

It wasn't fair. She could barely think—or breath—much less answer him in a reasonable fashion. But, oh, did her hand feel marvelous.

"I've hired you as an employee. It's the only way I can reach my father," she sputtered.

"So, that's why we're heading to Nevada?" He began tracing lazy circles along her palm and up to her wrist.

Jenny couldn't breathe at all now. Her belly tightened, unlike anything she'd ever known. She yanked her hand from his.

"I'll tell you, Miss McShanahan, tongues wag for sport. You do the right thing, whatever pleases you and what you can live with. Don't worry how others judge you."

He looked over his shoulder. "You refused to accompany me to supper so I've brought supper to you. Let's eat."

"In here?" she squeaked.

He nodded. "In here."

CHAPTER 7

Noah didn't have to coax Jenny for long. He tempted her further by offering to leave the door open and she readily agreed. The way she eyed the food on the tray let him know how hungry she must be. He figured she hadn't eaten all day. One look around the small room told him all he needed to know.

"Looks as if you've kept busy today." He eyed the dresses placed carefully across the neatly-made bed. "Are you a seamstress?"

She shrugged. "I've made my own clothes for many years. Fortunately, it's one thing I'm good at."

He began clearing the dresses from the bed. "I'll do that," she said and quickly took them from him, her cheeks flushed.

He wondered what made her so embarrassed. He had moved plenty of women's clothes out the way in his time. Of course, none of those frocks belonged to nice girls like Jenny McShanahan.

Noah brought the large tray to the bed and sat down. He indicated to her to sit opposite him, the tray between them. She looked uncomfortable but she did perch on the edge. Miss Prim and Proper must be awfully hungry to do that. Although her exterior seemed frosty at times, she definitely surprised him today with her actions. A trip with her would prove mighty interesting.

"Whereabouts in Nevada are we heading, Miss McShanahan?" He bit into a leg of cold chicken and then scooped hot mashed potatoes onto his fork.

She dabbed her mouth with her napkin. "It's a small town near the southern tip of Nevada." Her brow wrinkled as she reached for the name. "Prairie Dell."

He dropped his fork and it clattered noisily against his full plate. He nearly choked on the bite he'd just swallowed. He coughed and wheezed. Jenny didn't help matters by whacking him on the back between his hacks.

"Are you all right, Mr. Webster?" She poured a cup of water from a pitcher on the basin. "Here. Drink this."

He waved her away, feeling his face burning red. All he wanted was one good breath. She was a bossy little thing, though, and somehow she forced a few sips down him. It calmed him enough to where he croaked out, "Much obliged." The entire experience wore him out.

Prairie Dell.

When he'd heard her wanting to go to Nevada, he should've put two and two together. Well, at least he'd get to visit with Moira in person, at long last. Funny how the whole thing would come full circle. The scene of his one venture into crime would be the end of Sam's life as a career criminal.

Jenny relaxed and sat again but he could still see the concern on her face.

"A piece of meat went down the wrong pipe. That's all," he assured her. "Now, you were saying we're headed to a place called Prairie Dell?" He paused. "I may have heard of it before."

"I tried to purchase a map at the general store but

none were available of Nevada. In fact," she leaned in confidentially, "there weren't any maps at all."

He laughed. "That surprised you?"

She looked put out with him. "It most certain did! How are people to get around from place to place without a map?"

He shrugged. "You just do. Is this your first trip to the west, ma'am?"

"Yes, but I have studied the area extensively. I wanted to familiarize myself with it."

"How long have you been studying up?"

A shadow crossed her face. It surprised Noah how much that one look said. He guessed she'd read everything she could get her hands on about the west ever since Sam left her in that school back in Massachusetts.

He remembered the one time he had seen her in a picture Sam kept in his battered wallet. Sam had left it lying out. Noah stared at it a long time. It was hard for him to realize that Famous Sam McShan at one time had been a family man. He'd overheard Sam talking about his deceased wife with Pete and Noah supposed the little girl in the starched frock and wavy hair in the family portrait was their daughter.

Pete had been the one to tell Noah that Sam's daughter was in a boarding school in Boston. He'd warned his son not to broach the subject with Sam. Noah never asked why. He did as he was told. He had learned not to mess with Sam. Most of the time the outlaw oozed fun and charm, but every now and then one of his black-tempered Irish moods surfaced.

Noah thought about that little girl now, how happy and hopeful she'd seemed in the picture. She stood between her seated parents, both arms draped around their shoulders. She couldn't have been more than six or seven at the time. To think she'd lost her mama at a young age was tragedy enough for any child but then to be abandoned by her daddy for the next decade was a double loss.

He looked at her with new eyes and a little more respect than before. She appeared to be well-mannered and intelligent. It must have taken a lot of courage on her part to make it through the last ten years alone.

Jenny finally answered, toying with her fork. "Sometimes, I feel I've read about the west my whole life, Mr. Webster." She sighed. "Reading was my only means of travel for many years. When I was young, though, my papa moved us frequently, all up and down the eastern seaboard."

She paused. "Then my mother fell ill and passed away. Papa found the means to place me at The Thompson School while he paid off some debts." Her eyes glittered with unshed tears. "He has had many difficulties over the years and it is only recently he's been able to send for me."

Noah gazed into those shimmering green eyes. "You spent all those years at school. Did you ever see your daddy at any time?"

She shook her head and squared her shoulders. "No. but he did write to me some," she said defensively. "He thought to make his fortune out west. Papa believed there would be many opportunities for a man to take hold of there and he knew I was safely cared for at The Thompson School."

The look on her face told him the full story. He could see a lonely child left in a strange environment, no family to visit her and no friends to be had. He knew what it felt like to be an outsider. He wouldn't wish it upon anyone, least of all a slip of a girl.

Fishing a bit, he said, "You say he's sent for you. Does that mean he's made the most of his opportunities?"

She brightened considerably. "Oh, yes. His recent venture has paid off handsomely. He wishes for us to be together." She laughed. "I was only too happy to leave my position and come immediately to Texas."

"You were working?" The fact that Sam had left her alone all those years bothered Noah. He could imagine the infrequent letters sent, the empty promises and dashed hopes, but he couldn't believe she'd had to work, too.

"Yes. I graduated with high honors from school at eighteen. My teachers said I had great promise." She smiled sadly and his heart wrenched. "Papa thought it best for me to remain at the school, though. The headmistress, Miss Thompson, allowed me to teach classes to the younger girls for my room and board. I've been doing so for over two years now."

He tamped down the fury he felt toward Sam. Noah had already drawn a clear picture in his mind of Jenny's isolated life at school, a forlorn child who withdrew into her books and fantasies about a father who never came, a girl who longed more than anything to join her daddy, no matter what the dangers. Now, he saw her even further separated—not a student—yet not quite good enough to be a salaried teacher.

If Miss Thompson were here, he would have harsh words and maybe more with her, no matter what his sainted mama had preached about how to treat a lady. In his mind, this Miss Thompson was no lady at all. He guessed her to be a cold fish who saw a chance to string Jenny McShanahan along, while the headmistress raked in tuition and fees at an even bigger margin of profit.

"Well, Miss McShanahan, it sounds like you and your daddy will have a lot to catch up on." He lifted the buttered bread to his mouth and chewed thoughtfully.

"Yes." She frowned and took a sip of water. "He was to meet me in Apple Blossom but some unforeseen problem cropped up. I would have already been on my way to Nevada if not for the unfortunate demise of the guide that Papa arranged for me."

It amazed him that she could receive such bad news and then have the fortitude to stride into a saloon and try and scare up her own guide. Jenny McShanahan could be termed brave or foolish for trying to hire a stranger but she obviously wanted to see her father badly.

Guilt streaked through Noah's conscience for a moment, knowing that he would be the one to pull them apart again. This time forever. Sam had too long a record for it to be anything less than a hanging. Over ten states would line up quicker than lightning strikes to be the one to do the honors. He knew with certainty now that Jenny had no idea what Sam had been up to all these years.

"Why did you accept my offer, Mr. Webster?"

She pulled him from his thoughts. He hoped his face gave nothing away. "I need to head further west anyway, Miss McShanahan. I've got the consumption," he lied, laying the ground for the background story he would feed to her.

Her jaw dropped. "But . . . you're the picture of health. You're tall and robust, with strong muscles and a healthy glow. Why . . . " Her voice trailed off as she blushed furiously. She brought her napkin to her mouth and dabbed it daintily to hide her embarrassment.

This was the most modest gal he'd run across in his twenty-five years. He grinned at her, glad she'd noticed he cut a fine picture.

"It's in the very early stages," he assured her. "Doc says I can live for years and years if I'll just get myself out to some dry, desert air. That'll be the best medicine for me."

She recovered slightly and returned the napkin to her lap. "Still, it's a shame that you received such a harsh diagnosis. What will you do when you reach your destination?"

He shrugged. "Probably a little of this and that. Doc

says I'm in pretty good condition, due to my cowboying."

"You're a cowboy?" Her eyes danced merrily. "Have you driven cattle to market?"

"Yep. Started out in sixty-six when the first drives headed up to Kansas after the war. Had to ride drag at the beginning. That's when—"

"—when you must ride in the rear of the herd. It must be awfully dusty. And smelly."

"More of your book learning?"

"Yes," she admitted. "The cattle drives have always fascinated me. They sound so romantic."

Noah laughed. "You have a twisted idea of romance, ma'am. It's romantic to walk your gal home from a barn dance and spoon a little under a full moon with the scent of magnolias surrounding you. Riding for weeks at a time with a bunch of smelly cows and even smellier men is not quixotic at all."

"Quixotic? What an odd word choice for a cowboy." She scrutinized him carefully. "You must be very well read, Mr. Webster. Perhaps you studied your namesake's dictionary in your spare time around the campfire?"

It was his turn to blush. He was well-educated, thanks to his mama. Having been a newsman's daughter, she'd been taught the importance of words at an early age. She passed on that magic to all her children. Mark, his brother, now worked at a San Francisco newspaper. Last he'd heard, his sister, Elizabeth, was trying to get excerpts of her diary of life as a homesteader's wife published in some fancy ladies' magazine in New York.

"You could say that all the Webster children have substantial vocabularies, thanks to our mama."

Jenny rubbed her hands together. "I am delighted to hear it, Mr. Webster. I had thought I would be saddled with a dull cowpuncher for this trip. Instead, you make lively conversation and appear quite experienced, able to handle any difficulties we might encounter while on our journey."

"I'm experienced, Miss McShanahan." He gave her a wry smile and winked. "That you can count on."

Noah just loved seeing her blush.

Jenny splashed cold water on her face and shivered. It was still dark. She couldn't believe they were leaving at six in the morning. They wouldn't even be able to see the trail, much less stay on it.

She was an early riser so the early hour hadn't bothered her. She was used to stoking fires and helping Mrs. Smith with the beginnings of breakfast before she woke the girls on three different floors at The Thompson School. She hoped she hadn't given Mr. Webster any false impressions. Simply because she had attended and then taught at a fancy girls' boarding school did not mean she was not used to hard work. She would take their journey through rough country in stride.

She resolved to keep any complaints to herself while they were on the trail. Mr. Webster seemed more than kind and he was probably going out of his way to take her to Nevada. Jenny had read that many of those stricken with consumption went to Arizona Territory so he would eventually have to loop around. She appreciated his efforts on her behalf and would request that Papa give her guide an added bonus when they arrived in Prairie Dell.

As she finished dressing, a brisk knock sounded at

the door. The hotel owner's wife opened it and peeped in at her. "Glad to see you dressed, dearie."

"Mrs. Swenson? Why are you up at this hour?"

The small woman whisked through the door, a steaming bowl of oatmeal in her hands. "I couldn't bear the thought of sending you off without something hot sticking to your ribs. It's quite chilly out there."

"You are so thoughtful. Thank you."

The older woman shrugged. "Least I can do for you, Miss McShanahan. You've got a long ride ahead of you. I cain't understand why you have to go off so early, though." She handed Jenny the wooden bowl. "Eat up."

Jenny spooned a bite into her mouth. "Mmm. This certainly hits the spot on a cold morning." She placed the spoon back in the bowl. "Mr. Webster feels that we should leave early every day. I am not as experienced a rider as he and so he would like us to take a longer break in the afternoon once we eat, to give me some time to rest before we set out again."

She dipped the spoon into the oatmeal and swallowed another bite, looking back at Mrs. Swenson. "That seems to be a reasonable and sound plan, don't you think?"

Mrs. Swenson snorted. "I suppose. Though why you'd want to set off on such a back-breaking trip to the middle of nowhere is lost upon me. Won't find anything better there than in Texas, mark my words."

Jenny savored another bite of her breakfast. "I'm anxious to meet up with my father. I would do just about anything at this point to reach him."

As soon as she finished her oatmeal and gathered her things, she looked at the watch pinned to her bodice. Six o'clock sharp. Mr. Webster was to meet her in front of the hotel at any moment. She hurried down the steep stairs quietly, so as not to wake Mr. Swenson, and eased open the door.

She stepped outside, the cold air settling around her like a blanket. Thank goodness they weren't undertaking a long journey from Boston. She couldn't imagine riding in a harsh Massachusetts winter. Everything she had read, though, assured her that the day would warm up considerably this time of year. She thought back on her last few days in Texas and knew that to be true although her guide last night warned her about blue northers.

"Just when you think the weather is doing tolerably well, Miss McShanahan, a blue norther will whip down from the Panhandle and sweep across the state faster than lice jumping on a schoolboy's head."

"I assume that means it gets very cold."

"Colder than a witch's tit on a frosty day."

She remembered pinkening slightly at his turn of phrase but Noah Webster went on speaking as if nothing were out of the ordinary. She wondered if he said things to make her deliberately uncomfortable. She certainly did a lot of blushing in his presence.

Jenny brought her valise down the steps to the uncobbled road. She caught a glimpse of Mr. Webster and watched him come up the street. He was a very handsome man, almost too handsome for his own good. He was astride a beautiful black horse that had a touch of white on its forehead.

Come to think of it, her guide had a glib tongue, as well, and though she'd told him she enjoyed his conversation, she wondered about it now. He was probably what would be termed a charming rogue. She wondered again if she should trust going off with a total stranger. In her other life in Boston, the decision would have been against her better judgment but she was starting fresh now in the west. She was stuck with Mr. Webster and he with her.

He was leading an unfamiliar horse, as well as a pack horse laden with their supplies.

"Where is *my* horse, Mr. Webster?" She found she hadn't kept the snooty schoolmarm tone from her question because he raised his eyebrows at her.

"Your horse, Miss McShanahan, is back where it should be. In the stockyard. I had Whitey trade it for a new one."

"You had no right!" She slammed her suitcase to the ground for emphasis.

He dismounted from his horse and strolled the few paces to her. "I had every right, ma'am, seeing as to how I'm your guide. That nag you chose wouldn't have made it twenty miles before it keeled over. You have a nice piece of horseflesh now. She's even-tempered and should be fairly easy for a greenhorn to handle."

He walked to her new horse and brushed a hand along its flank. Jenny had to admit it was a lovely horse, a deep chestnut color. She moved closer and lifted a hand to stroke its silky coat. With one pat, she fell in love.

"Shall I help you mount this replacement and be on our way?"

Before she could reply, he placed his hands around her waist and lifted her onto the horse as if she were lighter than a floating balloon. Startled, she gripped the horn of the saddle. Then just as suddenly, he pulled her back to the ground.

"You look might fetching but that'll never do," he said, shaking his head.

"Now what?" she asked, frustration bubbling within her.

"You'll have to change, Miss McShanahan."

She gritted her teeth. "Not this again." She crossed her arms. "My outfit is perfectly fine this time. I felt comfortable wearing it for the limited time I sat upon my horse. Which, by the way, Mr. Webster—what is my horse's name?"

Noah looked surprised at her question. "Why?"

She blew out a noisy breath, not trying to hide her irritation with him. "This horse must have a name, Mr. Webster. How can you expect me to ride her without being able to talk with her?"

He wore a bemused look on his chiseled features. "She doesn't have a name."

She pressed him further. "Does *your* horse have a name?"

"This here's Star, ma'am," her guide said with pride.

"Then I'm sure you see my point." She leaned over and petted his horse. "Hello, Star," she cooed. "I'm Jenny and this is . . . " She eyed her mare speculatively for a moment. "Sassy. We're going to be traveling together. I know we'll have a nice trip."

She swept a gentle hand along her own horse's flank. "Hello, Sassy, dear. I know we will get along famously. I have always wanted a horse and you are a real beauty. I'm going to need lots of help, though. I know you'll take good care of me."

She looked to Noah. "Well? Are we ready to leave or what?"

"Not till you take off that corset."

Her face immediately flamed. "I beg your pardon! That is not a matter for discussion, sir."

Noah tipped his hat away from his forehead. "We'll discuss it and anything else I see fit to discuss. You simply cannot ride any length of time, especially as far as we need to go, in such . . ." he searched for the appropriate words, ". . . restrictive attire."

He had the grace to look a little sheepish. "It's just for your own good, Miss McShanahan. Besides," and he gave her a slow, heated look as he took in her tall frame. "You don't really need to wear one. Your curves are already in all the right places."

Humiliated, she stormed back into the hotel, past a confused Mrs. Swenson, and up to the room she had recently vacated.

How dare Mr. Webster talk about her undergarments! Jenny was ready to fire him on the spot.

Instead, she practiced a few of the choicer epithets from Mulholland's guidebook under her breath as she removed her clothing. She unlaced the corset and slipped it off, redressing hastily. And then she took a deep breath.

Freedom.

She took another. She couldn't believe how liberating it was. She couldn't remember ever having worn her clothes without a corset. She felt as comfortable as she did when she stepped into bed every night.

She scooped up the corset and flew down the stairs, passing Mrs. Swenson on the landing.

"Miss McShanahan. You can't carry about your corset in public! Miss McShanahan!"

She ignored the woman's outraged cries. She could and would take her corset anywhere she chose. She was a western woman now, with a mind of her own.

Her boots clomped down the front steps of the hotel. She didn't even feel the cold anymore. Instead, she flung the wadded up corset into her guide's hands and placed a booted foot into the stirrup. On sheer adrenaline, she hoisted herself into the saddle and smiled down at Noah Daniel Webster.

"Aren't you coming?"

He tossed the corset over his shoulder and remounted Star. She heard him mutter, "Women," under his breath.

◈

BY TWO IN THE AFTERNOON, JENNY MCSHANAHAN was hot, cranky, and saddle sore. Noah knew she was because she'd told him so every few minutes for the last two hours. He gritted his teeth for the umpteenth time and tried to ignore her prattle. Obviously, the woman had been on her sweetest behavior earlier. Now it was much later—and the real Jenny McShanahan had emerged. If he had known what she was really like, he might never have taken on this assignment.

She was the exact type of woman he intended to avoid for the rest of his life. She was a know-it-all, bossy, a complainer, and worse. He glanced toward her and tried to harden his heart where she was concerned.

It was difficult to do so. Jenny McShanahan had a simple beauty rarely seen. Her oval face displayed a beautiful complexion, as flawless as a white rose brushed with a trace of pink. Her neck was as long and graceful as those of swans he'd seen in a book once. Noah imagined starting at that soft mouth of hers and working his way down her jaw to her slender neck. Lord, he could spend a month of Sundays kissing that neck alone.

Where in the blazes did these thoughts come from?

He gave himself a good mental shakedown. Even though he continued to dismiss her complaints, he couldn't totally remove her voice from his head. When she wasn't squawking away, she had a low, sweet voice, soft-spoken and very articulate. He was definitely attracted to her. What fool wouldn't be? One look at those deep green eyes and any man he knew would be a goner.

Noah repeated to himself for the tenth time that day that Jenny McShanahan was forbidden fruit. She was the daughter of an outlaw, her blood probably as tainted as Sam's. There was no way he would get involved with Famous Sam McShan's daughter, no matter how delicious a curve her small, high breasts made and despite her tempting little waist and sweetly-rounded rump. She was bad news. Besides, she would hate his guts the minute he arrested her daddy right in front of her. No sense in borrowing trouble.

Nice girls weren't for the likes of him anyway. He

would never settle down. He had Pete's wanderlust in him but he'd curbed it by putting it to good use as a Ranger. Very few Rangers married. Any woman who married a Ranger would be filled with a life of disappointment and probable widowhood. No, Noah Daniel Webster was never getting married. Period.

"If you'll stop your caterwauling, we'll pause here and eat us some dinner," he said pleasantly.

Her eyes went wide. "I am not caterwauling, Mr. Webster. I am simply explaining to you the current state of affairs."

"Thank you for that note of progress, ma'am. You can bring me up to date again in say, two weeks."

Noah swung a leg over and touched the ground. As much as he loved to ride, it always felt good to plant his feet on solid ground. He patted Star's rump and walked around to Jenny.

She wore a desperate look.

"Having a problem, Miss McShanahan?" he drawled.

Her lips formed a thin line. "I'm having trouble feeling my legs, that's all. I fear they've gone to sleep."

"Let me give you a hand."

She took his hand and leaned forward, but nothing else happened.

"I think I may need more help than a hand," she confessed.

He grinned. "That's all you had to say."

Noah captured her waist and set her on the ground. She promptly crumpled. He caught her and held her up as her legs wobbled unsteadily.

Tears formed in her eyes. Oh, Lord, he'd be a lost soul if she cried. He'd always been a sucker for tears, his mama's in particular, but any woman's would do him in. Sometimes, he thought women turned them on and off just to get his goat. But as he looked at her, he could see Jenny's tears were real.

Noah tried to think back on the first time he'd

ridden a long distance. He recalled how stiff he was as he dismounted and how tired his bones felt, despite the fact that the horse had done all the work. His bottom had blisters rubbed on it and he'd been miserable for a week. A pang of sympathy sprouted in him for Jenny's predicament.

She gripped his shoulders with fingers that seemed to be made of steel. He could feel her nails slice into him through both her gloves and his wool shirt.

Damn, but he wanted to kiss her!

"Miss McShanahan?"

Her eyes met his. Fortunately, she held back the floodgate even though the tears swam in her eyes. He took a calming breath.

"If you'll let me carry you, I'll take you over to that rock." He motioned to it with his head. "I don't think you'll be walking there on your own between now and sunset."

She bit her lower lip and nodded slightly. He scooped her up and walked the few steps needed, concentrating hard on putting one foot in front of the other, doing his level-best not to think about the womanly package in his arms.

"I'm going to set you on the rock, then I'd like to help rub some feeling back into your legs."

Most ladies would be appalled but Jenny Mc-Shanahan looked grateful. He set her down as gently as he could and leaned back on his heels as he knelt before her.

"May I take off your boots?"

"Please," she whispered. She hiked up her skirt a little so he could better maneuver the boot from her leg. He figured about now her bottom and her legs would start stinging as the feeling returned so he kept up a constant conversation to distract her.

"These are awfully nice boots, ma'am. Not quite

what we have around here, but they're nice all the same."

She grimaced as he began working off the first one. "They're men's boots."

He stopped and studied her.

"Oh, go ahead. Don't stop. My legs are starting to feel like I've fallen in a bed of pine needles and decided to dance in them."

"That kind of stabbing sensation?"

"Yes!" she threw out as the first boot came off. "I have rather large feet for a woman. I suppose it's because I'm so tall. I've always had trouble finding shoes. When Papa sent me some money to buy a few new things, I knew from Mr. Mulholland's guidebook that I would need sturdy boots. The sales clerk told me that they made no sturdier—ouch!"

"Sorry." He eased off her woolen stockings and saw what she meant. She had feet longer than most men he knew, but they were perfectly shaped, each toe better than the one beside it.

He handed her the stockings and began massaging her legs. She moaned a few times and he began to grow hard. Oh, God Almighty, this would never do. Here he was in the middle of nowhere, stroking the long, alabaster legs of Sam McShan's daughter, and they were the best set of legs he'd ever had the pleasure of touching.

Noah turned until his back was mostly toward her and sat on his heels, placing her legs on his thighs. At least his front side was hidden from her view this way. He continued his circular motions for a few minutes and she quieted considerably. Thank goodness she didn't sound like a painted lady in the throes of pleasure anymore.

Jenny was in heaven. At the first touch of Noah's hands on her leg, she almost jumped six feet into the sky. No man had ever touched her before. All the rules of propriety that Miss Thompson ground into her echoed through her head. An unmarried lady did not spend time alone with a gentleman without a proper chaperone, much less let him massage her bare feet and legs.

But did Miss Thompson have a glimmer of how good it could feel? Through the stinging sensations that darted up and down her legs in a frantic dance, she sensed a marvelous warmth rushing along her, past her legs and into the pit of her stomach, spreading faster and faster. She had no control over it.

She wondered what had come over her to go off with a handsome stranger, much less let him stroke her intimately less than a day into their journey.

Jenny didn't care. She was a western woman now, one who was simply being practical in the situation. She may have crossed a line she'd never even considered existing before but the West was a radically different place. She could toss a bit of her pride aside and let Mr. Webster help make her a bit more comfortable. That's all it was. Besides, no witnesses to this spectacle meant no gossip would reach anyone's ears.

Her guide took one of the stockings from her and carefully slid it back up her leg. He repeated the action with the other.

"Thank you," she said quietly. "I know I must seem brazen to you. Normally, I would never allow a man to take such liberties."

"You're in a bad way, Miss McShanahan. Don't worry about it. I told you last night—do what you think is right and to heck with what others think." He looked around them. "No one's here anyway to think poorly of you." He smiled wickedly. "Well, maybe Miss Sassy thinks less of you than she did before."

Jenny stared at the horses a moment and then

laughed aloud, a deep laugh from her belly. He gave her a heart-melting smile and her laughter died as she focused on the dimple that creased one cheek. Suddenly her heart knew she was in for trouble, just as surely as the sun would set.

CHAPTER 9

"I can't believe you'd call this a meal."

Jenny wrinkled her nose as she held up the beef jerky for closer inspection. The dried meat had a smoky smell to it. She took a bite and had to really work to tear off a piece. The jerky had a hickory taste but she found chewing it tougher than trying to gnaw on shoe leather. Mr. Webster had said they would have dinner and then rest awhile before getting three or more hours down the road. A few swigs from a canteen and as many bites as she could stomach of the jerky was not the repast she had in mind.

"Don't we eat biscuits out on the trail? And red-eye gravy?" She waved the jerky around as she spoke. "Flap-jacks and strong coffee and—"

"Whoa, Nellie girl, just back it up." He eyed her with obvious amusement. "I never promised you a feast."

"But Mr. Mulholland said while on the trail—"

"There you go again," he interrupted. "You've mentioned this Mulholland fellow before. Just who in heck is he? Some expert on the west?"

She relaxed. "Why, yes. I would have expected you would be familiar with his work, living here."

He look perplexed. "What work?"

"Guidebook to the American West. Mr. Milton Mulholland is the author. It was recently published. I've read it from cover to cover several times and twice on the train coming out here, to be precise. He has fascinating information in it, more so than most books I've read."

Mr. Webster snorted. "I'll just bet. Exactly what did this Mister Fancy-Pants write about?"

She rolled her eyes at him, as one of her former students might. "His credentials are impeccable, Mr. Webster. Mr. Mulholland worked as a ranch hand and cowboy on the Goodnight-Loving Trail. He mined silver in Colorado and Nevada. He lived in Texas with the Comanche for—"

"Hold your sweet horses, Miss McShanahan. Ain't nobody foolish enough to try to live with the Comanche. Not that those wild Indians would let a white do that."

She caught the smirk he tried to wipe off his face unsuccessfully.

"You're telling me—"

"I would never presume to tell the likes of you anything, Miss McShanahan. I'm simply trying to inform you that Mr. Milton Mulholland and his *Guidebook to the American* West is a bunch of hogwash."

She gasped. "How dare you, sir! It is a legitimate book published by a reputable company. It can't be all lies."

"I'm calling Mr. Mulholland a bald-faced liar, ma'am. Sure, he might have traveled out west and picked up enough stray facts to write himself a book that only neophytes would read but I doubt he's done a tenth of the things he claims to have done in that book of his."

"How can you possibly say that when you haven't even seen his work, much less read it? Why would you believe such a thing?"

He gazed at her steadily. "Why would you?"

Jenny was speechless.

He took the chance to speak before she regained her senses. "We'll stop every day around one and have a light meal. Similar to the one we're partaking of now." He paused, daring her to interrupt. "We'll rest for an hour and then head back out. When we stop for the night, we'll build a fire and have coffee and something hot for our bellies. You do know how to cook, ma'am?" A mischievous light danced in his eyes.

"No." She glared at him.

"Then I guess you'll be happy to know that your trail guide is also a first-rate cook. At least we won't starve in the wilderness."

She reached for her canteen again. She felt extremely hot, too hot to keep arguing. The day had warmed up considerably and she'd been able to remove her cloak. Her face seemed warm, though, as if she had a fever. Her parched lips seemed dry as a desert. Every time she swallowed, it hurt.

Suddenly, her companion sat next to her on the flat rock. He pulled a bandana from his pocket and poured some water over it. He handed it to her.

"Wipe your face with this. You're looking a little peaked."

She did as he said and she did recover some. She guessed her hat hadn't protected her face as well as she'd imagined it would. She could picture herself as red as a Boston lobster tomorrow and shuddered.

"Here," he said and took the cloth from her. "Remember to moisten it every now and then while we ride from now on. Just dab it along here," and he touched the wet bandana under her jaw and slid it down her throat slowly, "and here," as he brushed it along the back of her neck.

If she seemed hot before, she was now on fire. She didn't understand at all why this intense heat grew, all the way to the pit of her stomach, unless it was acute embarrassment. She tried to take the bandana from him.

"Yes, well, thank you, Mr. Webster. I'll keep that in mind." But he didn't let go. His fingers brushed hers—and the flames in her stomach sparked and fanned out.

"Wait," he said softly. He dipped the cloth in water again and then lifted it over her head. She was engulfed as his arms went around her but didn't touch her. The space between them was very narrow. Jenny could not breathe.

"Wh—what are you doing"? she stammered.

He looked down in her eyes. "You'll see." Noah tied the bandana loosely around her neck, knotting it at her throat. "This should help."

He stood and slowly backed away from her. "I should have thought to tell you a bit before we set out. You still look mighty thirsty, ma'am. Every time I take a sip from my canteen, I'll remember to tell you to take one, too." He smiled at her. "Don't worry, Miss Mc-Shanahan. We'll get you through this in one piece."

With that, Noah Webster stretched out his tall frame on the ground and plopped his hat over his face. She heard a mumbled, "Just give me an hour now." Within a minute, light snores echoed in the air.

It amazed Jenny that anyone could fall asleep that fast. How could he even be comfortable sprawled on the rock-hard ground like that?

She rose and started to peek under his hat to see if he were pulling her leg. No, that would never do. Mr. Mulholland said cowboys needed to be very light sleepers, in case someone tried to steal their cattle at night. She could imagine lifting his hat and being shot in return, strictly on his honed instincts.

Instead, she sat again and proceeded to study him. The man cut a fine figure. That was one fact she could attest to. She had no involvement with men. The

Thompson School possessed no male instructors or students besides the lone janitor.

The only man in her life had been Dr. Randolph, unless she counted the men she encountered at the clinic he ran. Jenny had been exposed to some hardened types there. The clinic offered free services for the most part, as Dr. Randolph only had patients pay what they could afford. That usually amounted to little if anything at all. She saw all sorts enter with injuries too numerous to count.

Most of them had been in too much pain to bother her as she assisted the physician in his ministrations. She helped tend to broken bones, cuts, stab wounds, burns, infections, and even a few gunshot wounds. Some of the rough clientele frightened her, but her conversations with them were limited, and always with Dr. Randolph present. She learned several useful skills over the years concerning medicine. She wished her guide knew that side of her. She feared Mr. Webster thought her a simple-minded, fluffy-headed, prissy little creature. She was so much more than that.

Maybe he was right in calling her bossy, though. She did have a lot of book knowledge and wasn't shy about sharing it. Most of the time Jenny knew her information to be correct. Normally, she acted with confidence, especially when she was in control of a situation. That was when she felt most comfortable. So much of her life hadn't been in her power and so she strove desperately to be in charge—no matter what—whenever she could. She had learned from teaching spoiled little rich girls that she always needed to show those around her that she was in charge. Perhaps she had taken it a step too far with her hired guide. After all, Mr. Webster was supposed to be the expert.

She watched as his chest rose and fell with a regular rhythm. He did look like she imagined cowboys on cattle drives would. He was tall, with the Stetson that all men here seemed to favor. She looked at his hands crossed on his chest, the fingers long and lean. She shivered as she thought about those tanned fingers running along her jaw, guiding the wet bandana down her throat.

She knew deep in her soul that she wanted to kiss Noah Webster.

Why? She wasn't sure. All she knew was that she had never been kissed before—and she was ready now. But she didn't really like him all that much. He oozed charm with his Texas drawl and catlike grace. He was exactly the kind of man that ladies stayed away from.

But she still wanted to kiss him. A lot.

She imagined his lips on hers. The heat in her stomach burned as before.

"Miss McShanahan?"

She jumped as a shadow blocked the sunlight. She raised her eyes to look into his. Though she knew it wasn't quite appropriate—at least by east coast standards—she *was* in the west now. And a western woman wouldn't stand on ceremony.

Especially if she might find a chance to kiss this man somewhere down the line.

"Why don't you call me Jenny?"

His lips twitched. "All right. Miss Jenny. Ready to go?"

She nodded. She pushed off the rock. She couldn't believe she'd been so wrapped up in her woolgathering that she hadn't even seen him awaken. He was quieter than a cat stalking a mouse.

❧

NOAH THOUGHT A WOUNDED ANIMAL HAD WANDERED into their camp. The low, guttural noise threw him a moment. Then he realized it came from his traveling companion.

"Having problems, Miss Jenny?"

She threw him a murderous look. "Other than the fact I can't walk and dread putting my sore posterior into that saddle? No, Mr. Webster. No problems at all."

He laughed heartily. "Just call me Noah, ma'am." He helped her mount her horse. She cooed to it and patted its neck lovingly. He wished she would cozy up to him like that.

"I'll try to set a slower pace than before. This has been a hard first day for you." He looked at her with admiration. "I don't know of many women who could've done what you have already, Jenny. You just hang in there."

She beamed at the compliment and her smile kicked him in his gut. Maybe he should just be a surly cuss from now on. He didn't need any more of Jenny Mc-Shanahan's sunny smiles putting foolish notions into his head.

They rode a few more hours and talked as they went.

"How long do you think it will take us, Noah? To reach Prairie Dell, that is."

He thought about it. "I'd say about three weeks if we don't encounter any problems. Maybe a bit longer. It depends on how long you can stay in the saddle each day."

She frowned. "What kind of problems?"

"Oh, something like floods, fires, angry Indians. Poisonous snakes. Outlaws." He deliberately cut himself off when he saw the look of horror grow on her face. Nothing like putting his foot in his mouth.

"I'm sorry I asked." She fell silent for a few miles.

"I will be happy to see my father," she finally said. "It's been such a long time. I can't think of anything in my life that could be more exciting than seeing Papa in the flesh."

She grew quiet again. They rode several more miles before he heard her humming softly to herself. It was a sad tune, probably Irish by the sounds of it. He'd heard Sam sing plenty of Irish ballads in the past.

Noah glanced sideways at his traveling companion. She had a beautiful profile. Flawless skin. A few blond tendrils escaped from under her hat and floated in the breeze.

She finished the song and launched into another one.

"Sing it."

"What?" She looked up at him, startled. "Sing what?"

"The words to whatever tune you were humming."

She blushed. "I'm sorry. It's a bad habit of mine. I have a tendency to hum like some people doodle."

He smiled at her. "I don't mind you singing. Wish I could join in."

"I wish you could. I'd teach you the words if I knew them." She sighed. "I don't remember any of them. Papa used to sing me a litany of songs every night before bed. I remember all the melodies and even some of the titles but I never can seem to remember the words. I guess it's been too long."

He saw those green eyes begin to glisten and had to swallow hard. Either the shade of those magical eyes or her tears would do him in. He better toughen up fast before he lost his head.

And his heart.

"Noah, what if he doesn't recognize me? The last time I saw him, I was a little girl. Only ten years old. Now, I'm a giant of a woman." She shook her head. "Why I grew so tall is a mystery to me."

He almost blurted out that Sam himself was tall, about six-four, but he caught himself. He had to be careful and not slip up. She was a bright woman and would pick up on any small mistake. He had too much at stake. He couldn't let Sam get away.

As they rode, he thought back about how he'd worshipped Sam at first. The witty Irishman was much more interested in him than Pete ever was. Noah had loved listening to all Sam's stories of life back in Ireland and his trip over the Atlantic to New York. Sam told him of all kinds of scams he and Moira pulled before she was hurt. He thoroughly enjoyed being around Sam.

Until that day at the bank.

At least he would get to see Mo again. Wouldn't she be surprised at him riding up after all these years? He had a lot of catching up to do with her, things that hadn't gone into the many letters he'd written to her over the years.

He still had conflicting feelings about Sam. Part hero-worship mixed with contempt for the man who committed crimes against others. It didn't matter to Noah how much of the loot Sam gave away. Stealing was wrong.

He had conflicting feelings, too, about Jenny. He pitied her. He hated how Sam promised to send for her all these years and never did. He knew how bad Sam could be. He wondered how Jenny would take it when he arrested the old man. Then she would learn who Noah really was and why he'd been willing to escort her so far.

He didn't want to kill Sam. He was determined to take the outlaw in alive so he could stand trial and be punished for his many crimes. But what if Sam didn't give him a choice? He wondered if he should use Jenny as bait somehow to flush Sam out when the time came.

That thought made him feel lower than pond scum. No, he would try to keep her out of it as much as he could. He sure didn't want to be around when she realized her daddy was a famous criminal but Noah couldn't see any way around it. Maybe he would figure something out on the way to Nevada.

"Noah, have you ever met any outlaws?"

CHAPTER 10

Riley hustled through the depot, his rucksack tossed casually over one shoulder. He didn't want to miss this train. He gave a quick glance at a pretty girl and regretted he couldn't stop to make her acquaintance.

"All aboard!"

The conductor's cry sounded through the small station. Riley stepped onto the platform just as the train was ready to pull away. A billowing black cloud of smoke erupted from its smokestack, scattering ash and soot through the crisp morning air.

He took the last few yards quickly and bounded up the steps as the train departed, walking through a couple of cars before he found a seat to his liking. He plopped down and tossed his bag next to him.

He should have figured Sam would head up to Prairie Dell, though why he wanted to take the haul to such a dump baffled Riley. There was nothing to spend the money on and nowhere to go for fun. Maybe that's exactly why Sam decided to go to such a godforsaken piece of dirt. It would be the perfect place to lie low and let the excitement of the robbery die down. Sam also had a built-in safety net. Moira McShanahan would protect Sam from the fires of Hell itself, so fierce was her love for her only brother.

Riley shivered involuntarily. The thought of Moira and her eye patch gave him the creeps. Of course, better that than seeing the hole in her socket. No, he didn't like Moira at all and the feeling was mutual. He'd caught her staring at him several times when Sam took the gang to Prairie Dell once, years ago. Riley didn't trust her—and he could tell she sure didn't trust him. He was glad Sam never used the place again while Riley was a part of his crew.

He stared out the window as the train began to pick up speed, thinking about how he would spend all that money. Having it would make a huge difference. He could retire from being on the run. Gamble and whore all he wanted. Never have to lift a finger again.

All his life he'd been on the outside, looking in, even in the McShan/Webber partnership. The two outlaws called on him on occasion throughout the years when they needed an extra hand. He'd grown weary being on the fringe of things. He'd thought it through carefully and knew this was his one shot at the big time.

It helped that the bank had been unusually crowded. Confusion rang supreme as they attempted to escape after the robbery. Nothing went as planned. He would have liked to shoot that woman with the piercing shriek but was grateful that she added to the chaos. He'd thrown a quick upper-cut to Bill, their lookout, and knocked Bill from his horse as he'd mounted. Frank had to swerve to avoid trampling his brother, Bill. Riley shot the horse from under Frank to make certain nei-ther man followed. He figured with fewer men he'd get a bigger cut, which he richly deserved.

He hadn't counted on Pete seeing what happened, though. He'd thought Pete too far ahead but the son of a gun must have had hawk's eyes in him that day. They'd ridden hard for almost ten miles before Pete pulled up short and blocked Riley's way. The posse wasn't that far behind but Pete decided then and there to confront him all the same.

Nobody yelled at Riley Withers.

Pete got shot just south of his heart for his efforts. He was dead before he hit the ground. Sam had circled back and seen the confrontation. Sam shot Riley—and his horse—in the process. Of course, Sam had never been a great shot. He'd killed in his time but Riley suspected half of those dead were due to Lady Luck, while the other half Sam hadn't meant to kill at all.

Famous Sam grabbed the reins of Pete's horse, which held part of the plunder, and took off like a lightning bug being chased by a kid with a jar. Riley, sporting a bullet in his shoulder, fell back on foot and missed being found by the skin of his teeth.

Now, he was out for the money. All the money.

And revenge.

Shifting in his seat, he cracked his knuckles slowly as he thought of what he wanted to do to Sam McShan. And his daughter. That gal was a mighty sweet morsel. Maybe he'd have his way with her and make Sam watch.

Riley chuckled to himself. The man across the aisle looked at him questioningly. "What the blazes you looking at?" he barked.

The stranger hastily returned to his newspaper. The young man's hands trembled. Riley smiled at that, pleased at his ability to frighten a stranger. He liked people a little bit afraid of him.

He stretched his arm and grimaced at the tightness still in his shoulder. Luckily, Sam's bullet hadn't done much damage.

Riley was able to get fixed up and head out in record time. He racked his brain as to where Sam might go. He wished he'd thought of Prairie Dell but it had been years since he'd been there that one time. Sam had been pretty attached the last few years to hiding out in Texas and Arizona Territory till the heat wore off. That was why Riley hadn't imagined the outlaw heading anywhere else.

This was Sam's last haul, though. Riley made it his business to listen when people thought he wasn't around. He learned plenty that way. He'd perfected eavesdropping to a fine art and was proud of his hidden talent. He'd overheard a conversation between Sam and Pete two days before they pulled the job. Sam said he would call it a career after this and send for Jenny—if she still wanted to see him.

Riley slipped into Sam's saddlebags late that same night and found a few letters from the girl. It was obvious Sam's precious daughter had no idea what her daddy did for a living. Jenny did long to see him, though. That rang loud and clear. So when he didn't know where to look for Sam, Riley decided to look for Jenny instead. He took a train to Boston and waited her out. He knew Sam would send for her, especially since he had all that loot and no one to share it with.

She'd been too skittish on the way out. He tried to behave as a perfect gentleman and make her acquaintance but she was wary of him from the start. He'd aimed to throw her off by slipping off the stagecoach right after it left Apple Blossom. He'd learned all about her attempts to hire a guide to Nevada when hers turned up dead from a knife fight just before she'd arrived. Knowing she'd have nothing to do with him in that role, he didn't bother to volunteer. Once she headed for Nevada, he figured Sam had to be in Prairie Dell, so he didn't need to tail Jenny McShanahan anymore.

Let her and that cowboy go the overland route. Riley would admit he was lazy. He hated traveling across the empty prairie. Instead, he'd take the Southern Pacific to Yuma and head north by horseback from there. It would probably take about the same length of time and he'd be a whole lot more comfortable.

He settled back and began to daydream of the ways to spend his fortune.

❧

"WE'LL STOP AT FORT GRIFFIN. THERE'S NOT MUCH after that, least until we reach New Mexico Territory."

"Do you think I can telegram Dr. Randolph from there?"

Noah hooted. "You want to send a cable to that quack guidebook writer, Jenny?"

"No," she said primly. "I'm not personally acquainted with Mr. Mulholland. I am referring to Dr. Randolph. He is from The Thompson School. We are special friends."

He got a funny look on his face. "Just how friendly are you?"

"Dr. Randolph has been like a second father to me. I look upon his family as my own."

Noah adjusted his hat. "You'll be able to get word to him from the fort but I'm pretty sure you'll be sending him a letter. Last I was there, they still didn't have a telegraph."

They rode in silence for an hour until Fort Griffin came into sight on the horizon.

"It'll certainly be nice to see other—"

"Don't say that," he interrupted.

She was puzzled. "Say what?"

"That you're already bored with the pleasure of my company."

She sensed her cheeks begin to burn. In just a couple of days, she'd grown to enjoy Noah Webster's company immensely. He was knowledgeable about the area they traveled and pointed out all sorts of interesting things along the way. He knew so many stories, too, probably from his days on the cattle trails. Surprisingly, he'd been considerate, as well. She couldn't have asked for a more congenial traveling companion.

Moreover, the man was definitely easy on the eye. Her stomach gave another of those flutters as she looked into his clear blue eyes. She saw they held a teasing light in them. *Oh, Lord, guard my heart from this man with the princely looks.*

He smiled that lazy smile of his, the one that made the butterflies do a double-time march in her stomach.

"Bother," she said under her breath.

"Beg pardon?"

She looked at him in exasperation. "Never mind."

He laughed and spurred Star. They picked up their pace and soon reached the fort.

The military post bustled with activity from all directions. Noah called a greeting as he led them to a hitching post. He dismounted and came to assist her. His hands went firmly about her waist as he lifted her off Sassy. She thought he hesitated a bit too long before he released her. No, she refused to let her imagination run wild.

"I'll take care of the horses and pick up a few supplies we might need along the way. Check over there." He pointed to a clump of wooden buildings. "You'll find the post office. They might have a telegraph by now. If not, it'll be where you can post a letter to your Dr. Randolph."

"Thank you."

Jenny took her reticule and slipped it from her saddle horn to her wrist. She gave Sassy a love pat and headed in the direction Noah indicated. She was glad to be off her horse for the short time they would be at the fort. Her bottom remained sore but she knew she'd begun to get a feel for how to ride. Noah even complimented her on how she handled her horse. Sassy was a sweetheart and would have been a dream for any inexperienced rider but Jenny cherished his comment all the same. She was eager to fit into this new land. She hoped her father would be proud of her new riding skills.

As she made her way across the open area, Noah's words echoed in her mind. He'd tried to prepare her for what Fort Griffin was like.

"The worst of the worst," he'd said. "It's the last outpost of civilization before you hit nothing but desert."

Her trail guide had been more than correct. She passed buffalo hunters, their skins to be traded slung over donkeys that looked too thin to make it a step further. She couldn't decide which smelled worse—the donkeys or the hunters themselves. She skirted as far away from them as possible, only to run straight into a painted lady.

Jenny recognized her not by her paint, for this woman had none on her face, but by the hard look in her eye. It was the same she had seen in the women who had come into Dr. Randolph's clinic and her heart went out to them each time. The fact they had to sell a piece of themselves to put bread into their mouths—or those of their children—was too horrible to dwell upon.

"Watch where yer goin'!"

"I'm terribly sorry, ma'am," she apologized and hurried away.

She spotted the post office and entered quickly, glad to be out of the afternoon glare. As her eyes adjusted to the dim interior, the postmaster stepped from a back room and greeted her.

"Good afternoon, ma'am. What brings you through Fort Griffin? You need some writing paper or stamps? Have you stopped for supplies?"

She focused on the jovial character before her. He was the very image of Saint Nicholas, minus the red suit. His cheeks shined as polished apples and his eyes disappeared into slits as he smiled at her.

"Good afternoon, sir. I am looking to send a telegram to Boston."

"'Fraid a letter will have to suffice, ma'am. Fort Griffin is the end of the world, so to speak. The fact we get mail delivery at all is a minor miracle and not to be taken for granted."

"I see," she said, trying to hide her disappointment. "I suppose I will jot a brief note then." She glanced around and spied the high counter designed for that purpose.

"Let me get paper and pen for you. I'll be right back."

"Thank you."

She leaned against the counter, which was pushed against a wall, and glanced up at the notices that filled every inch of wall space. Her eyes traveled quickly over the many announcements and handbills. Then she spotted the poster.

Her father's face stared back at her.

Jenny gripped the counter for support. Surely, she was mistaken. It was a wanted poster for an outlaw. The list of crimes proved too numerous to read but she got the gist of it as her eyes skimmed its contents.

She looked back up at the face that stared out at her. He had aged since she'd last seen him but he was still a handsome man. The Irish mischief she remembered so plainly had been captured by the artist's sketch.

Her eyes went to the bold letters above the picture.

WANTED DEAD OR ALIVE: FAMOUS SAM MCSHAN, THE ROBIN HOOD OF THE WEST.

Jenny grew lightheaded as the room swirled violently. Darkness rushed up and enveloped her.

CHAPTER 11

The acrid scent of smelling salts filled her nostrils. Jenny sat up quickly and pushed them away from her nose.

"You all right, ma'am?"

She stared up at Saint Nicholas, no sign of joviality on his face. Around her were three other men, all dressed in army blues. She struggled to stand.

"No, ma'am, you just sit a spell," one young soldier told her. "We'll find your husband for you and things'll be just fine."

She opened her mouth to protest that she didn't have a husband and thought better of it. She didn't think it wise at this point to advertise that she was a single female traveling with a consumptive guide to the far reaches of Nevada.

Jenny took a deep breath. "Could you please find Mr. Noah Webster, sir? He's about six feet tall, with dark hair and the bluest of eyes." She wanted to add that he was the best-looking man in the state of Texas but she had already embarrassed herself enough by fainting. She didn't need to add to her misery.

The young soldier said, "I'll be back in a jiffy with your Mr. Webster, ma'am." He tipped his cap to her and hurried off.

"This is my first trip out West," she explained. "I guess I'm a little overwhelmed."

The men all nodded as if they knew of the delicate nature of females.

She tried to keep her tone casual. "My, what an awful lot of criminals pictured up there." She indicated the wanted posters covering the wall to her left.

"Yes, ma'am. You could say Texas is a real breeding ground for outlaws," a red-faced soldier told her. "We got your horse thieves and cattle rustlers and bank robbers, to boot. Everybody tries to make the most of his opportunities in Texas. Of course," he added apologetically, "some of those opportunities ain't quite legal."

She pointed to the center of the wall. "I noticed this Robin Hood of the West. I've never heard of him before."

All three men's eyes lit up. "You're talking 'bout Famous Sam, ma'am," said the Saint Nicholas look-alike. "Everyone from here to California knows about Sam's exploits."

"Sam's the most famous bank robber in the west," said the oldest of the group. "Why, he's stolen from banks and stagecoaches, from trains and from those on horseback. There's not a man out west ain't heard of Sam McShan."

"And generous, too," said the postmaster. "Gives away almost everything he takes. The widders and orphans and poor folk alike, they've all been recipients of Sam's charitable spirit. I'd bet my boots he's got the biggest heart in the whole west."

Bitterness mushroomed inside her. A generous heart with everyone—except his own daughter. Why had he turned to a life of crime and then given away the money from his robberies? Why had he written her time and again and told her the time wasn't right and he didn't have enough funds to support her?

Jenny thought of all the letters she had written, begging to come and live with him. That hardly could have been possible if he lived out of his saddlebags, going from one robbery to the next with a price on his head. She ached at the rejection of the past decade. True, he put her in a place that educated her and turned her into what polite society would term a lady. Her physical needs had been met—but her emotional needs were more numerous than the stars. She strained against the emptiness that rang through her, fighting the tears that threatened to spill.

She decided he wasn't worth crying over. She didn't know what he was worth. What puzzled her is why had he sent for her now, after all this time? Was it guilt? Or had he really loved her and wanted to keep her ignorant of the man he'd become?

"Has he ever killed anyone in these robbery attempts?"

The postmaster shrugged. "Well, there have been a few people who've gotten in his way. But Sam's not known for being a *murdering* thief."

"A thief with honor," she said hollowly.

All three men grinned. "You could say that, ma'am."

She stood. Her action surprised the trio. The oldest grasped her elbow to help support her. She shook it off.

"I'm fine now, gentlemen. I thank you for your patience with me. I need to be off." She straightened her skirt and took a few steps.

"What about your letter? Ain't you going to post it, ma'am?" asked the postmaster.

Jenny looked at him with hard eyes. "It doesn't matter now."

She stepped from the small building and stopped to get her bearings as the two men who'd ministered to her left, as well. The soldiers tipped their hats to her as they passed. She had a thought and decided to double back. She slipped inside the building again. The postmaster wasn't in sight.

She removed the poster of Sam from the display board and folded it in half, tucking it into her reticule and easing back out the door. She wasn't sure why she wanted it but it seemed important.

જી

N OAH HURRIED ALONG WITH THE YOUNG SOLDIER who had located him. The man babbled something about his wife fainting in the post office. He could understand the innocent mistake and didn't bother to correct it. All he knew was that something was wrong with Jenny.

They rounded the corner only to see Jenny herself coming their way. Noah knew immediately that something had happened in the short time they had been apart. Her face was set in stone. As he got closer, he saw those green eyes glittered darkly with some hidden knowledge.

Then he knew. How could he have been so blind? She'd gone into a post office, for God's sake. He would bet a penny to a pound that Sam's picture had been splashed all over. After all, he was Famous Sam McShan and he'd earned that moniker like no other outlaw in the West. Sam was practically a living legend in most folks' eyes. Even a hero to some.

He tried to remember the last poster he'd seen of Sam. From what he recalled, it wasn't good. There'd been a price on his head and a big one, at that. It must have shocked Jenny to her core to see her daddy larger than life amongst all those hardened criminals.

"Jenny? I—"

"Have you gotten everything you need, Mr. Webster? I'm anxious to be off."

He stared at her in disbelief. The woman had received the biggest blow of her young life and she acted as if nothing were out of the ordinary. Boy, she had grit.

If he ever thought about taking a wife, Jenny Mc-Shanahan would be the one. She had beauty and brains and was tough as a magnolia made from steel. He decided to let her run the show for now. She would tell him what she had learned in her own time.

"That's Noah, or have you forgotten?"

She gave him a cold smile. "Of course. Noah. Shall we move along?"

His mama hadn't raised any fools. With that prim schoolmistress voice in place, warm butter wouldn't melt in her mouth. He'd best leave it alone. For now.

They took their leave and rode without conversation. Not for lack of effort on his part, but every time he tried to get her to talk, she shut him down. He knew she was angry and yet she kept it bottled up tightly inside. If this were a small dose of her fury, Noah didn't ever want to be on the receiving end of her full wrath. This kind always, but always, exploded like a volcano in the end.

He had them stop a little earlier than usual and explained it away by saying he felt like rabbit for dinner. She'd learned quickly during the last couple of days and he left her going through the motions of making biscuits.

"Be sure to get the coffee on, Jenny. I'm going to need a strong cup when I get back."

She looked at him but he didn't know if she had heard him or not. Her eyes had a faraway look. It worried him.

Noah wasn't gone fifteen minutes. Jenny wished it had been fifteen hours. Her heart ached more than she had ever thought possible. It was a physical hurt that threatened to drag her down to the bowels of Hell. She had never been more miserable in her life. She hadn't cried. She didn't want to. She'd learned years ago that a crying jag didn't do a soul any good. It didn't solve anything. All you ended up with were red, puffy eyes and a lumpy throat—and the problem didn't go away. No, she refused to shed tears over Famous Sam McShan.

But how could he? How could her father have kept her on a string all these years? He hadn't been working toward any goal at all, other than acquiring money that didn't belong to him. So many lies for so many years. And for what? Why had he even bothered to send for her now? Surely an outlaw like Sam McShan wouldn't feel guilt.

Jenny swore that she would never trust a man again. If a girl couldn't trust her own papa, whom could she trust? She was ashamed to be related to him. Then it hit her—what if this bad blood ran through her veins? She shuddered and forced the thought away.

What she'd learned about her beloved father caused her to miss her dead mother even more. Jenny had lost Mama at such a young age. The truth was, she remembered very little about Suzannah. From the start, Jenny had been a daddy's girl. Samuel McShanahan dominated all her memories of childhood. She only had a vague notion of her mother, wrapped in shadows. She could barely picture Mama anymore and when she did, it was how her mother was at the end, thin and sickly. Jenny prayed that her mother's sweet nature would cancel out any evil that might run through her, due to her father's wickedness.

Noah's return bothered her. She knew she shouldn't be angry with him, but he was a man, and the only person around for miles. He had oodles of charm as Sam did, that easy, affable way about him. He'd probably broken a few hearts in his time and that made her all the madder at him. She stood, arms akimbo, on the defensive.

He sauntered up. "We'll have to settle for a prairie chicken. I'm hungry and it's the first thing that came along."

"I'm releasing you from our agreement, Mr. Webster."

He gazed at her steadily. "Noah."

"Noah," she echoed through gritted teeth. "Something has come up and I no longer have need of your services."

He shrugged. "If that's what you want, Jenny, it's fine by me." He pushed his hat back on his head. "We'll start back to Apple Blossom at first light."

"I won't be returning to Apple Blossom."

His eyebrows shot up. "Oh? Well, then, where are we headed?"

"*We* aren't headed anywhere. You may make your way to Arizona Territory as you originally intended."

"And you?" His eyes had gone as cold as a winter's day.

"I'm still going to Prairie Dell." Her chin went up a notch as she tossed out this challenge.

"The hell you are!" he roared. "You're crazy to think I would leave a defenseless tenderfoot of a woman alone on the prairie, much less let her think she could make it hundreds of miles thr—"

"Then escort me to the nearest town. You will be relieved of your duty to me then."

"No. I see things through. Unlike my daddy."

She immediately recognized the pain in the few words he spoke. She realized she hadn't been the only one disappointed by a parent. She wondered who Noah's father was and why Noah seemed so bitter. Jenny wished she knew him well enough to ask but Miss Thompson always drilled into her girls how polite society would never pursue such a personal conversation.

"I'm sorry, Noah." She softened her tone. She wanted to ease him down gently. "I have more problems now than I realized." She moved closer to the fire. As the sun set, the night grew chilly and the warmth of the blaze comforted her. She pulled her cloak tightly around her.

With her back to him, she continued. "I moved around so much when I was young. I didn't realize it then because my papa made it all seem like fun and games. It was a miserable existence, though. My mother must have been terribly unhappy but I don't remember her letting her feelings show."

She sighed. "Papa always had a new scheme to play out or an old friend to look up. He constantly promised something up ahead would make things better for us. But my mother grew ill and began to waste away." Jenny wrapped her arms around her. "She grew so painfully thin. We never had enough money, especially not for a doctor. I always felt so helpless. Hopeless.

"And then she died."

Noah placed a hand on her shoulder and gave her a gentle squeeze. A lump formed in her throat.

"Papa left me at The Thompson School right after that. He vowed we'd be together soon but one year turned into another. All his words became empty promises." A single tear slid down her cheek. "You don't know what lonely is until you've spent years with no one—no family, no friends. No one. I cried until I had no tears left in me. And then I never cried about it again."

She placed her hand atop his and pressed it in return before she stepped away. Just the physical contact with him made this harder to say. She had to put some distance between them.

Jenny turned and saw pity on his face. It almost did her in but she had to get through this. She had to be strong. For herself.

"I found out today that Papa is . . . an outlaw. He's Famous Sam McShan, the Robin Hood of the West." She swallowed hard, unable to go on.

"Jenny, you don't—"

"No. Let me finish. I already feel guilty enough as it is for dragging you out to the middle of nowhere. I don't want you involved in this anymore, Noah. You are too good a man to be caught up in this web of deceit. I'm tired of feeling helpless. I want to make a new start —for myself and with Papa. There must be some good in him if he's given away so much money. Surely, he can't be all bad. Maybe I could make the difference in his life."

But the thought that it had been done at her expense was almost too much to bear. She was unloved, unwanted, and the daughter of a wanted criminal. What would society think of her if they knew? All her hopes —of being reunited with her papa, of them sharing a home together, of one day finding a good man to marry and raise a family—were now dashed. Who would want to marry the daughter of a thief and murderer?

Jenny had never felt more alone.

A sob choked from her. She crumpled into a heap on the hard ground. Her weeping turned into harsh, guttural noises.

CHAPTER 12

The sound of Jenny's sobs broke Noah's heart. He knelt and scooped her in his arms.

"There, now. It's okay, honey. It'll be fine. You'll see," he murmured.

She buried her face against his shoulder. He sat on a stump near the fire and stroked her hair over and over. He whispered mostly nonsense to her, in gentle, soothing tones, trying to quiet her sobs.

Noah hated it when a woman cried. Yet if anyone had something to cry about, it was Jenny McShanahan. He hated Sam in that moment more than he'd ever thought possible. The outlaw abandoned this sweet woman when she was but a child and spun her dreams of future happiness. Now, those dreams had splintered into a thousand pieces. Sam needed to be punished.

"Jenny?"

She raised her tearstained face as she clutched his shoulders for support. He still held her on his lap, an arm about her waist. She bit her lower lip as it quivered uncontrollably. A fresh wave of tears cascaded down her cheeks.

"Damn him." Noah brushed his knuckles across her soft, wet cheek. "I'm so sorry, honey."

His hand slipped to the back of her neck and drew

her close to him. He needed to comfort her—and so he did it the only way he knew how.

He kissed her.

Her lips were softer than he'd imagined. He'd had trouble even looking at her the last few days because he had wanted to kiss her so badly. And now he was.

It was the sweetest kiss in his life. It made him want to protect her from everything bad. He wanted to keep Sam and the world at bay for a few minutes.

Instinctively, he deepened the kiss and felt her tentative response. He realized she had never been kissed before and the thought pleased him. He tightened his hold around her waist. She melted in his arms.

Noah wanted her. More than he ever wanted a woman he'd held. Gently, he coaxed her mouth open and pushed his tongue inside. He caught her hesitation and pulled back.

"Trust me," he whispered as his mouth came down again on hers. This time, she eagerly accepted him. It sent a warmth rushing through him.

The kiss turned from gentle to possessive. His hand went up to caress her face and then pushed into her upswept hair. The pins fell away. Honeyed curls cascaded about her shoulders. His fingers ran through the waves as he deepened the kiss and strove to make them as one, if only for a few moments.

He pulled away from her mouth and pressed his lips along her jaw to her ear. He nibbled lightly on her earlobe and was rewarded with her shiver of pleasure. Noah claimed her mouth again, a fierce tenderness racing through him. She made the most delicious sounds in the back of her throat.

His hand fell from her hair and went to fondle her breast when he stopped himself. *What on God's green earth was he doing?*

A man kisses a nice girl like this too much and it leads to an end of his freedom. If there was one thing he wasn't interested in, it was settling down. Passion be damned. He could find this kind of pleasure with any crib gal.

He abruptly broke the kiss and pushed Jenny from his lap. He stood up, his knees weak, but his resolve strong. Until he looked at her.

She was more tempting than any female he had ever laid eyes upon, and he'd seen his share of beautiful women. Her lips were swollen and full from their passion, her moss green eyes misty. The hair tumbling down her back gave her a wild look. This was no sexless schoolmarm. Instead, Jenny McShanahan was a tigress waiting to be awakened. He had just messed with fire. He needed to put it out before it raged out of his control.

"We can never do that again," Noah said flatly.

Jenny looked up at him in confusion. Damn, if he didn't want to sweep her up and do it all again. He dug down deep for his resolve, hoping he'd still find it there.

"I only wanted to comfort you. I never meant for things to go as far as they did." He paused and she looked as if she would speak. He didn't need any womanly reasoning now. Every time a woman got logical, it was a lost cause. A man never knew what hit him.

"You're a nice girl, Jenny. Real nice. I took advantage of you in a weak moment. It can't mean anything, though. You're as pretty a girl as I've ever seen. You'll probably kiss plenty of fellows before you settle down. But this is one man who's never going to get married. So don't go looking at me all moonstruck now because we spooned a little. Let's just forget it happened and continue on our way."

JENNY STILL FELT DIZZY FROM NOAH'S KISSES. IN fact, she compared it to Dr. Randolph's patients that had taken laudanum. Even as they awakened from a laudanum-induced sleep, they acted as if they moved underwater, their words and gestures slow and languid. She behaved the same way now. Her limbs were heavy. It made it difficult to focus on what Noah said. He had a stern look about him. She tried hard to listen to his words.

When she finally comprehended their meaning, they devastated her.

For a few stolen moments, she belonged. She had been safe. She was wanted. The kisses she'd shared with him had been beyond her understanding but it hadn't mattered. She needed him and he returned the feeling. In his arms was the security she had longed for her entire life.

She hadn't had time to conjure dreams of white, picket fences and children at their feet and he certainly didn't let her. Couldn't he have at least indulged her in that fantasy for a few minutes? This man awakened new feelings in her, a powerful wanting of something she barely grasped, and here he had already torn it down and shoved it aside.

Jenny recalled the note she had received. Its single line ran over and over in her thoughts.

Watch the man following you.

She regarded him closely. Noah Webster remained a mystery to her. His effortless charm and easygoing nature hid deeper waters, she was sure. She was suddenly suspicious of him. Weren't consumptives prone to lethargy and coughing fits? The few that came into the clinic were always short of breath. Noah hadn't displayed any of these symptoms though he said his disease had been caught in the early stages.

Despite her doubts, it was his words that hurt her almost as much as the knowledge her papa was a common thief and murderer who had passed up numerous opportunities to send for her.

Rejection ran through her again. She was unwanted and unloved. But she was strong. She would survive this—and whatever lay ahead.

In a calm, detached tone even a cold fish such as Miss Thompson would have found hard to voice, Jenny said, "It's already forgotten, Noah."

She leaned down to pour herself a cup of coffee. She let the bitter brew push away the thickness in her throat. With each swallow, she closed her heart to the world.

And Noah Webster.

⊙⊗⊙

NOAH STUCK TO HER LIKE A CHIGGER ON AN ANKLE. Jenny had tried to cut him loose after they reached a tiny dot of a town but he refused to say goodbye.

"I'm in this for the long haul, Jenny. You agreed to pay me a certain fee to escort you to Prairie Dell. I'm counting on that income, to be paid upon our arrival. I won't give away your secret," and he'd watched her eyes go a deeper green than he thought possible, "but I aim to finish what we started. Shake a stick at me if you see fit, but you're not about to turn me loose."

Instead, she'd simply given him the cold shoulder.

They had spent three days in silence now. It was about to eat Noah alive. He started more than his fair share of conversations but she froze him out each time with that teacher stare she'd mastered.

Now, they were into New Mexico, close to Fort Bascom, and he'd spent those three days in misery. With nothing to keep his mind off it, he couldn't help but dwell on their kiss.

He couldn't forget that kiss.

Noah had never been so affected by a plain kiss—though there had been nothing plain about it. He could look across at Jenny as she bounced along on that prissy

Sassy and taste her. When he helped her to dismount, he smelled the subtle scent of lavender that clung to her. His senses would reel. It took every ounce of concentration to prevent from locking lips right then and there.

And then there had been the nights. Normally, he fell asleep faster than a hundred men put together. The last couple of nights had been the longest in his life, though. He had to fight from tossing and turning. He didn't want Jenny to have a clue as to how restless he was. Especially when she lay within an arm's reach of him, next to the fire.

So, he lost sleep as he daydreamed about her. His heart would start to pound. His fingers would itch as he saw them run through that mass of curls again. His tongue tingled as he imagined it mating with hers. It became more than desire. He was afraid he'd go out of his head.

And the more Noah wanted her, the more she withdrew from him. He understood she had been dealt a harsh blow with the instant knowledge of Sam's true occupation. She needed time to think about it, process it, and come to an understanding about it. All he did was confuse her more. Eliminate him from the confusion and she might handle things better.

But how he ached for just one more pass at that lush mouth.

He knew it was incredibly foolish. They were both from bad blood. Bad blood would tell in the long run. Things never could work between them—even if he did ever think about settling down. They might put their best faces on for the world, but deep inside, they both hid their darkest secret. They had no future, especially one together.

"That's Fort Bascom," he told her as it appeared on the horizon. "We'll need to resupply ourselves."

It surprised him when she spoke. "I have a letter I'd like to post while we're there."

Noah had watched her write it last night by the light of the fire. She concentrated so hard, her brow wrinkled at times. The flame caught the golden highlights in her hair. He had to tamp down his desire to remove the pins and bury his face in it.

Instead, he settled against his saddle and closed his eyes. He pretended to sleep as he listened to the scratching she made on the page. He supposed it was to her doctor friend at that fancy school. He didn't know of anyone else she had to write. He wondered what she revealed in it.

He pointed her in the right direction as they entered the fort's gates and went to find the post's commander. The man welcomed him warmly.

"Good to meet you, Mr. Webster," said the colonel, after Noah introduced himself. "A Texas Ranger is always welcomed in New Mexico territory."

The man was in his late forties with eyes sharp as steel. Noah couldn't see much getting past him. "I'm hunting down a man named Sam McShan."

The colonel laughed heartily. "Ah, the Robin Hood of the West. Don't we all wish we could find Mr. McShan and collect on the sizable reward?"

"I'm not interested in the reward, sir. I'm after the man himself."

"Maybe you could donate the reward to a worthy cause, in Sam's honor, once you bring him in." The army officer smiled at his own wit. "*If* you bring him in, that is. McShan's been a slippery eel for a long time, Mr. Webster. I wish you luck in your endeavor."

"Any sight of him in these parts?"

"No, son. If he did come this way, I would've heard about it. Nothing gets by me. Absolutely nothing."

Noah nodded. "Just as I suspected, Colonel." He thanked the officer for his time and quickly purchased the few supplies he thought they would need during the remainder of their trip to Prairie Dell.

Jenny joined him and they left the confines of the post. They traveled another couple of hours before he called a halt to their progress.

"Let's make camp here for the night."

She shrugged and brought Sassy to a halt. Noah felt his temper rise. Three days with only one sentence from her was long enough.

He leaped from Star and strode toward her. Grabbing her around the waist, Noah yanked her from the saddle. Her eyes widened in surprise.

With his hands holding her firmly in place, he said, "Enough is enough, Jenny. You've punished me for my lack of respect toward you. I'm sorry for that. I'm sorry about your daddy, too, but you've got to get past that. Now, quit trying my patience. I'm no Job and never claimed to be." He softened his tone. "I wish you'd talk to me, is all. I've missed that. Us talking."

He gave her waist a little squeeze and dropped his hands because he didn't trust himself to touch her any longer. He stepped back to place some space between them. He adjusted his Stetson and waited on her, his hands balled into fists by his side.

She took a step toward him and placed a gloved hand on his forearm. A jolt passed through him at the contact. He knew she felt it, too, by the way those green eyes danced for a moment, but she ignored it.

"Forgive me, Noah. I've been out of sorts. I didn't mean to punish you for . . . for just being here." She took a cleansing breath. "I retreated into myself. I wanted to find an answer to my problems and I didn't need any distractions. Of any kind," she added.

Jenny gave him a weak smile. "I promise to be better company during the remainder of our journey." She removed her hand from his arm and held it out to him.

He took it and shook with her. He held her hand longer than called for but he was so glad she'd spoken to him again, he didn't care.

"It's a pretty cool night," he said cheerfully as he released her hand. "Better get a fire started. I could use some coffee."

"Me, too," she agreed.

They both busied themselves with the domestic tasks of setting up camp for the night. He was happy they lingered over coffee after supper. Things seemed right again between them. He still wanted to kiss her senseless but he'd happily take conversation with her instead.

She leaned back against her saddle. "The stars are beautiful tonight. You can never see them this clearly in Boston."

He looked up at the dark night sky. "I guess some people begin to take them for granted if they've been on the plains long enough."

"Not me." She stretched lazily. "I think I'll write in my journal for a while." She leaned over the saddle to reach inside the bag that contained her book as she continued to look at him.

"Noah, do you ever th—"

He sensed the snake right before it struck. Somehow the atmosphere changed, charged with evil. As he heard the familiar rattle sound, he dived to knock Jenny aside.

Noah felt sharp fangs sink into his calf.

CHAPTER 13

Jenny heard the rattler as Noah slammed into her. She knew immediately what the noise signaled. She landed face first on the dusty ground, her left cheek sliding across gravel in the hard soil. The pain stung instantly. Before she could react, a shot rang out in the desert quiet. She flipped over. Her eyes went to Noah.

He held a smoking pistol in his hand as he rolled away from the deadly snake. She stared at it in fascination. The light from the fire danced along its length. The patterns along the viper's back almost hypnotized her with their beauty.

"It's a Western diamondback," she said in wonder. "I recognize it from Mr. Mulholland's book." She gasped. "It's poisonous!"

"Don't touch it," he warned. "It can jab by reflex even after it's dead." He grimaced as he spoke.

"You're hurt." Her eyes flew to where he held his hand against his calf. "It bit you."

"Bring me my saddlebag," he ordered.

She retrieved it and brought it to where he sat. A fine sheen of sweat had broken out across his forehead.

"Tell me what to do."

"Nothing. I—"

"Tell me."

Jenny looked at him calmly. A peace descended upon her. She was now in her element. She had assisted Dr. Randolph in dozens of emergencies through years of working at his clinic. The physician teased her about how she grew old before her time. Still, he impressed upon her the need to refrain from panic in a time of crisis.

"You can fall apart all you want afterwards, Jenny girl," he had said, "but your patient needs you placid as a pond on a summer's afternoon if you're to do any good."

She took Dr. Randolph's words to heart. Sometimes after a particularly difficult experience, Jenny found her hands trembled as she washed up—but she always remained unruffled during whatever procedure took place.

As she gazed steadily at Noah now, she remained composed. She recognized the moment when he decided to trust her. She went to the pack horse and lifted out a pot from a side bag. She filled it with water and put it on to boil.

"I have a razor that will need to be sterilized," Noah told her. "We don't have time to cleanse it in water."

"I know. That's for later." She focused on him. "Mr. Mulholland said the diamondback's venom is quick-acting. Walk me through what to do. If we act quickly, we'll save you."

He gave her an admiring glance as she found his razor. "Hold the blade in the fire. Ten seconds should do it."

She did as told and came back to his side, handing him the razor. She then reached over and slipped his knife from his belt. She cut away the lower portion of his wool trousers and peeled the material away from the bite. She also pulled off his boot and tossed it aside before claiming the razor again.

"You'll need to make a small cut through both fang

marks. Go through both. It has to be lengthwise to my leg." He stretched out his legs but leaned on his elbows so he could watch her work.

Jenny knelt, concentrating as she made the slits. Noah flinched as the hot razor scorched his skin.

"Press the blood from the cuts."

She followed his directions and applied pressure to the wound. The blood spurted then oozed down his calf.

"Good. That's good," he praised her. "You didn't go all woozy at the sight of blood. I guess my quick little prayer helped." He tried to sit up.

"What are you doing?"

"I need to draw my leg close to suction out the venom. It's the—"

"—only way to keep the poison from circulating. I know." She bent to his calf.

"No!" He grabbed her chin and pushed her away. "I'll do it."

She shoved him back. He fell flat against the ground. She poked him the chest with her finger.

"I'm in charge here, Noah Daniel Webster. I know what I'm doing. I don't have any cuts in my mouth where the poison could leak. I also have a better angle at this than you do. Behave yourself."

She leaned close and cupped her mouth around the bite marks, sucking hard to draw the venom from him.

"That's good, honey. I can feel the pressure. You're doing it."

Periodically, she raised her head and spit to the side before she returned to the task at hand. After several minutes, she stopped and examined his leg again.

"Do you have any whiskey?"

"Check the side flap of my . . . saddlebag."

From his voice, she figured he was beginning to feel lightheaded. That meant the poison had begun to enter his bloodstream.

She poured whiskey over the wound and then pulled two clean handkerchiefs from her pocket. She tied them together before dipping them in hot water and making a compress from them.

"I wish I had some salt," she muttered.

He grunted. Tried to speak. No words formed.

"I can't move you, Noah. Any kind of movement or stimulant can speed up your heart and circulation. That would allow the poison to run through you—what's left of it." She brushed the hair from his forehead. "We'll make you as comfortable as we can. Rest now."

She watched him begin to drift in and out of consciousness. She wrapped him in blankets to help prevent shock from setting in.

And began the long wait.

Jenny worried about more than shock. She was afraid Noah would die. She kept trying to second-guess herself. Had she acted quickly enough? Had she let out enough blood? Did she remove most of the venom?

She spent the night by his side. Every few minutes she awakened him and forced some water down his throat. She hoped that would dilute any remaining poison and keep a fever away.

Fever came anyway. She knew it would. He kept up a constant chatter the entire night. She had been around patients who, when in the grips of fever, carried on entire conversations with her that they never remembered afterward. She hoped Noah wouldn't recall much about what he told her. He was a private man. She doubted he would be happy if he realized what he had rambled about during the night.

"He is the sorriest excuse for a parent that God every put on this planet."

"Who, Noah?" she asked, humoring him.

He snorted. "My daddy. That's who. The most selfish, egocentric, narcissistic man who walked the earth.

His dang partner's even worse. The two of them to-gether made Mama miserable."

"Uh-huh." She knew to indulge a patient on a tirade and continued to minister to him, bathing his face in cool water.

"He lied to her, you know. Thought he was getting a rich woman, but her daddy cut her off quicker'n a cat's sneeze when they eloped. Never had a thing to do with her—or us kids. That broke her heart, for sure."

He tossed about and Jenny tightened the blankets around him. Since the sun set, the night grew cold. She didn't want him taking a chill.

He raised his head, his blue eyes burning as he looked at her. "Moved us here. Moved us there. We never had a real place to call home. Hurt us all real bad. Wanted me to work with him. Hah! I left as soon as I could. Was fifteen when I hit the cattle drives. Sent money home to Mama." He shook his head. "She was a pretty woman once. She's a broken one now, in body and spirit."

Noah fell into a fitful sleep after that rant. She didn't think his father physically hurt his wife and chil-dren but his abuse ran along the same lines her own papa's had. It was an emotional kind of ill-treatment. She experienced a kinship with Noah at that moment.

He awoke again shortly, thrashing and pitching from side to side, tangled up in the folds of the blankets.

"I'm worthless. A feckless, nugatory, undeserving vagabond. Not any better than my daddy. Pete's a good-for-nothing and so am I."

She noticed how his vocabulary seemed to expand as the fever climbed. She wondered why he hid his book learning from others. With his guard down, though, his phraseology expanded considerably.

"You talking migratory? That's me and Pete. No-madic? Just show us a door and we're through it, lick-ety-split. Can't trust us 'cause we aren't trustworthy. I've done all I can to put distance between him and me and it's to no avail. I'll never be a better man. It's all his fault."

He continued to ramble through the night as she nursed him. At one point he went completely out of his head as he shivered and babbled. Most of that tirade she couldn't understand. She continued to bath his face and dribble water down his throat in her efforts to fight his fever.

It bothered her that he thought he was a worthless excuse for a man. Noah seemed to believe he was tainted with whatever wrongs his father had done and he'd spent his entire life trying to be a better man than Pete Webster. She could have told him he was a good man, better than most, despite her limited contact with his gender. She prayed she would have that chance.

Toward dawn, the fever began to break. Noah mumbled a few more comments that indicated he was very down on the practice of marriage. Not that he hadn't made that perfectly clear to her before, she thought wryly.

"Mama told me never get married. Said I wasn't to be a disappointment to any woman. I'm not. I will not disillusion or disenchant any female. Ever. I promise you that."

After that last diatribe, he fell into a restful sleep. No more blathering on. No writhing and twisting. His breathing slowed and became deep and regular. She touched her hand to his forehead and found it damp but cool.

By the time the sun had been up for a few hours, he awakened. Shaky, but she knew he was out of the woods.

"Jenny?" he rasped.

"Yes, Noah?" She ran the wet cloth across his forehead tenderly. Her feelings for this man were so mixed.

She tossed them into the back of her mind. She couldn't think about them now.

⚜

NOAH TOOK IN HER EXHAUSTION. DARK CIRCLES shadowed her eyes. Wisps of hair had come undone sometime during the night and fell in tendrils about her face, which had a tired, drawn look.

"You really stay composed in a crisis, Miss McShanahan. I might have to take you along on all my cross-country trips." He smiled weakly. "Now, let me get unraveled from all these blankets. We need to get on the road."

Jenny looked at him in amazement. "We aren't going anywhere. You almost died last night, Noah! Besides, as much as you jabbered away, you need to rest your mouth as much as your body." She shook her head. "Lord, I never heard someone talk as much nonsense as you did. Couldn't understand a word you said—and you said a lot of them."

She stood and grimaced, her hands going to her lower back. "I need to figure out how to rig some kind of covering for shade. It looks like today's going to be unseasonably warm." Her mouth set in her schoolmarm look. "We're staying right here."

He'd learned not to argue with her when that look occurred. Besides, he didn't have the strength to do anything but breathe and even that took more effort than he'd thought possible.

"How about you just drag my sorry carcass to that rock overhang?"

She looked to it and then him. She bent and grabbed an end of the blanket.

"I'm joshing you, Jenny," he protested. "Just get me out of this cocoon. I'll walk. It's not that far."

She helped unravel him. The cool air rushed against

his sweat-soaked clothes, causing him to shiver. He was grateful it wasn't as cold as it had been for the past week. He started to take a step and found he couldn't, instead leaning on her the thirty paces to the overhang.

"I guess I'm punier than I thought," he amended.

Noah dozed off and on for most of the day. Every time he opened his eyes, Jenny was there, pouring more water down him. He knew she hadn't slept in thirty-six hours and was dead on her feet.

"You can quit playing guard dog now," he told her as the sun began to set. "I think I'm going to make it."

She sighed. "I am pretty tired."

"Then stretch on out and saw some logs."

She scooted away from him and settled at the far edge of the open blanket. He suddenly seemed lonesome with her so far away.

"Jenny?"

"Hmm?" She didn't even open her eyes.

"Could you come back over here?"

She opened one eye and looked at him questioningly.

"I might need you," he said weakly. It was all he could think of on short notice.

"All right," she said testily and came closer to him.

"Come on, now." He motioned her to draw nearer. When she crawled within his reach, he grabbed her and hoisted her up next to him, slipping an arm around her shoulders.

"Noah, I—"

"It's okay. Just stay by me. That's all I ask."

He shut his eyes and held his breath. She was tense for a couple of minutes. Then her body began to relax. Her head dropped onto his chest. He heard her slow, even breathing.

Noah opened his eyes again. She was fast asleep. Despite the scrape on her cheek from when he'd pushed her from the snake's path, she had to be the most beautiful sight he had ever seen. She was warm and soft against his side. Having her next to him felt right.

Jenny was different from any woman he'd ever known. If he didn't know better, he'd think he was falling in love with her.

He laughed quietly to himself. Besides his mama and Elizabeth, he didn't even know any decent women. Mo and the sporting gals were all he had to compare Jenny to—and that wasn't right.

Anyway, what would a man like him know about love?

CHAPTER 14

"We'll leave on one condition."

Noah suppressed a grin. "And that would be?"

"That we take things at a leisurely pace."

He clucked his tongue. "You mean no buffalo hunting? No scalping Comanche? No—"

"You know what I mean, Noah." Jenny glared at him from under her bonnet, her green eyes turning a dark emerald. "Although I am anxious to reach Prairie Dell, I won't let my haste be at the expense of your health."

"Yes, ma'am."

He began to break camp. He doused the fire as she rolled up the blanket on which they had lain. He watched her movements from the corner of his eye. Lord Almighty, Jenny McShanahan was one fine woman.

She had slept through the night without stirring, all her womanly curves pressed against him. He, on the other hand, had not slept much at all. He had never been confused by a woman before but this little schoolmarm was about to do him in.

Noah saw Jenny in a new light since the snake incident. He respected her fortitude and character. He even questioned his quick judgment of her. Maybe she wasn't like Sam at all. Maybe she was more like her mama, who seemed to be a fine lady that had gotten mixed up with the wrong varmint. It was much like his own mama had done.

He finished loading the packhorse and turned to help her mount Sassy. She chattered away to the proud filly.

"Hey, sweet girl. Ready to ride today? We'll get to take it nice and slow. I hope you and Star enjoyed your little break yesterday."

She gave the horse a hug and bumped into Noah as she stepped back.

He caught her before she tumbled to the ground. "Wouldn't want you to sprawl face first."

She touched the raw place self-consciously. The skin on her cheek had begun to scab over. He took her wrist and pulled it away.

"Don't, honey. You look just fine." He placed his hands around her waist and tossed her into the saddle.

They rode a ways in silence before she asked, "Where will we pass through next?"

He tipped his hat back and looked out across the desert. "We'll cross the Pecos. Then head to Albuquerque. I'd like to go south around the mountains into Arizona Territory."

She nodded. "Mr. Mulholland says that Arizona has a natural beauty all its own. I can't wait to see mountains." She paused and apologized. "I've only seen pictures of them in books."

He whistled low. "You'll be in for a treat. It's like looking at the water from the ocean the first time. Only better."

"Are the mountains in New Mexico the only ones you've ever seen, Noah?"

"No."

He thought back to his childhood. Pete never wanted to stay in one place for long. Not that he was ever around much. Mama had them try farming and horse breeding but they'd never been able to meet with success, much less plant any roots. Noah had enjoyed fishing the most. He and Mark tried their hand at it for a short while in San Francisco and they both took to it faster than when they had learned to hunt. He envied his brother being about to stay in Frisco. He wondered what it would be like to remain in one place and make it home.

"I've seen mountains in California. Nevada, too. I heard Utah has some nice ones. Never made it that far. My friend, Patch, likes it up Wyoming way." He shook his head. "Too cold for me there, I think."

"I've always wanted to travel," she said in a pensive tone. "Many girls at The Thompson School traipsed up and down the eastern seaboard between terms. Some had even visited Europe. They used to tell the most marvelous stories."

"Travel's not all it's cracked up to be." He left it at that.

They passed a good-sized creek the next afternoon. The day had turned quite warm for early January, almost like the days of Indian summer in the Texas fall. Noah was used to a harsher wind this time of year but today was calm. No breeze stirred the air. He'd already shed his coat and rolled up the sleeves of his white, cotton shirt.

"Let's stop and water the horses. Maybe make camp here for the night." He looked out over the spot. "Seems too pretty a place not to sit a spell and enjoy it."

"Noah? Do you think . . . that is, would it be possible for me to . . . you know?"

He looked at her in bewilderment. "What?"

"Take a bath?" Her voice held a pleading tone, the one his sister always used when she wanted her way about something. The one to which he had no immunity.

"I suppose," he said, hoping he sounded as properly disgruntled as a man should.

"Oh, thank you!" she cried. "You don't know how I've been dying for a real bath."

"Now the water'll be plenty cold, I hope you know. Just because the day's turned mild as spring doesn't mean the chill's gone from the water."

She nodded enthusiastically. "I don't care. I'll pretend I'm a penguin who's gone astray but I've simply got to get in that water with a bar of soap."

He led them down close to the creek where a nice patch of flat land lay. "We'll make camp here. I promise you a hearty stew tonight, Miss McShanahan. We've got the time for it."

He flung a leg over Star's back and went to help Jenny dismount.

"Just think, Sassy. I'll be a new woman." She eyed her filly speculatively. "It wouldn't hurt if you went in, too."

"I think Sassy might draw the line at bathing with her mistress." Noah looked up at Jenny with his hands outstretched. She pursed her lips in that prissy teacher way of hers. He lifted her to the ground. She did have the tiniest waist.

"Betcha don't miss that corset one bit."

"Mr. Webster!" She pretended to look taken aback but she couldn't keep the laughter out of her voice. "A gentlemen doesn't discuss such topics as undergarments with a lady."

"I'm a simple cowpoke, ma'am." He cocked his hat back off his face. "Don't go in for those fancy-smancy gentleman ways."

She placed her hands on her hips. "I won't hear such talk, Noah Webster. Being a gentleman has to do with good manners and a heart in the right place. Why, Mr. Mulholland says that most all cowboys are gentlemen to their core. His guidebook even said that—"

"Give it a rest, Jenny. I don't need to hear about Mr. Know-It-All today."

She rolled her eyes at him. "Hmmph! Maybe I've misjudged you. Maybe you aren't a gentleman after all."

"Maybe I'm not." He flashed her a devilish grin. "Let's get unloaded. Then you can have that bath. Although as cold as the water will feel, I think you'll do an in and out." He ran his tongue along the inside of his cheek. "I think I'll give you under a minute."

"I accept your challenge. I'll venture to say that I will be in there longer than five minutes. Possibly ten— if I feel like it."

"You, my girl, have a smart mouth on you."

Her eyes sparkled as her reply.

Noah told her he would stand guard while she was indisposed. "Wouldn't want a stranger coming to steal your clothes," he quipped.

"As long as you keep your back turned, Mr. Webster, I'm sure we will be fine."

He plopped near the water and extended his hand to the creek beyond. "Be my guest, Miss McShanahan."

He heard a rustling of clothes as he drew his heels close. The thought of Jenny McShanahan naked just a few paces behind him had him in a cold sweat.

He sensed as she moved into the water since his back was to her. He closed his eyes and imagined her gliding slowly through the water.

"Oh. My."

He chuckled. He pulled his pocket watch from his vest. "Clock's on," he called out.

"No need for that," she responded but he heard the surprise in her voice. He imagined her unmarred flesh covered in goose bumps. He longed to yank her out of the water and wrap his arms around her. He would rub every inch of her smooth, alabaster skin until those goose bumps disappeared.

Her timid splashes grew bolder. He pictured her

rubbing a cake of soap into a fine lather and running her hands along her arms and shoulders. He couldn't help it. He was a man, after all. Wasn't it his mama who'd said that all men would burn in Hell? He stole a glance over his shoulder. If he were going to Hell, he might as well enjoy the ride there.

Jenny concentrated on her ministrations. Her cheeks were flushed a dewy pink. Her hair cascaded down her back. The sunlight caught shades of amber and gold as she turned in the water. Her back was a milky white and tapered into her waist. The rest was hidden from view.

He ached to see such perfection. No soiled dove ever looked as good to him as Jenny McShanahan did at this moment. He imagined his tongue running along that creamy back and beyond.

Noah whipped his head around. He could just hear what she'd say if she caught him snatching a look at her. He knew he'd be dressed down but good with her quick tongue and quicker temper. He grinned at the thought of Little Miss Hellcat on his case. Yes, deep waters ran through his traveling companion. He almost decided it might be worth getting caught just to get her riled up.

He sneaked one last glimpse. Her eyes were closed as she rinsed the soap from her hair, a contented look on her face. This woman was sheer perfection. He hungered for her in a way that he couldn't comprehend. They were from such different worlds. He didn't understand why he possessed this fierce attraction to her.

He had to keep in mind that he was after Sam. His mission had to be what drove him. Jenny would instantly hate his guts the minute Noah whipped out his handcuffs and arrested her papa on the spot. He couldn't afford any emotional entanglement with this woman. He had a job to do and his reputation as a Texas Ranger to maintain.

But, oh, did he ache right now.

"Brr." He heard her come closer to the bank through the water, sloshing mere yards behind him.

"I do believe I outlasted your one minute estimation of me, Noah." She snapped her drawers—or what he imagined were her drawers dancing in the breeze. "Although if I catch the pneumonia, it will be from my own stubbornness, I'm sure."

He stood without moving, willing himself to look straight ahead. "I'm sorry. I should've made a fire for you. Guess I took this guard duty a little too seriously."

❦

JENNY WATCHED NOAH LOPE OFF AND FELT A TUG AT her heart. All the strange feelings she had experienced the past few days bewildered her. She hadn't been able to get his kisses out of her mind, no matter how hard she tried. Then when he risked his life for her, she knew he would die because of her stupidity.

As she'd sucked the poison from his calf, she prayed over and over that he would live. Now here he was, merely days later, and he looked as if nothing terrible had happened to him at all. She supposed Mr. Mulholland was correct when he said that cowboys were a breed apart, tougher than the tumbleweeds that rolled across the plains. That certainly seemed to be true of Noah Daniel Webster.

She finished buttoning her dress and decided to unpack some of their supplies. Noah soon returned and had a fire going.

"Sit by the fire," he instructed. "It'll dry your hair faster."

She removed her comb from one of the saddle bags and began to work on the tangles. "I may be clean but I think I have a rat's nest in here," she joked.

He moved to her and took the comb from her hand.

"What—"

He crouched behind her and ran it through her hair. "I used to help get out my little sister's tangles all the time." He reached a knot and began patiently working on it.

"Noah, really, I can—"

"I know you can, honey. Just let me help." He sighed. "I sure miss Elizabeth. I taught her to ride and read, both when she was barely out of diapers." He chuckled. "She was a spitfire but she's a real sweetheart, too."

She heard the pride in his voice. "Where is she now?"

"She's married and homesteading out in Arizona Territory. She and Bill have a herd of ponies. Turned a profit for the first time last year."

"Will you live with them?"

"What do you mean?" He finished with the knot and she sensed him separate the strands.

"You said that because of your health you were moving to Arizona Territory. I wondered if you'd stay with family once you arrived."

He laughed. "No, though I'll sure go visit some. Elizabeth and Bill have two of the loudest boys that walk the earth. They can grate on my nerves but good after about twenty minutes. I guess I'm not much for little ones underfoot."

"Oh." Jenny wondered why his words caused such melancholy within her. She fought to concentrate on that feeling instead of on what he now did. His very nearness drove her to distraction, more than two small boys ever could.

Noah rested one hand on the crown of her head as he combed her hair in long, smooth strokes. Whenever he hit a rough spot, he worked patiently until the curl unsnarled, then he continued on. She found herself short of breath, her heartbeat erratic, her throat dry. More than anything, she wished he would kiss her again. She knew that must make her wanton. Noah had already explained he wasn't the marrying kind—and yet all she wanted to do was kiss him anyway.

"There." He handed her the comb over her shoulder.

She turned and gazed at him. "Thank you," she said, her voice small and tight.

He gave her a funny look and shook his head. "I think if a woman can brave it, so can I." He rose, his knees popping loudly. "I'm going to get me a bath, too, right after I find us a rabbit and get some stew going." He picked up his Winchester and tipped his hat to her as he left.

Good to his word, Noah returned with the said rabbit in hand. He skinned it, cut it into small pieces, and placed it in the pot with water. He took out his spice bag, as he called it, and shook a little of this and that into the pot, stirring it well.

"Why don't you sit and nurse this now while I get cleaned up?" He smiled at her. "And no looking, either. What's good for the goose is good for the gander."

Jenny nodded and watched him walk down to the creek. She moved so her back was to him. She had never seen a man fully naked before and had no intention to start now. She had seen parts of naked men at the clinic and none of those parts ever really appealed to her. Of course, those body parts usually had been shot or stabbed or diseased.

She had heard some of the whispers of the girls at The Thompson School as they gossiped about men and what went on between a woman and a man in the privacy of their bedroom. She knew it involved having sexual relations and that you had to take off your clothes to do it—whatever *it* was. Some of the girls said it hurt and some claimed it didn't. That was the extent of her knowledge.

Mostly, she knew the results. She thought of the

poor fallen women at Dr. Randolph's clinic, many no older than she, their bodies swollen with unwanted children they would leave at the doorsteps of an orphanage. Dr. Randolph worked with these pitiful women and tried to give them ways to prevent such happenings. Some listened to him; the majority didn't. Jenny never asked what information he shared with them. She didn't feel it was her place to know about such things.

A fly buzzed around her nose and she tried to swat it away. It was persistent, though, and she found herself snapping her head back and forth to avoid it from landing on her nose as she waved her hand wildly in front of her.

Then she caught sight of Noah. Her hand fell. So did her jaw. He was already in the water, which reached his waist. His shoulders were broad. Even from this distance, she could see the muscles that rippled across them and his bronzed back. His arms were sculpted as if an artist had hewn them from rock. She didn't know a man's bare arm could be so mesmerizing.

He rotated in the water and dipped his head, wetting his hair to wash it. He squeezed his eyes shut as he ran the cake through his dark, wavy hair. The lathered soap drizzled down his face to his imposing chest. It, too, was bronzed by the sun and covered in a mat of thick, dark hair that tapered into a thin line that disappeared into the water.

Jenny couldn't breathe. At all. She'd heard the expression of something taking your breath away and now she knew what it referred to—Noah Webster's muscular chest and flat belly. He was like something out of one of Miss Wilson's Greek art books—only better—because he was flesh and blood. She felt wicked staring at him but she couldn't bear to look away. She'd never thought of the word beautiful applying to a man but that adjective barely began to describe him.

Noah plunged his head under water to rinse his hair.

That broke the spell. She reached to stir the stew. Her mind wandered all over the place but every time it came back to Noah. She resolved to push all thoughts of this handsome cowboy from her mind. She must concentrate on reaching Prairie Dell and straightening out this woeful situation with Papa. Maybe he could give the money back and they could start fresh. But in her heart, she knew that was nothing more than a naïve fantasy.

What would she do or say to him once they arrived in Prairie Dell?

CHAPTER 15

Noah knew something was different the minute he stepped up to the fire. Jenny looked at him like a hungry wolf would a plump sheep, naked desire painted across her face. It took him aback. He didn't think nice girls had those kinds of urges. The painted gals had all led him to believe that nice girls married and simply tolerated their husband's ways in the bedroom. He'd even heard that after a few children, many husbands spent themselves with the crib girls and left their wives alone entirely.

Here was the most innocent girl he'd ever laid eyes on with a yearning on her face that was strictly for him. His manhood stirred, ready to leap to attention for her. And he wanted her. Badly. More than badly. He wanted her more than any man could ever have wanted a woman.

How had the Good Lord ever gotten him into such a mess?

Despite his fresh bath and clean shirt, Noah felt the trickle of sweat run down his back. He glanced up at the late afternoon sun, which had nothing to do with his problem. As his gaze fell, it landed smack dab on Jenny McShanahan. She made him nervous. He acted like some wet-behind-the-ears schoolboy around her, not the grown man he was. He probably started a sentence seventeen times, but as he looked up at her, he couldn't for the life of him remember where that sentence was supposed to head.

Instead, he'd said he needed to do some laundry. So did she. At least she took her things farther down the way. He gathered her upbringing did not include washing out her undergarments next to a man.

Noah heard her humming *The Irish Rover.* Funny how he'd gotten use to her humming and picked up the names and tunes of over a dozen songs since they'd been on the trail. He'd always thought of himself as tone deaf but he could recognize each melody after only a few bars.

He kept her in sight, though. All day long his neck had that tingling feeling it got when something wasn't right. Nothing had been out of the ordinary today but the bristling had showed up, all the same. He watched for a sign of anything unusual, any glimpse of men on horseback in the distance, but nothing appeared.

As they'd set out, he explained the rules of the road to her. She knew that those who camped on the prairie often shared a fire or a meal together if they came into contact. Jenny even began quoting that obnoxious city dandy again about life on the trail. Noah thought if he ever met the all-knowing Milton Mulholland, he would cram his *Guidebook to the American West* so far down the man's throat, it would never see the light of day again. Maybe then Jenny would quit citing the offensive moron at every turn.

He finished rinsing his last shirt and twisted the water from it, placing it flat on a nearby rock to dry and then walking back to their camp. The stew's savory aroma greeted him as he approached. His mouth watered instantly. He couldn't wait to fill his belly. Maybe that would fill other needs in him, as well.

Jenny returned minutes later. She hadn't been very talkative since they'd settled in for the rest of the day.

He found himself drawn to those lash-fringed eyes. The depths of her green orbs made him feel like a drunken sailor responding to a siren's call. He dropped his gaze but only saw her rosebud of a mouth. No, that wouldn't do at all. Noah fixed his hat low on his brow and focused on the gliding spoon as he ran it through the stew.

"That smells heavenly. I'd read about things such as rabbit stew and beef jerky. I never imagined myself eating them, though."

He glanced up at her sharply.

"Oh, but I really like your stew, Noah. You are an excellent cook."

Slightly mollified, he looked away—but not before catching her flirtatious smile. Didn't the girl know she played with fire?

He had to stop himself from pulling her up against him and kissing her senseless. He realized she didn't have any idea of what she did. He'd kissed her but good, and even though he let her know there could be nothing between them, she still must have thought about those kisses as much as he had.

This poor slip of a girl had never been kissed—probably never had any man show her attention—but she responded to him in that way women had. Jenny may not know what she did but she did it all the same. He didn't know whether he should say something to her or not. One more smoldering look might drive him over the edge.

"Are we going to eat that or are you going to stir the night away?" she teased.

"Get the bowls, Miss McShanahan. We'll dine at the top of the hour."

The sun was setting as they settled down with their steaming supper. Jenny had put biscuits on to accompany the stew and she'd done a nice job with them. Between the bread and the stew, he couldn't have asked for a better meal. Except every bite he took, he wished he tasted her instead. He knew he wore the hungry wolf look now because she was as skittish as a colt.

More long looks passed between them. Noah shoveled in bite after bite, not aware he ate, so intent was he on staring at the lovely creature before him. He was so wrapped up in Jenny that the whinny of a horse close by startled him. He lowered his bowl, on edge, angry that he hadn't heard anyone approach.

Star and Sassy both answered the other horse's greeting when two men rode up over the rise. Both sat the same horse, which looked as if it had seen better days. Noah winced at the weight the nag carried.

The taller man dismounted first. He had a long, string-bean build with shaggy hair and a frayed hat. He wore a hard look. Noah's mama would say the man had a lot of miles on him.

A shorter, stout man followed the first to the ground. He looked like a mean cuss that had spent many a night in a bar fight. Noah had no other reason than instinct to distrust these strangers. The way the taller one looked at Jenny, though, was all he needed to tell them to move on.

Jenny beat him to it by greeting them instead. "Welcome, gentlemen," she said brightly. "It's so nice to have some company. It can get awfully lonely out on the trail."

He saw the uncertainty in her eyes but she must think they should be hospitable to these men, as he had explained earlier.

"Why, hello to you, ma'am." The tall outsider's mouth smiled but Noah saw the smile didn't quite reach the stranger's eyes. "Could smell that stew the last three miles, I'd reckon."

"No, Ned, I betcha it was four." The other man moved closer to them. He swept off his hat, baring his bald head. "Homer Perkins, folks. This here's my brother Ned."

Ned nodded curtly. "Do you think you might spare us a bite or two?"

"We'd be happy to have you join us," Jenny replied.

At least the tension between them had been broken but it was traded for a new kind of stress. He didn't like these men. He knew his eyes and his body language told the pair that much.

They ignored Noah in favor of staring at Jenny. She scooped stew into the cups they pulled out. She chatted with them, playing the perfect hostess. He suppressed a smile at her eager hospitality.

His neck twittered again and began to itch. That was a really bad sign. The itching let him know the danger was real. His itch never steered him wrong.

"Mrs. Webster and I would be happy to let you fellas partake of our meal but we wouldn't want to hold you up in your travels."

He'd told Jenny when they set out that if they encountered anyone on the road, it would be better for her reputation if they thought her his wife. It was a pretense she argued about at first until he persuaded her to its logic. The men stationed at the first fort they passed had assumed that to be the case and he had been pleased that she didn't correct them.

Homer slurped his stew and wiped away the juice that dribbled down his chin with the back of his hand. "I know you might be wary of strangers, Mr. Webster, but we was hoping to share your fire tonight." He looked hopefully over to Jenny, who glanced tentatively at Noah.

"My wife is a little bashful around strangers, Mr. Perkins." Noah glared at Ned, who couldn't seem to take his hungry eyes off Jenny. "I'm sure you won't mind camping down a ways from us."

Homer laughed and looked to Jenny. "Oh, Miz Webster, we are as harmless as bedbugs. Maybe a little pesky, that's a fact, but we won't be causing you no trouble." He looked to his brother. "Will we, Ned?"

Ned Perkins snorted. "Wouldn't cause you no grief at all. What d'ya say, Miz Webster?"

Jenny bit her lower lip and turned to Noah again. He could tell the men had begun to frighten her by the look on her face. Still, she lifted her chin a notch. "What do you think, Noah?"

Maybe it would be better if he kept his eyes on these two. As dark as it got on the prairie, if they slept twenty yards away, he'd be hard pressed to see them.

"I think we'll be fine, gentlemen. Feel free to throw down your blankets over there."

He ignored the unspoken question in Jenny's eyes. "Let's settle our things this way, honey. We want the Perkins brothers to have plenty of room."

He busied himself in getting out their own blankets and motioned for Jenny to clear away the supper things. She took the dishes to the creek to rinse them. Noah watched both men as they stole furtive glances at her and then between themselves. No, he wouldn't be getting any sleep tonight.

She returned with the dishes and dried them with a dish towel. She placed them back in a saddlebag and secured it before she turned to him.

He rested his hands atop her shoulders. "Honeybunch, I think you got a bit of dirt on your cheek. Let's go get it cleaned up."

Jenny touched her face as Ned snickered. Noah took her hand firmly and pulled her along behind him. He led her back to the creek so he could speak to her alone.

"I don't like those men," she whispered. "Why did you ask them to stay?"

He leaned down and dipped his handkerchief in the water and brought it to her cheek. As he wiped away the imaginary dirt, he said, "Because I *don't* trust them, darlin'. I'd rather them be close by than sneaking up on us."

"Oh." She shivered and pulled her cloak more tightly around her. He touched his hands to her shoulders and rubbed them lightly up and down her arms to warm her.

"Don't worry, Mrs. Webster," he quipped. "I'll protect you." He brushed his lips against hers quickly for reassurance and then took her arm in his and led her back toward the fire.

As they reached it, she said, "It was nice meeting you, gentlemen, but we've had a full day. I think I will retire for the evening. Hope you like strong coffee and cold biscuits because that's all breakfast will be." She nodded to them and went to the blankets Noah spread out.

JENNY DIDN'T THINK IT WISE TO ARGUE WITH NOAH about sleeping so closely to each other. She didn't want these two men to know that she and Noah weren't husband and wife. In fact, she was grateful he would be so close to her with strangers in their camp.

She made her nest for the night and smiled up at him when Noah pulled an extra blanket over her. He bent to kiss her cheek. "It'll be cold tonight, honey. Sleep tight."

He certainly knew how to put on a show for strangers. First, he kissed her as he wiped at her cheek, and now this. She found it hard to sleep as she was worked up over his solicitous behavior. She listened for over an hour as Noah tried to draw the two men out in conversation but they didn't take any of his bait.

Despite her nerves, she fell into a fitful rest.

Jenny awoke sometime later. She wasn't sure how

long she'd slept. The fire burned low. She could feel the cold air on her face and knew the temperature had dropped considerably since her afternoon bath. Noah had said that it had been a freak day for the warmth they'd experienced. She supposed tomorrow would be cold again if tonight was any indication.

She was lying on her side, facing the fire. She could see two shapes on the other side and knew it to be their company.

She suddenly realized she rested against Noah, which explained why she was so toasty, despite her face being cold. He was pressed up against her, his arm wrapped firmly around her waist. She could feel the hard muscles of his chest against her back. He emanated an immense heat. Why, if he were always this hot, he had no need of a coat!

The twinge hit her and she knew why she'd awakened. She had forgotten to relieve herself before she turned in for the night. The strangers had made her so nervous, it slipped her mind. There was no way she could go back to sleep unless she took care of this pressing matter.

Gently, she picked up Noah's hand so as not to wake him. She lifted it from her and slipped out from under the blanket, gathering her cloak about her. The chilly night air caused her to shudder. Already, she longed to be back next to Noah's heat but nature called.

She tiptoed from the campsite and made her way over the rise. She wouldn't need two minutes of privacy before she was back under her blankets. She attended quickly to her business and started toward the glow of the fire in the distance.

An unexpected hand gripped her waist and yanked her back, hard. Another hand covered her mouth as cold fear nestled around her heart.

"You are a sight for sore eyes, Miz Webster," breathed someone on her neck, his arm pining her to him. "A sweet morsel like you shouldn't run around alone in the dark."

A rough hand worked its way under her cloak and grazed against her breasts as she squirmed.

"No corset?" the voice whispered. "You are a brazen one, Miz Webster. No wonder your husband's so taken with you."

The man pinched her nipple and twisted it. Jenny tried to scream behind the hand but it died in her throat. She began to struggle.

He clutched her more tightly, choking the breath from her. He twisted her head to the side, his hand still over her mouth, and nuzzled the back of her neck. The stiff whiskers rubbed into her delicate skin as his lips and tongue ran across it. She thought she was going to be sick.

His hand traveled from her breast, moving to the collar of her dress. He locked his fingers inside the neckline and jerked down, ripping the bodice to her waist. The cold pierced her skin, with only her shift now between her and her assailant. Fear paralyzed her but she knew she couldn't turn coward now. She did the first thing that came to her mind.

She pretended to faint.

CHAPTER 16

Noah feigned sleep as Ned got up and shuffled through a saddlebag. Through squinted eyes, he saw a match light in the dark. Moments later the smell of cheap tobacco drifted through the air. The cigarette floated along, away from the campfire, as Ned Perkins moved quietly in a northeast direction. Noah hoped a quick smoke was all the man desired.

He tried to relax again and enjoy being next to Jenny. Before he could take any pleasure in that, she gently raised his arm and scooted away from him. Where in tarnation did that woman think she was headed? He had enough to worry about with those Perkins boys around. He didn't need to traipse after her in the dark. Lord knew what would happen if he did.

He was already certifiably insane as it was. Lying next to her soft curves for the past hour drove him thus. He had done it for show to begin with but it was funny how it showed him a thing or two. While he'd lain close to her, his arm around her to demonstrate to their company what a happy, loving couple they were, he realized this was how he'd like to spend the rest of his nights. With Jenny in his arms. And that was plain foolish.

She was just a woman and he'd had plenty of women

in his time. Some homely, some pretty, some downright beautiful—but a woman was a woman. You were polite and treated her right but you used her for what she was good for and then left. He was a Ranger. He refused to settle down. Ever.

Especially with a woman who'd go slip away from him when two dangerous strangers were ten feet away, even if she had headed in a different direction than Ned. She didn't have a lick of sense in her pretty little head, a head filled with book knowledge and the sayings of that pathetic Milton Mulholland. No matter how much Noah desired her, it could never be. He couldn't get involved with a lady like Jenny McShanahan.

He eased the blanket away from him, ready to go drag her back from whatever she thought was so important. He'd wait until morning and their guests were miles down the road before he gave her a piece of his mind that would make her ears sore just from listening to it.

Noah paused, his senses honed to every shift in noise around the campfire. Through slitted eyes he watched Homer sit up and stare in his direction. He breathed steadily, allowing his chest to rise and fall in the rhythm of sleep, wondering what the bald man was up to. He must've played possum well because Homer was satisfied enough to rise silently and go to Noah's saddlebags. With the grace of the best of thieves, the man began to rifle through their contents.

Noah reached for his Walker Colt and rolled in a blurred motion to the same spot. In a matter of seconds, his cocked revolver rested behind Homer's ear.

"Feeling a bit nosy, Mr. Perkins?"

The older man stammered an excuse that Noah chose to ignore. Instead, he slammed the bunt of his gun into Homer's scalp. The big man grunted but didn't go down. He turned and threw a wild punch at Noah, who ducked it and tossed back an uppercut. Homer wobbled a bit and made an effort to try again but Noah drove a fist into his gut. The man doubled over and then lay still.

He took Homer's pistol and tucked it into his pants. If one brother was a thief, he could imagine what the other might be. Noah found Ned's gun under his blanket and pocketed it, as well. He quickly went through their gear and found no more weapons. He didn't want any available to the duo.

Jenny.

It hit him that she was still out there—and so was Ned Perkins. Noah ran up the short hill and looked across it. He spied both of them. They weren't more than fifteen feet from him. A blinding fury tore through him as he saw the man's hands on her. He drew his gun as Ned ripped open her dress front. Jenny went limp and he supposed she'd fainted.

With dead weight in his arms, Ned struggled to pull her around. As he did, Noah aimed and fired just as Jenny leaned forward and slammed her head back but good into Ned's face. Noah didn't know if the high-pitched scream was from the man's broken nose or bleeding shoulder.

The man dropped her. Holding his shoulder, he scampered away, only to run smack into Noah.

He grabbed Ned's shirtfront and growled, "Touch her again and the next bullet goes through your heart."

He shoved Ned from him. The man fell and hurriedly jumped back to his feet. He ran toward the glow of the campfire.

Noah didn't pursue him. Ned blubbered like a baby and didn't seem a threat at the moment. Instead, he went where his heart led him.

To Jenny.

She sat on the ground, hot tears spilling down her cheeks. He knelt and put his arms around her and kissed her briefly. It was a kiss of comfort, not passion, and it made her cry all the harder.

Jenny tugged at the fabric that hung in front of her, trying to cover herself. He pulled her cloak around her, as much to keep out the cold night air as to protect her modesty.

"Stay here, honey," he said gently and smoothed her hair. "I need to go check on those men."

She clung to his shoulders, her nails digging in. "Don't go," she whispered.

"I have to, darlin'. I'll be right back. I promise."

He looked at her wild eyes and trembling mouth and leaned in for another kiss. She clutched his shirt-front as he stroked her cheek a moment. He broke the kiss and headed back to the Perkins boys.

Ned had bound his shoulder by ripping a blanket into strips. Blood still flowed from his nose, which Noah noted with pride that Jenny had indeed broken. Ned shook Homer hard and his brother finally opened one eye.

He walked straight to the pair. Whipping out his badge, Noah said, "I'm a Texas Ranger, boys, and not in a mood to be messed with."

The men looked startled. Both inched away from him instinctively.

He fought to sound matter-of-fact, when he longed to crack their skulls open. It was a fight to keep his temper under control. He hoped his obvious rage was a warning as he spoke to the two scoundrels.

"I'm on special assignment and don't have time to deal with the sorry likes of you now. You can each take your canteen and then I want you to start walking in the direction I say, else I'll take you in. And I wouldn't be happy about that interruption." He glared at them. "Understood?"

Both men nodded. He went to their lone saddle bag and tossed out items till he came to their canteens. He threw them at Homer. "Fill 'em. Now. Be quick about it."

Homer rushed to the stream. All his swagger was a thing of the past. He completed his task and returned, handing one to his injured brother.

"It's time to hit the trail, boys." Noah's eyes burned with anger. "And if I ever see you again?" He paused. "I'll shoot first and guess where you want to be buried later."

He pointed and the men struck out in that direction, canteens hung over their shoulders. He didn't think they would come back for him without a gun between them but he wanted to be sure. He waited several minutes with his Winchester cocked, just in case.

The crack of thunder sounded throughout the quiet night. He glanced up. It was too dark to see any gathering clouds but he smelled the rain. It would hit soon. He needed to attend to Jenny.

He crossed the rise and saw her hunkered down, her head resting on her knees, her arms wrapped around them. At his approach, her head snapped up, then she relaxed. As he came to her, the first sprinkles hit his face.

"You want to pack up and move on?"

She nodded. He held out a hand. She took it and he pulled her to her feet. She dropped his hand and crossed her arms over her chest, holding the torn gown close to her.

"May I change clothes first?"

"Sure." He wanted to put an arm around her. He wanted to protect her from the ugliness of what had just happened. He didn't think Ned hurt her too badly, probably just bruised her with his rough handling. Still, he knew a big part of the hurt wasn't physical.

Noah followed her as she briskly returned to the camp. She paused at her saddlebags and removed a fresh dress, unrolled it, and shook out the wrinkles. A moment of panic hit her as she looked around.

"You can stay right with me. I'll turn around and you can change here. You don't have to go anywhere."

She nodded stiffly. Noah turned away and presented her with his back. He felt a few more drops of rain on his face as he waited.

"I'm finished," she said.

He turned around and saw how she tried hard to keep from giving into the tears that glistened in her eyes. He cursed the Perkins boys and wished he'd just shot both of them dead and been done with it.

Closing the gap between them in three strides, he placed his hands on her shoulders. She jerked away from him, fear on her face.

"It's all right, Jenny. You're safe." He wrapped her in a bear hug and held her close to his chest, feeling the tremors course through her. She tried to pull away again and he kept her against him.

"Noah," she said weakly, "you're scaring me."

He eased up on his grasp and looked at her. "Now, why in hell would I be the one scaring you? Dammit, woman, I'm trying to un-scare you."

She attempted a feeble smile but it failed to materialize. "It's your eyes, Noah. They've gone all . . . cold. They're like dark storm clouds." Her face puckered. One fat tear slid down her cheek. "You don't look like you."

"Ah, honey." He held her to him again, more gently this time. "Don't be alarmed. It's just my mad face. Believe me, I'm plenty mad right now."

They stood together a few moments until her shaking subsided. He hoped she could draw strength from him. He finally released her.

"I'm darn proud of you, Jenny. You thought fast and broke that buzzard's nose. I don't think you needed me at all. You were smart and protected yourself. Like a true western woman."

Her smile almost lit up the entire prairie.

"It's time to put on your poncho now. We're in for a soaking."

Hurrying to their saddlebags, Noah removed a slicker for each of them. He lifted it over her head and smoothed it out, then did the same for himself.

"What do you say we press ahead and see if we can find us some kind of shelter?"

She shrugged.

"I promise we'll still get some sleep. Besides, it's too dark to travel very far. Let's go."

He lit a kerosene lantern and doused the campfire before he saddled their horses as the rain began to pelt hard. He hesitated at the nag that had been left behind. He didn't think that the poor creature could make it very far. He was tempted to slap its behind and shoo it away.

"Noah, you can't leave him here."

He heard the ache in her voice. Without a word, he tied the animal to their packhorse and climbed on Star.

"I've tied our horses together but I want you to keep talking to me. I'll guide us with the lighted lantern but I don't want us to get separated. Understand?"

"I've never had anyone tell me to keep talking, Noah. Usually, the teachers at The Thompson School asked me to *stop* talking."

He shot her a grin over his shoulder. "That's my girl."

He led them slowly in the opposite direction from Homer and Ned Perkins. Flashes of lightning cut across the sky in bright, jagged lines, followed by thunderous booms that made the horses skittish. Jenny kept up a constant stream of conversation to which he paid no heed while he concentrated on Star's footing.

"I see something," he called out a few minutes later.

She fell silent, seemingly talked out. He glanced over his shoulder and smiled encouragingly. He knew she was running out of steam.

He got off Star and held the lantern high. "Don't move an inch, Miss McShanahan," he said lightly. "I will be joining you again momentarily."

He bowed formally and walked away from the horses to investigate. He scanned the rock formation for an overhang or some kind of opening in the rocks that might offer shelter. The driving rainstorm had picked up momentum. Between it and the sudden wind, he was chilled to the bone.

He finally spotted what he'd wished for and returned to Jenny. "We're in luck," he said as he eased her down from Sassy. "I've found a good-sized opening."

"A cave?"

"Not exactly, though I didn't go in far enough to explore that possibility."

Securing the horses, he grabbed a few of their bags and slung them over his shoulder. He hated to leave the animals out in this raging storm, but except for their new addition, they were hardy. The storm might spook them some but they could survive being out in the elements more so than Jenny.

Noah took her hand firmly in his. "Come on." He guided her with the help of the lantern until he spotted the entrance again.

"In here."

They took a few steps inside and he dropped the bags. "Sit here. I'll be back in a jiffy."

He returned with two blankets he had wrapped in oilcloth before they set out from Texas. This area wasn't known for rain at this time of year but he always liked to be prepared. He unwrapped the blankets and spread them on the ground.

"Don't think we'll able to have a fire just yet but we can wrap up and aim to get warm."

Noah heard Jenny's teeth rattle. Her jaw danced up and down despite her efforts to control it. She was deathly pale and soaked to the skin. Her hair had come undone from its single, long braid and was tangled around her face.

"Let's get you out of those clothes, honey."

Her eyebrows lifted a good two inches. "I'm *not* going to take off my clothes, Noah Webster. Despite the circumstances, I am a decent woman."

He gave her a stern look. "You're drenched. Either you'll take them off or I will. Your choice."

"Noah! That's not proper."

"Respectability is for places like Boston, Jenny. I'm trying to be practical here. You've got to get out of those wet clothes or you'll catch the pneumonia." He gazed at her steadily. "I signed on to be a trail guide, not a nursemaid. Now, what's it going to be?"

Jenny flung off her poncho in reply.

CHAPTER 17

Jenny shouldn't be cold, not when she was this angry. Who was this cowboy to boss her around? She clamped down on her jaw. She refused to allow any more chattering teeth. No more shivers or shakes or chills. She would remove her wet clothes, wrap up in a blanket, and be done with it. When her clothes dried, she'd put them back on as if she did this kind of thing every day.

She avoided looking at Noah by pointing her gaze toward the low overhang. Oh, that man rubbed her the wrong way.

Except when he rubbed her right.

She though back to how scared she'd been when Ned Perkins grabbed her in the dark. She'd caught his suggestive glances all night long. Why hadn't she exercised more prudence? She could have awakened Noah and explained her dilemma. Certainly, it would have been embarrassing, but he was a gentleman. It might have inconvenienced him some but he would have protected her all the same.

She removed her gown, then her single petticoat, and laid them out in the corner, along with her stockings and boots. She wished she could retrieve her one remaining dress but it was outside with most of their equipment. Noah had already been so kind to her tonight. She wouldn't dream of asking him to go out and look for it in this violent storm.

She couldn't stand the thought of being without her shift, though. It was damp, but not overly so. Truth be told, she'd rather take on a raging head cold tomorrow than be without her shift tonight.

She took one of the dry blankets he had provided and wrapped it snuggly about her. She backed against the solid wall and slid down, her knees tucked under her. She would lean against this wall for support. In her own little corner, she would try to forget the events of tonight.

"I'm finished," she told him.

Jenny closed her eyes. She could hear Noah going through the motions of undressing. She dared not peep. No matter how much pleasure she'd received in watching him bathe, she couldn't chance a glimpse up close. He would no doubt tease her unmercifully if he caught her at it.

But it was hard keeping her eyes shut. The pictures that ran through her mind at an astonishing pace all included Ned Perkins—his sly looks, his tall, skinny body, his soulless eyes. She bit the inside of her cheek, trying to focus on anything but the ugly stranger and his roaming hands.

The only time a man touched her before in an intimate way had been when Noah kissed her. She enjoyed his touch—had in fact craved it ever since—but now all she could feel were Ned's roving hands on her, clawing at her waist, his hand over her mouth, his lips against her nape. Even though they had come through a blinding rainstorm, Jenny felt dirty. She longed to sit in a scalding bath and scrub the places Ned pawed.

She didn't know if she'd ever feel clean again.

Her chilled body begged for warmth. She thought if she lay down and curled up, she might be warmer. It was hard to believe that only hours ago she'd enjoyed a bath in the deep creek. She tipped over onto her side and balled up as a kitten might, her head tucked low.

"Jenny?"

Noah's voice startled her. She opened her eyes. The lantern was turned so low, it barely flickered. He stood close by it, a blanket around him. It didn't cover his long legs. The muscled calves bespoke of his strength.

"I've opened the oilcloths. If we get on top of them, they'll give us some protection." His eyes pleaded with her. "Come on over, honey."

She loved the way he had slipped into calling her that. Somehow, it seemed so natural rolling off his tongue. She knew he didn't mean it as an endearment. She had read that many westerners used *honey* or *sweetie pie* as easily as a person's name. Still, when she heard it in that low, deep voice, it made her knees go weak.

"All right." Jenny got to her feet and moved to where Noah motioned. "Right here?" She hovered next to him.

"Yes." He took a deep breath. "I have my tinder but I doubt I could find a dry stick anywhere. We'll just have to hunker down and get through the rest of tonight as we are."

She settled herself on the ground and rolled onto her side, away from him.

"You should take off your shift, Jenny."

"I beg your pardon! How did you know I still had it on?" She glared at him over her shoulder and then snapped her head away.

"I could see a glimpse of it when you came over, is all. I'm just concerned about you catching cold."

"It is only slightly damp, Noah. I prefer to leave it on." She fell silent. The ground seemed harder than it had any night since they'd started out for Prairie Dell. She was still deathly cold. Her body began to shudder. She couldn't stop it. She did not want Noah Webster's sympathy. Or body heat.

"Put your feet on mine."

"What?"

"Your feet. Slip 'em on my legs. If your feet can warm up, maybe the rest of you will."

She was proud—but not too proud to pass up his offer. It was too tempting. She remembered how warm he'd been earlier, radiating heat. Even now she could feel that heat close to her. She inched her feet onto his legs.

"Jesus, Mary, and Joseph!" he cried. "They're blocks of ice."

He sat up and took her left foot in his large hands. He began to rub it briskly. "No wonder you've been shivering."

Noah continued to rub first one foot, then the other, until she knew she'd died and gone to heaven. Something about this man's hands did her in.

"Okay. Now rest 'em here. Good."

They lay in silence. As tired as she was, she didn't know if sleep would be possible. A fresh wave of tremors ran through her. Would she ever get warm?

Noah sidled up to her back. By now, she was too cold to protest. He slipped his arms around her and tucked her head under his chin. "You are a living glacier, Miss Shanahan. Let's try to fix that."

The man practically glowed like embers. Even through the blanket and her damp shift, she was soon warmed. But it wasn't enough. She wanted more. Much more.

"Noah?"

"Mmm?"

She turned her head toward him. "I forgot to say

thank you. I don't know what would have happened if you hadn't shown up when you did. That man—"

She broke off. All the awfulness she'd tried to block out resurfaced in a rush. She burst into fresh tears.

"Oh, honey, I'm sorry," his deep voice rumbled. "You're safe now." He tightened his hold on her. "Nothing happened." He continued to murmur soothing words as he brushed his lips against her hair. He turned her so she faced him. He kissed her brow and the tip of her nose. Somehow, he was kissing her mouth.

Oh, God, the sweetness of his mouth. Jenny had been drawn to it ever since the first kiss they had shared. His lips brushed against hers tenderly. Never had there been a more enticing mouth than Noah Daniel Webster's. It was even better than she remembered.

He ran his tongue from one corner of her mouth to the other, along her full, bottom lip and back again. His lips pressed against hers, gently at first, then more demanding. She sensed that he wanted to possess her, protect her, be a part of her always. She responded to him and opened her mouth.

He plunged in his tongue, mating with hers as if they were meant to be since Creation began. Each kiss bettered the one before it but all were hot, enticing, heady. He kissed her until she couldn't breathe, until her heart almost leaped from her chest.

Noah trailed kisses along her jaw and down her neck, circling her pulse point. He parted the blanket and moved lower, easing her shift from her shoulders. She knew she should stop him but she'd never experienced this kind of magic before.

He touched his tongue to her breast and she jumped, trying to pull away from him. He steadied her, silencing her alarm with another deep, drugging kiss that left her shaken to her core. His mouth gradually moved again to her breast. He rotated it around her nipple until the bud stood taut for him. He placed his mouth over her breast and suckled her as he kneaded the other one. The fire building within her threatened to rage out of control.

She lifted her hands and ran her fingers through his dark, wavy hair, pulling him closer. He moved to her other breast and repeated the ritual until the intense pleasure made her think she'd lost her mind.

"Oh, Noah," she called.

He lifted his head to smile at her, a smile she ventured had broken a thousand dance hall girls' hearts.

But tonight it was for her. Only her.

He kissed her mouth again. She didn't know for how long. As he kissed her, he ran his fingers through her hair, massaging her scalp with a delicious slowness. He pushed her shift lower, removing it, and placed his hands at her waist, encircling it with his long, lean fingers, stroking her stomach with his strong thumbs. He nuzzled her neck and all thoughts of Ned Perkins and his vile hands fled. Only Noah existed in her heart. Her mind. Her soul.

His hands moved to her hips, his thumbs continuing their circular motion as he rained kisses along her jaw. He slipped his hands lower, along her thighs, and then parted them slightly. The throbbing that she'd been aware of now demanded attention. She wanted—no, needed—his hand there.

And then it was. He cupped her gently, slowly stroking her, while he kissed her ear. She found it hard to concentrate on anything. So many different sensations at once confused her.

Noah gently pushed a finger inside Jenny. He heard the catch in her throat and felt the slight tremble as he caressed her. Her hips rose instinctively to meet each stroke. God, she was beautiful. He looked into her eyes, glazed with passion and desire, and was overwhelmed.

Every curve, her scent, the tousled hair—he was moved beyond words by this woman.

He kissed her hard, wanting her more desperately than he'd ever wanted any woman, anywhere, at any time.

She moaned softly as his fingers continued their motion. She was ready for him. He needed to be inside her —now—but he couldn't. As much as he wanted her, this was one woman he could never have, much less take. Jenny might think she wanted him but when she learned who he really was and what his mission meant, she'd be beyond betrayed.

He also knew a simple, unchangeable fact. He wasn't good enough for her. A girl like Jenny needed someone reliable, a man she could always count on, with a steady job and a past with no regrets. He could never be what she needed—or deserved.

Noah could picture her in front of a white house surrounded by a trim picket fence, children playing tag in the yard. Maybe a dog or two running around. A man would stop at the gate and study her for a moment as she hung a load of laundry out to dry. The man would admire her trim figure and her creamy skin, the curve of her breast as she reached and clipped the clothespin around the clean sheet. He would swallow hard and thank his lucky stars that she was all his, in every way.

The children would spot him and cry out, running to meet him—but he'd meet Jenny's eyes first. She would smile at him, her eyes flashing mischief, glad he was home again like clockwork, every night. He'd be a man she could love. A husband she could depend upon.

Not a wanderer. Not a man who'd be there only part of the time—and when he was there, longing to be somewhere else.

It wouldn't be Noah Daniel Webster.

Tears stung at the back of his eyes. A bittersweet feeling washed over him. Maybe he did have a little bit of good in him, for as much as he craved this woman, he'd do right by her. He wouldn't take her virginity. Let that privilege be for her future husband. The man who would be the steady rock she needed. The man who would love her for all time.

But Noah could pleasure her and enjoy that small part of her. Here. Now. Just for a little while. It would be a memory he could carry with him always, being the first to help her realize what desire was and a way pleasure could satisfy that desire.

He continued to make love to her with his fingers while he listened to her moans and gasps.

He kissed her again, so thoroughly that Jenny was confused. And all the while he kept that rhythm going. It was almost like a dance. Not that she'd ever danced before, but she imagined it was something like this. She found herself urging him on, breathless now, wanting each thrust of his fingers as they became faster, longer, harder. Suddenly, a shower of stars exploded from inside her.

Waves of pleasure ran through her over and over, like the tide coming in and out again. She wanted to tell him what happened but he still kissed her like there was no tomorrow. He rolled over, taking her with him, his arms strong and sure about her. She could hear his heart pounding wildly as her ear nestled on the soft matting of hair on his chest. She was sure her heart beat in time with his.

"Noah?"

"Mmm?"

She didn't know how to put into words what she wanted to say. "That was nice," she managed primly.

Noah looked at her and grinned. He kissed the tip of her nose. "It was right nice, honey."

He possessively tightened his hold on her, his hand rubbing her back. She yawned and snuggled closer to him, happy to be in his arms. She had never imagined being married to a cowboy but she was a western woman now. She couldn't wait for her papa to meet Noah. She was positive they'd get along famously.

Jenny fought to stay awake so she could enjoy lying in Noah's arms. She lasted twelve seconds.

Jenny awoke instantly to a scream that tore from her throat. Noah shook her and then held her close, his hands running through her tangled, golden curls.

"It's fine, darlin', you're with me. No one's here but us. Go back to sleep."

Sleep eluded them both. At first it was Ned Perkin's face that bothered her, then the quivers that ran through her body which kept her awake. Noah simply held her fast. His very nearness comforted her.

Gradually, though, she became more aware of that nearness. She realized he wasn't asleep either.

"Noah?"

"I'm here, Jenny." The low voice and gentle tone made her feel safer than she ever had.

"Kiss me, Noah."

"I am always pleased to oblige a lady." He pressed his lips against hers tenderly. As he moved away, she leaned up and caught him around the neck. She brought his lips down on hers again. He needed no further invitation. His mouth touched hers hungrily.

He feasted on her mouth, her earlobes, her neck, and her breasts. His unshaven face ran along her belly as he placed fervent kisses on it. His hands roamed over her shoulders and up and down her arms.

Finally, he stopped, his breath ragged in her ear. "Go to sleep, honey." He pulled her next to him so that her head rested on his chest. Soon, she heard his breathing slow and knew he'd finally fallen asleep.

What a world of discovery had gone on this night. She cuddled close to him, basking in happiness. The act of love had surprised her. She hadn't really known what to expect but Noah seemed talented at everything. It didn't really surprise her that he was an expert at this.

She wondered what it would be like, being married to a cowboy. She remembered he spoke of giving up his cowboying ways, due to his consumption. She wondered what they would do in order to make a living. She was an excellent seamstress and could always get work that way. Despite his dark, dangerous looks, Noah was very knowledgeable. She knew he was much smarter than he let on. Maybe he could take a position as a teacher. Because the territories were growing so fast, she was sure they could find a community that needed one. She'd watch over him and make sure that he didn't tax his health. Maybe they could even teach together, her taking on the younger pupils while he handled the older students.

Jenny would love to have a garden, too. She had never planted a vegetable or flower in her life but the idea appealed to her. She'd make curtains for the windows and slipcovers for the sofa. She sighed in contentment, ignoring the light snores that came from him. Well, no one was perfect. Not even Noah Daniel Webster.

Still, she needed to find Sam. Funny how she'd begun to think of him as Sam and not Papa. It had been that way ever since she saw his wanted poster in the post office. She was grateful Noah knew the circumstances and still accepted her anyway. Perhaps they could talk, man to man, and Noah could convince Sam to give up his outlaw ways. Maybe Sam could retire from his life of crime and come to live with them. If he chose not to, at least she still would have Noah in her life.

She laid her palm against his chest. He was a good man at heart, despite his gruff ways. She fell asleep wondering where they would be married.

Jenny awoke to the smell of freshly-brewed coffee. She stretched, one bare arm leaving the warmth of the blanket. She looked around for her shift and saw it folded neatly next to her. She smiled. Noah was so thoughtful. She couldn't ask for anyone sweeter. A tenderness rushed through her. She couldn't wait to have his babies.

She reached for the shift and pulled it over her head. She finger-combed her hair and groaned. It would take a lot of work to get her tresses untangled. She rose and slipped on her petticoat and dress. Both were almost dry to the touch. Only her stockings remained a bit damp.

As she stepped out from their shelter, she shielded her eyes against the sun. She wondered for a moment where her bonnet was. She would hate to have a flood of freckles spill across her nose and cheeks, in time for her wedding day.

"Good morning," she called to Noah. His back was to her as he poured coffee into a tin cup.

"Morning." He handed her the cup. She cradled it between her hands and dipped her head to smell the brew.

"Did you sleep well?" she asked sweetly. She figured it was the kind of question a wife would ask her husband. Or in this case, her future husband.

He shrugged. "Suppose so. Best I could under the circumstances."

She frowned. He was being awfully abrupt with her.

She had expected a little more . . . well, she didn't know what she'd expected but it wasn't this.

"Did you wake up on the wrong side of the cave, Noah?" she teased.

He looked up at her blankly from where he sat by the meager fire. "No."

"Noah!" she exclaimed, exasperated by his lack of conversation. "I expected—"

"Nothing to expect, Jenny. Let's get some grub in us and head on out. We've lost a little bit of time. I'd like to hit it hard for a few days."

"Pick up the pace? Is that all you can talk about this morning? Noah Webster, we had *relations* last night." She stamped her foot for emphasis. "The most beautiful thing that's ever happened to me passed between us last night—and all you want to do is hop on a horse and ride out?"

He shrugged. Again.

It infuriated her.

"When are we going to get married? Or where? Do you have any preferences?"

His face was unreadable, almost empty of emotion.

"Where is the man who protected me last night?" she demanded. "The man who loved me tenderly and completely. Where is he, Noah?" She heard the rising hysteria in her voice and tried to calm herself. She wrung her hands in front of her.

"We're not getting married."

Her jaw dropped. It seemed as if she were drowning. No words came out. Jenny couldn't think. Couldn't breathe.

"I do regret how far things went last night. I know you'll understand why we can never do that again. I—"

"We have been *intimate*, Noah. I'm not some fallen woman who dallies about. You're supposed to *marry* me!" Her outrage showed despite her shaking voice.

"We didn't even make love all the way, Jenny," he interjected. "No one need ever know what went on between us last night. Don't worry. No baby will come from what we did together."

His words confused her. *There was more to it?* And then a thought occurred to her. "You don't want me. Because of my father."

She caught the guilty flush that crossed his face. She saw it in his eyes. He thought her no good—because of Sam.

"You're wrong. I just can't marry you. I won't ruin your life."

"You've already ruined me," she said dully.

Jenny sank to the ground, her throat dry, her eyes hot and itchy. She wanted to cry but she was so stunned, no tears came. She had given everything a woman had to give to a man to Noah. At least she thought she had. Had he taken her virginity? She didn't really know. She did know she loved him. She thought he had felt the same about her.

Suddenly, his rejection poured through her. Why didn't he want her? Why did men constantly find her inadequate? Her papa abandoned her for a decade and found more satisfaction in a life of crime than in providing a home for his only child. Now the man she had come to trust—*to love*—also found her lacking. He'd discarded her faster than a used handkerchief. She wished she could crawl in a hole and die. How could she look at him after what they'd done together, much less continue on as if nothing had occurred?

She jerked when he put a hand on her shoulder. "Don't touch me," she said icily. She met his steady gaze. "If we weren't in the middle of the desert, I'd be through with you, Mr. Webster. As it is, I'm stuck with you. For now."

She rose and angrily dusted off her skirts. "Don't expect me to be a sparkling conversationalist for the remainder of this trip, sir. And when we reach Prairie

Dell, I want you gone from my sight." She raised her chin a notch and tossed out her coffee.

His eyes narrowed. "Have it your way, Miss Mc-Shanahan."

THE NEXT FEW DAYS WERE BY FAR THE MOST miserable Noah ever spent. Jenny scarcely spoke to him, only the bare minimum necessary to communicate.

He couldn't blame her. He knew she was hurt. Bewildered. Feeling betrayed. He, too, was in a state of shock. He could have kicked himself to Hell and beyond. He should have fought his attraction and been done with it.

Instead, he acted on it—not once, but twice—and they would be the sweetest memories he'd carry with him till his dying day. Jenny was more than a man could ever dream of having. She was passionate and intelligent, with a spirit within her that seemed to bring out the best in him.

But Noah couldn't see her saddled with him the rest of her life. He wasn't good enough for her. Oh, he might pretend to be as good as the next man but he knew he was tainted by Pete's bad blood. He owed it to himself and his sweet mama to fight against it. That's why he had to keep at Rangering. It was all he had to try and help him make a difference.

Besides, even if he wanted to settle down with Jenny McShanahan, she wouldn't have him. In less than a week his deception would play out. She would know he had used her to get to Sam so he could bring the outlaw to the authorities. She wouldn't have a blessed thing to do with Noah after that—and he wouldn't blame her.

No, he had to give up any fantasies of being with her. It was for her own good. He cared more for Jenny in this short time than he could have dreamed possible. It was best for her that he squash any feelings she had for him now. Better that she hate him.

And yet each time he looked at her, the memories of what passed between them threatened to bring him to his knees. The ache inside was physical, stronger than a bullet wound. His heart had broken in two. He knew when they reached Prairie Dell that it would shatter into a thousand pieces when she learned the real truth about him.

They reached their destination around ten in the morning. He told her the night before how close they were. Noah thought he might finally see some kind of emotion—excitement or happiness—but her face was void as a blank slate. She didn't even acknowledge that she'd heard him, though he knew she had.

She continued to spoon beans into her mouth, chewing slowly, no words passing between them. He wanted to shake her from her damn complacency but didn't trust himself to touch her. He longed to but he had to be strong now. For her. He couldn't have anything more to do with her.

Prairie Dell was much as he remembered it, which meant there wasn't much to it at all. It consisted of a few broken-down shacks, most empty now. No saloon, no church, no school—just what passed for a general store, though from the looks in the window, it didn't seemed well-stocked.

A lone geezer sat outside the store in a rickety chair. As they approached, he rose on unsteady feet and grinned at them. Most of his teeth were missing.

"Hey, there, folks. Welcome to Prairie Dell, a thriving town in the State of Nevada." He swept off his sweat-soaked hat in a courtly gesture. "Whereabouts are you from?" He eyed them up and down with curiosity.

"Do you have any crib girls around?" Noah asked.

The man cackled. "Hoo-ey, boy, you don't go wastin' time, do you?" He glanced at Jenny, who sat silent and straight in the saddle. "You'd be lookin' for Mo, I'd imagine. Go down this main thoroughfare, now, till you git to the end. Mo's the last on the left, son."

The old man loped back to his chair and sat, ready to watch the show unfold. He even waved congenially as they passed by him.

Noah sensed Jenny's eyes on him. He decided to answer her unspoken question. "I figure your daddy being who he is, if he is here, he would be with the local whore."

She stopped Sassy. "Then if that's the case, Mr. Webster, your services are no longer required."

Jenny reached into the reticule that hung on her saddle horn and pulled out an envelope, forcing it upon him.

"You may count it if you like but the agreed upon payment is all there," she said crisply, her teacher voice back in full force. "Thank you for your assistance."

She gave Sassy a slight nudge. Noah reached over and caught her reins. "Just wait a cotton-picking minute. I said I'd take you to your daddy. I am not going to ride off now. What if he's not in Prairie Dell?"

They held a staring contest for a good two minutes before she finally backed down, taking the envelope from him and placing it back inside her reticule.

"All right. You may come with me."

Noah gave her back the reins and they proceeded down the pitifully short street. They reached the end of the road. He threw a leg over Star and went to help her from her horse. As he lifted her down, he let her body slide against his. He had to feel her one last time, inhale her lavender scent, hold her the only way he knew how. They looked at each other a long moment before he released her. She stepped back, her eyes still on him. He saw the sparkle of tears in her moss green eyes.

Noah knew Jenny ached as much as he did. He mentally kicked himself for the umpteenth time for allowing things to have progressed as far as they had. More than anything, he wished he could sweep her into his arms and ride fast and far away to where nobody knew who they were.

Jenny broke the spell. She turned and lifted her reticule from the saddle horn and slipped the cord around her wrist. When she faced him again, she had full control of her emotions.

"Shall we?"

He nodded and walked her to the shack's ramshackle door. He raised his hand to knock but the door opened with his hand in mid-air.

Mo stood there. She was certainly older than when he'd last seen her almost half his life ago but he would know the warm smile anywhere.

"Hello, Noah," Mo said in her rich, husky voice. "It's been a long time."

He tried to warn her off of being too friendly as she spoke her greeting and saw the confusion on her face.

Jenny said, "You seem to know all the whores between here and Texas."

He looked at her sharply. He didn't even recognize her voice. It was so cold, so remote. He knew in that moment how deeply he'd hurt her.

"We're looking for an outlaw by the name of Sam McShan, Mo," he said formally. "We have reason to believe he is in Prairie Dell."

Mo shook her head. "He was here, honey, but Sam's dead. He died nigh on a week ago."

CHAPTER 19

Jenny gasped. "No," she moaned as she fell to her knees. A wail came from the pit of her soul, echoing throughout Prairie Dell. She collapsed into a heap. All the years gone by. All the miles she had come—only to have the ultimate disappointment. Through her flood of tears she experienced heartache, regret, sorrow, longing. She sobbed as if her very heart would break. She wished it would. She didn't want to live anymore.

First, Noah's betrayal. Now this. It was more than she could bear. She cried until no more tears came. Then all that was left was a vast emptiness, a hollow void in which she was certain was Hell.

The old whore had dropped to the ground next to her and put an arm about Jenny, rocking her to and fro. Jenny looked up at Noah.

"I'm sorry," he told her and walked over to the horses.

The woman he'd called Mo pulled her to her feet and steadied her. "I'm Moira McShanahan, dear. You must be Jenny. I've been expecting you. My, you've certainly got the McShanahan height." She glanced down at the ground. "The big feet, too." A hearty laugh passed her full lips.

When she remained speechless, Mo said, "I'm your aunt, Jenny."

Jenny gazed at the woman in disbelief. She also was tall, which was a McShanahan trait, but there the resemblance ended. Moira was stout, with long, faded red hair that fell to her waist. A black patch covered one eye, giving her the look of a pirate. Her face was rough and leathery, as if she'd spent many years out in the sun.

The large woman propelled Jenny through the doorway and closed it behind them. Her cabin was dilapidated but neat. Jenny saw a cot, two chairs and a table, and newspapers stacked in piles that practically reached the ceiling.

"I have a fondness for reading," her aunt shared, if in fact this were her aunt. "I collect newspapers from anyone passing through. Even turned a few tricks for some of 'em."

Jenny walked toward the stacks and glanced up. She turned to look at the woman behind her, speechless.

"Oh, you have the look of yer dear ma, that's fer sure."

She heard the lilt in the older woman's voice. "You're Irish."

"Aye, and proud of it, gal. County Cork, me and yer pa. Yer ma was from County Kerry. We were practically neighbors and didn't know it." She took a seat and motioned Jenny to do the same. "Call me Mo, dear. Everyone does. Moira is too fancy a name fer the likes o' me."

Jenny seated herself and stared at Mo in wonder. "You really *are* my aunt."

"And proud o' that, too, dear. Sammy sent me letters all the time 'bout you. He was proud o' you to the bone, all yer fancy schooling and ladylike ways."

Her chin went up. "Then why didn't he ever send for me?"

Mo sighed. "It's a long story. O' course, we got all

the time in the world for me to tell it." She settled back in her chair. "I think I'll start from the beginning. I don't know how much you actually know. What do you recall about your pa?"

Jenny shrugged. "Not much, really. I remember his big, booming voice and the sandy hair that always fell across his eyes. He was forever pushing it back off his face."

"Well, he lost a lot of it. Mostly after yer ma died."

She tried to recollect the sketch of Sam on the wanted poster but already it was fuzzy in her mind. She would have to look at it when she was alone. The poster had remained stuffed inside her reticule since she and Noah had left Fort Griffin.

Jenny turned to Mo, wondering why Sam never told her she had an aunt. Probably because she would have clamored to come and live with Mo instead of being stuck at The Thompson School all those years. Mo didn't look much like Sam but the Irish in her voice seemed familiar and comforting.

"I remember that he laughed a lot," she continued. "He would come home and sweep Mama off her feet and twirl her around like she was a rag doll. Then he'd pick me up and do the same." Her lips trembled at the sweet memory.

"We didn't stay in one place for very long. We constantly moved around. As time passed, Mama got sicker. Papa would be gone more and more." She looked Mo directly in her one, good eye. "There was never enough money for food or medicine. He made a game of everything but I realize now how bad things must have been."

Mo patted her hand. "Go on, love."

"The night Mama died she coughed and coughed. She couldn't stop coughing. Her fever went sky high. I tried to soak a cloth in water and keep it on her forehead. She kept thrashing and throwing it off. She mumbled a lot. I couldn't understand much of what she said."

She hurt at the memory she had suppressed for so long. "When Mama died, I didn't want to let go of her hand. I thought if I kept holding on, she would be all right." A sob escaped her lips. Mo handed her a handkerchief and Jenny wiped at her eyes.

"When Papa finally came home, it was late. After midnight. He had a merriness in his step that had been missing for a long time, but when he saw Mama . . ." Her voice faded away. She cleared her throat and continued. "When he saw Mama, he broke down and cried like a baby."

"And then he put you in that school?"

She nodded. "He had a fine dress made for Mama, much nicer than anything she'd ever worn. I remember how smooth the casket was as I ran my hand along the wood. Then he took me to The Thompson School. It was located outside Boston. He left me there. I never saw him again."

She blew her nose. It seemed she had cried more tears in the last few weeks than she had in ten years. Her body felt depleted and tired. She decided then to shed no more tears for Sam.

Or Noah.

"I think I'll put on some coffee for us, sweetie." Mo busied herself for a few minutes while Jenny composed herself.

"Let me tell you about yer pa." Mo brought her chair close to Jenny's and wrapped her large-boned hands around Jenny's smaller ones.

"We came from County Cork. I think I already told you that. We left Ireland after the potato blight of forty-five. I don't know how Da scraped enough together for passage to America but he did. We got here in forty-six. Sammy was fifteen. I was a bit younger by less than two years."

Mo paused and gazed into the distance as if she saw them at that age. "Our parents were weak. Too weak from the blight and the starvation. They'd always given us whatever food they had. They were too puny to make it. They died on the voyage over and we buried them at sea." Mo wiped away her own tears on her sleeve. "Funny, it happened so long ago. Yet I can still see them like it was yesterday."

"Did you love them very much?"

"O' course I did. Love was about all we had in Ireland. Wasn't much of anythin' else. Still, Sammy and I had each other. He was always one given to gettin' into scrapes. I hadn't a brain in my head and followed his lead.

"We traveled far and wide, that we did. He hated the cities. He missed the open fields of Ireland. That's why we headed out west first chance we got. Gamblin', wheelin' and dealin', thievin'—whatever it took to get by—we did it. And we were good, too, if'n I say so myself. We became quite a duo back in those days. A right good team, we were."

Mo paused and looked at Jenny. "I was pretty back then, Jenny dear. Not as pretty as you, but I had gorgeous red hair and smooth skin and the bluest eyes you done seen this side of the ocean. It helped us in many a situation, that it did."

Jenny stared in fascination at Mo. It was hard to imagine her aunt ever being pretty. Her weathered face was lined with wrinkles and her hair was dull and lifeless. Mo did have a kind smile, though.

"Well, I'm rough as they come now. McShanahan women were always tall and feisty."

"I hate being taller than most men."

"As long as you don't let yourself go, you'll be fine, love. Yer young and pretty and thin as a rail. Just don't go eating yerself into something like me."

Jenny wanted to protest that she wasn't pretty. Her

feet were too big, her breasts too small, and her smile too wide. She didn't have to worry about the last one, at least. Smiling figured to be absolutely last on the list of things she planned to do.

"Go on, Mo," she encouraged.

Her aunt sat back in her chair. "We weren't doing too badly, I suppose. We made enough to eat well and dress nicely. The people we scammed were usually those who wouldn't miss a little extra anyway. At least that's how Sammy justified it to me. I even turned a few tricks on the side."

Mo paused, shaking a finger in warning. "And don't go judgin' me for it, missy. I provided a needed service to a few lonely men. For the most part, they treated me right nice, too. Except one."

"Is that how you lost your eye?"

"Hmmph." Mo adjusted her patch slightly. "I didn't lose anything. It was taken from me. I don't want to sully yer ears with the details. Let's just put it down to a minor disagreement that turned into a major brawl." She grinned triumphantly. "He looked the worse for wear than I did when it finished, I'll tell you that and wouldn't be braggin' if I did."

Jenny was amazed. In the matter of two weeks she had learned her father was a notorious outlaw and her aunt a scheming, one-eyed prostitute. What would The Thompson School think of her now? She stifled a giggle and nodded for her aunt to continue.

"Well, I decided to stay here in Prairie Dell, where it all happened. I knew no one would mess with me, seein' as to how things turned out. For the most part, I have a good life here. I've made friends. I have my privacy. And I have all the time in the world to read."

Mo leaned back in her chair. "Poor Sammy, though, was another kettle o' fish."

Jenny sat up expectantly. As interesting as Mo's life appeared, Jenny wanted to hear more about Sam.

"Sammy decided he was goin' to go straight. I guess what happened to me left him pretty shook up. He went back east to find a job and become a decent man. He met Suzannah there. Yer da was twenty-four and yer ma only sixteen. She wound up expectin' you. Sammy had lost his heart to her and wouldn't leave her, so they married, despite the disapproval of her parents.

"He tried his best to go the respectable route but all those efforts never panned out. Sammy couldn't hold a job and he didn't feel he was good enough for either of you. He wanted to give his gals the world and all he succeeded in doin' was drivin' poor Suzannah to an early grave."

A wave of sadness washed over Jenny. How hard it must have been for Sam to keep failing the two people he loved. She wished he were here so she could tell him that she loved him, no matter who he was or what he had done.

"The night she died, Sammy done pulled off a robbery of a house he told me he'd passed a dozen times. He hadn't committed one act of wrong since he'd married Suzannah but he was desperate to help her. He netted a nice stash of jewels."

Mo pointed a finger at her. "That's how yer ma could have a nice funeral and yer pa could put you at that fancy boardin' school. But he had to hightail it outta there so he wouldn't get caught by the law.

"He came visitin' me right afterward. Said he'd missed the wide-open spaces of the west. He admitted he'd also missed his life of wanderlust and crime. Livin' by his wits. Flyin' by the seat o' his pants. He fell in with Pete Webber not too long after that. Pete had just lost his partner and Sammy always worked better with someone. They were together, off and on, for years. Until Pete got himself killed a few months back."

Mo stood and shuffled around the tiny room. "They were a great team, honey. Famous Sam McShan and

Pistol Pete Webber. Sammy gave away most of the loot he stole. I think it made him feel better about himself."

Mo crossed her arms. "He always wanted to send for you but he didn't want you exposed to his way of life. He knew how happy you were at that nice school. He didn't have much to offer you in the way of stability. And if'n he did ever try and settle down, he wanted a nice place for the two of you, the best for you, since he never could get it for yer ma. He always did want to do right by you, Jenny."

"Oh, Mo." She stood and fell into her aunt's arms. "I was miserable at school. I told him how nice it was and how I liked it because that's what I thought he wanted to hear. More than anything, I wanted to be with him. I never thought he wanted me, though."

Mo hugged her tightly. "Sure he did, hon, but he didn't know how to go about it." Mo pulled away and held out her hands. "But look at you, how fine you've turned out. Sammy' would be mighty proud of you. Mighty proud."

Her aunt went to a corner and knelt beside a battered, wooden chest. She opened it and pulled out a box. She brought the box to the table.

"Sammy left a few things for you. He wanted to meet you in Texas but he learned he was dyin' o' the cancer and the law was closin' in on him. He came here to Prairie Dell, where he'd always felt safe."

Mo brushed Jenny's cheek with her rough, callused hand. "He wanted to spend his last days here. With you. He just couldn't hold on, though."

Jenny reached for the box. Carefully, she opened the lid and pulled out the few items, one at a time. She found a silver locket with fine filigree, so delicate and intricate. Inside was a lock of hair. She held it up to Mo.

"That's yer ma's necklace and a lock o' yer baby hair."

She nodded and looked down, too choked up to respond. Next, she pulled out a picture of her family she had never seen before. She couldn't have been more than three years old. Sam was lean and handsome, her mother breathtakingly beautiful. Until seeing this, Jenny had only remembered the thin, sallow, sickly woman. This reminded her of who her mother really had been.

"She's stunning," she whispered.

"You favor her quite a bit."

Jenny shook her head. "No, I don't look anything like this." She touched her fingertips to her mother's face, as if she could feel her in the flesh. Her eyes met Mo's. "But I thank you for the kind compliment all the same."

Putting down the framed photograph, she reached into the box again. This time she brought out a battered copy of Poe. She opened the slim volume and fanned through the pages. *To Helen. Romance. Lenore.* The names jumped out at her. The book of poems was well-worn.

"Irishmen love their poetry," Mo told her. "Sammy was no different. He felt an affinity with Mr. Poe, he said."

So had she. She always related somehow to the sorrow and melancholy that ran through all of Poe's poetry. It was poignant that she and her father shared this love though they were miles apart.

The last item in the box was folded, a hand-drawn map. Or at least half of one. She recognized the parchment paper and familiar black scrawl. Sam had entrusted her with the other half. She checked daily since she received it to be sure she still had it. She hadn't understood its significance, as it seemed to be in some sort of code, but Sam wrote to her that it was very important she keep it safe and bring it with her when she met up with him in Texas.

Puzzled, she turned to Mo. "Did Sam give you any

instructions as far as interpreting this? Or say anything about this map at all?"

"No. It's the first I've seen of it. When he arrived, he was beaten down. He was dying and knew it. He told me he'd just pulled a big job, the biggest he'd ever done, and that it was time he retired. He mentioned he'd hidden something before he came to me, then he collapsed. I nursed him for several days before he died." Mo's face puckered. "He did tell me that you were on yer way here and to give you the box. It was his last wish."

Her sorrow ran deep. If only she could have left Boston earlier. If only she had found her way to Prairie Dell sooner.

"The letter!"

Mo flew across the tiny room and reached under the cot. She pulled out an envelope and handed it to Jenny.

"It's not in his hand, I'm sorry to say. But he told me what to write and I recorded his every word. He knew he wouldn't live to see you but he wanted you to have this."

Mo went to the door. "I'll give you some time to read it." She opened the door and walked outside, closing it quietly behind her.

Jenny braced herself and opened the letter.

CHAPTER 20

My dear sweetest Jenny,

How very sorry I am that you will be reading this and not be in my arms, my darling child. I am dying of the cancer inside my body. Mo knew the moment I walked through her door. You can't pull any wool over her eyes, as you will soon learn.

If I had my life to live over again, I would change things, Jenny dearest. I would be a better husband to Suzannah, a better father to you, and simply a better man. But I can't do that. I can hope to make some amends for the past, though.

Know that I loved you and your mother. I wasn't a good enough man to deserve either of you—but I did carry that love in my heart till the end. I left you safely in polite society and though I have hungered for your presence every day we were apart, I have never regretted that decision. You have been well-educated at The Thompson School and it seems to me your Dr. Randolph was a fine substitute for this sorry excuse of a parent.

I thought to assuage my lack of decency by giving much of what I took to the poor, the downtrodden, and needy. No more of that now, I'm afraid. When I finally took it in my head that I could selfishly no longer live without you, I decided to pull one last score that would be enough to live comfortably with you. I am smart—not book smart—but in my own way, and I proved successful beyond my wildest dreams with this final job.

Unfortunately, by the time I sent for you, I learned I was dying. I had felt poorly for some time and a physician confirmed my worst fears. It was too late to reach you by then, as you were already on your way to Texas, and I selfishly wanted to see you one last time. Now, it looks as if I will be cheated out of even that.

Be good, Jenny, my love. Know I always loved you and your mother more than life itself. Say a quick prayer for old Sam McShan and please take care of Mo. Give her some of the money. Be happy. Find yourself a good man, one with honor and courage, one who will love and respect you all the days of your life.

You are a smart girl, Jenny. You'll figure out the rhyme and reason of things. The secret is in the map. Learn from it and guard it well. It is your key to security and all I can give now.

I love you, dear heart.

Your loving papa,

Samuel McShanahan

🙚❧🙙

MO STEPPED OUT INTO THE BRIGHT DAY. IT WAS COLD and crisp, just as she liked it. The sleepy town of Prairie Dell was quiet, as usual. She looked up the street for Noah. No sight of him. She turned and looked beyond her shack and saw him under the shade of the only stick that could be called a tree for forty miles around. He leaned against it, his long legs sprawled in front of him, his hat pulled low.

She walked the thirty yards to him. Lord Almighty, she loved this boy. She'd never had children of her own, though she would have given her very soul for one. Noah Webster was the closest thing she had to kin now, next to her niece. Although it had been years since she had seen him, he'd grown up exactly as she expected.

They made a connection during the short time he spent with her in Prairie Dell long ago, one that she hoped would continue to her dying breath. It had until now, thanks to their many letters written over the years.

As she approached him, he pushed back his Stetson. She saw abject misery on his face and had a pretty good idea why it was there.

He rose and greeted her with a tight hug. They stayed that way for a long moment before she pulled away.

"Let me look at you, boy." She admired his tall, muscled frame, the cool blue eyes, and unruly hair. "You've turned into quite a fine man, Noah. Fine indeed."

"You haven't changed a bit, Mo." He smiled and her heart melted at the beauty of it.

"So, are you a real lady-killer now, Noah?" she asked lightly.

He shrugged. "No more than the next lawman, I suppose."

"I was sorry for your loss. I liked Pete."

His face turned to granite. "Not much of a loss, if you ask me."

She glared at him. "Well, I didn't ask you now, did I? I was tellin' you how bad I felt when I heard the news."

"From Sam?"

"Yes, from Sammy."

He shuffled a booted foot in the dirt. "I am sorry for your heartache, Mo. I know you and Sam have been tighter than doodlebugs since you were kids. Even though I never could condone his lifestyle, I was sorry for you when you told us about his passing."

She sniffed, slightly mollified. "How long have you been in love with her?"

"What?" His eyes pierced hers. An angry flame burned in them. She was right. There had been trouble in paradise.

"You heard me, Mr. Texas Ranger. How long have you been sweet on my niece?"

"I am *not* sweet on your niece," he ground out.

"Deny it if you want, Noah Webster, but I have a lot of experience. I am stickin' by my story. You love that gal."

Mo turned and picked up her skirts, flouncing toward her cabin. Let him pout if he wanted. She would go comfort Jenny.

Noah caught up with her as she reached her hovel. He grabbed her elbow and twirled her around.

"I am not sweet on your niece!" he shouted.

She threw off his hand and placed her fists against her abundant waist. "I heard you the first time, Noah Webster. You didn't have a lick o' sense as a boy. I don't know why I thought things woulda changed when you became a man." She looked him up and down, gauging his temper. "I guess yer more like Pete than I thought."

"You are so wrong, Miss High and Mighty Mo." He took a calming breath and lowered his voice. "I only came here to bring in Sam and recover what he stole. No one else ever had the guts or gumption or smarts to do so. I left it alone as long as I could but I couldn't stay away from it any longer. When I heard Pete had bit the dust, I knew it was time to put an end to the long and infamous career of Famous Sam McShan."

"At the expense of Jenny?"

"No. Yes. I don't know!" he said, raking his hand through his hair. "Sam dropped off the face of the earth. His daughter was the one link I had to find him. Jenny was bound and determined to come to Prairie Dell. I couldn't let her come all this way alone."

Mo glared up at him. "So, you wanted to use my niece to trap her da?"

"It wasn't like that." Noah shook his head. "Jenny wouldn't have made it two miles before trouble found her. You should hear her, Mo. Spouting off wisdom from some guidebook she read about life in the west. I figured I'd do the gentlemanly thing and get her here safely. Let her spend an hour with her daddy, then do my duty as a Ranger and take him in."

"You used me!"

Jenny stood in the doorway, an avenging angel, her eyes full of fire and brimstone, her mouth quivering ninety to nothing. She stalked over and slapped Noah hard. Mo entered her shack and closed the door.

"How dare you pretend to be some consumptive cowpoke that happened to be headed this way!"

His face stung where she struck him. "Boy, you pack a wallop," he said lightly.

Noah had known this moment would come, had played it out in his mind a thousand times the last few days, but reality hurt more than he could have imagined.

"You took advantage of me!" Her voice rose louder with each word. "You exploited me!"

"Now, Jenny, don't go airing your dirty laundry. Prairie Dell can't take all this excitement at once."

She glared daggers at him. "Don't ever, ever think you have the right to tell me what to do. You are a disgusting, low-down, sorry excuse for a man."

He knew she was dealing with her grief and his betrayal in the only way she knew how. He decided to take whatever she tossed his way. It was the least he could do.

"Jenny, I—"

"No. Don't. Nothing you can ever say to me will change anything between us. Do you understand? I don't have to listen to you. You don't own me."

But she did own him, heart and soul. Noah's insides cracked with every word she hurled at him. He'd never hurt so much in his entire life. He wanted to cry out that he loved her, that what had passed between them meant more to him than she'd ever know. That it didn't matter about Sam or Pete.

But she was right. He was despicable. Bad to the bone. He didn't deserve her. So he held his tongue.

He let her rage on for a few minutes. She was all red in the face as she spewed her venom. He knew it would soon be over and she'd be spent. He wanted to walk away but he savored the last looks he had of her. It would carry him through the rough times that lay ahead.

Finally, he couldn't help it. Her words wounded him more than he thought possible. He wanted to strike out at her, hurt her as she did him.

"You know," he drawled, "Sam's biggest crime wasn't stealing all that money. His biggest crime was abandoning you."

Noah knew he'd cut her to the quick. Her face crumpled. Her shoulders sagged. Hot tears poured from her eyes and ran down her cheeks, dropping onto her bodice.

"I can't wait to get back east. Where people treat each other with decency and respect."

"Then go, why don't you?"

"I'll be happy to, Mr. Webster." She hollered one last remark at him. "Just go to Hell, Noah Webster. Straight to the Devil, why don't you?"

"I'm already there."

CHAPTER 21

Jenny stalked into Mo's dilapidated shack. She wanted to collapse on the lone cot and cry herself into oblivion. Not only had she lost her father, but she'd lost the man she'd given her heart to. Noah's betrayal stung deeper and sharper than the snake's fangs that had bitten him.

"Jenny?"

She whirled and saw Mo standing there. Her aunt held open her arms. She ran into them and latched onto Mo as if the older woman were a life preserver and she a drowning sailor. Jenny bawled like a lost, blind foal looking for his mother. Her sobs lasted so long that by the time they ceased, her legs wobbled. Mo had to lead her to a chair and push her into the seat.

"Do you love him?"

Jenny turned up her face to her aunt, knowing it was still wet with tears and full of woe. She didn't trust herself to speak so she shook her head furiously. She hugged her arms tightly about her.

Mo took the chair opposite her and placed a rough, warm hand on Jenny's knee. "Did you?"

"I thought I did. And I thought he felt the same, Mo." Jenny squeezed her aunt's hand. "He never said it in so many words but . . ."

"I know, honey. That's just how men are. They let their actions do the talkin'. They're not so good with the words."

Jenny wanted to weep again at the sympathy she saw written across Mo's face. She wouldn't, though. She had to remember that Noah Webster wasn't worth another tear.

"Noah was a good boy, Jenny. I think he's grown into a fine man."

"An unscrupulous, unprincipled man. Isn't that what you mean?"

"Ah, Jenny, my dear. He was just doin' his job as a Ranger. His task was to bring in Sammy. No one's been successful before. In fact, no one has ever come close, if'n I can believe Sammy. Noah had a personal history with Sammy, honey. One that goes back a long way."

Jenny frowned at that unexpected information. "What do you mean?"

"I met Noah when he was a boy. Must've been at least twelve, thirteen years ago. His daddy and Sammy came here to Prairie Dell, on the run from the law. They had Noah in tow with them."

"Noah . . . was an outlaw?"

Mo sighed. "Not exactly. His daddy was Pistol Pete Webber, Sammy's partner. Sammy took a shine to Noah. Thought him smart and all. Talked Pete into takin' Noah along on one of their jobs.

"The two men robbed a bank and Noah was to stand lookout and hold the getaway horses. The town's sheriff got shot in the middle of the robbery and it turned into a real fine mess. Noah got left behind in the escape. He almost didn't catch up with them, with a posse of angry men right on his tail. By the time they reached me, the boy had been scared pee-less. He vowed he'd never indulge in a life of crime."

Mo's words finally sank in. "Sam's partner was *Noah's father?*"

"Yes. Pete Webber was a career criminal, same as Sammy. Nice lookin' fella, quick with a gun and a joke. Moved his family around lots and was gone for long periods of time. Noah's ma did all the raisin' of her children. Pete had very little to do with how well they all turned out."

"Where is Pete now? Did he come to Prairie Dell with Sam?"

Mo looked startled. "No, I guess you wouldn't know. Noah's hurtin' too, sweetie. His daddy done got killed durin' this last big score he and Sammy pulled. Sammy told me all about it. They'd gotten away clean, though they lost a couple of men before they cleared the town, when one of their own gang shot Pete point-blank."

"Oh, no!"

"Oh, yes, and your da shot that man. Sammy always was too nice for his own good, though, and not the best of shots. He told me he only wounded Riley. Not too bad, just enough to slow him down. To be honest, Sammy was scared Riley would show up here 'cause he'd been here once before, years ago. He's a slimy snake, that Riley Withers."

Bells buzzed in Jenny's head. "Withers?" No, it couldn't be. She sat forward and took Mo's hands in hers. "Describe this man, Mo."

Mo's eyes almost disappeared as she squinted at her. "What's wrong?"

"A Mr. Withers introduced himself to me on the train from Boston to Texas. Something about him bothered me."

"Well, Riley's probly mid-thirties now. An oily type, if'n you know what I mean. Wears his hair all slicked back. It's dark and he has a dark mustache. Coldest, meanest eyes I've seen this side o' the ocean."

Jenny shivered. "It was Withers. I'm sure of it. Why would he follow me?"

"Sammy had all the loot. Somehow Riley Withers

learned about you. He always was snoopin' around. I guess he figured you could lead him to Sammy and the money."

"He did disembark at the same train stop I did. He even boarded the same stagecoach to Apple Blossom. But he didn't get off there. I haven't seen him since then."

"Riley is a clever one. If you didn't see him, it's because he didn't want to be seen. He probly shadowed you yer entire time here."

She gasped. "The note! I'll bet it was from Noah."

Mo narrowed her eyes. "What the tarnation are you talkin' 'bout?"

"When I was at the hotel in Apple Blossom, someone pushed a note under my door. It contained a single sentence—*Watch the man following you*. I thought someone was warning me about Noah because he was everywhere I turned."

"As sharp as that boy is, he musta seen Riley trailin' you."

She nodded. "I'm sure you're right. It sounds like something Noah would do. And all along I thought I had to be wary of him." She paused. "But I still have good reason now to be furious with him. He lied to me, Mo. I could never trust him. He's a blackguard, just like his father was. And it's his father who got mine—"

"Don't go there, Jenny. Sammy made his own choices, honey. Noah was doin' his job. He protected you from Riley Withers and he brought you safely to me. I'm grateful to him for that."

Mo hugged her. A warm rush of love poured from Jenny to her aunt. They hadn't known each other twenty-four hours, yet Jenny already thought of Mo as family.

"We'll need to be on the lookout for Mr. Riley Withers. We'd best warn Noah, too. I think he needs to know how serious that scoundrel is. If'n he followed you from Boston clear to Texas, it wouldn't be anythin' for him to show up here in Prairie Dell."

"I'll let you tell Mr. Webster, Mo. I have no intention of ever speaking to him again. Besides, I have more important things to attend to now. I've got a riddle to solve."

❦

NOAH MOUNTED STAR, READY TO RIDE BACK TO Texas. He didn't want to waste another moment in this godforsaken place. He was mad at himself. At Jenny. At Pete for getting killed. And at Sam for dying on him. He was mad at the world. He was even mad at Mo. Just by looking at her, he could tell that she'd take Jenny's side on anything. Blood did run thicker than water.

Sassy whinnied as he pulled on Star's reins. Star tossed his head back in his companion's direction and answered her. Then he snorted. Loud. Noah didn't like the sound of that snort.

"What do you want me to do, Star? I can't take her horse. She'll need to leave here, whether it's in one day or one year. She's burning to get back to civilization in her precious Boston. I can't let her walk there."

Star snorted again in reply.

"Hell and damnation." He threw his hat onto the ground. With clenched teeth, he leaped off his horse and looked Star in the eye.

"Why I'm talking to you, I haven't the foggiest notion. It's not like you understand the situation. You're just a fool horse."

Star turned his head away. Noah grabbed the reins and pulled them so Star faced him again.

"You're all taking her side is the problem." He reached down and picked up his worn Stetson and placed it back on his head. "And I guess my job here's not through. I've got to calm down and think rationally like the Ranger I am."

Noah returned to the tree he'd been cozied up to when Mo first came to visit with him. He planted his back firmly against its skinny trunk and crossed his ankles in front of him. He wished the world would go away.

Uppermost in his mind was guilt. Part of it was from Pete's death. He should have brought Pete in years ago. If he'd done so, at least Pete wouldn't have been killed in a bank robbery.

Even though Noah had no respect for his daddy, he couldn't help but feel some love for the man. After all, they were kin. Pete gave him and Mark and Elizabeth life. Even if that was all the good in him, it was still something. His brother and sister were two of the best people Noah knew. They made this world a better place. They brought joy to his and his mama's lives.

The rest of the lingering guilt belonged to what he'd done to Jenny. He'd hurt her and had no way to right that wrong. Oh, sure, she thought if they got married, it would solve everything. He didn't think so. He had enough of Pete's wanderlust in him. He didn't think he could ever settle down in one place, much less be true to one woman from now through eternity. Besides, everyone knew that a Ranger made a poor husband. He wouldn't be willing to take the kind of chances it took to do his job correctly if he knew Jenny waited at home for him.

God, he'd never want to *leave* home if she were there. He could feel his hand skim the satin smoothness of her alabaster skin, smell the subtle scent of lavender that clung to her, taste the sweetness that was all her own. If he left Jenny to chase outlaws and Comanche, his mind would be nothing but mush. Thought of her would spill out every minute of every day.

No, it was no good. It could never be.

But, oh, how his heart wished it could. He wished he were more citified and educated. A better match for her. All he could do was bring about her ruin. He refused to do that.

Noah pushed Jenny McShanahan from every nook and cranny in his head. He had to be logical. He had a lot to accomplish.

First, he would check out Mo's story. Not that he didn't believe her. She'd turned into one of the best friends he'd ever hard—but he would have to speak to witnesses for his report. He would ask who had seen Sam in Prairie Dell, both alive and dead. He'd have to cite where Famous Sam McShan was buried. The authorities were always interested in those kinds of details.

Then there was the money. Actually, the Treasury bonds. Sam had gotten some cash but the real haul lay in what he'd taken from the government. If Sam had truly made it to Prairie Dell, Noah would bet his last nickel that the bonds had, too. He hoped Sam shared with Mo where they were hidden.

Finally, he had to find out why that sly stranger had been following Jenny. He hadn't seen the piece of pond scum since Apple Blossom but Noah's common sense told him the man was out there somewhere. Maybe not in Prairie Dell yet, but he would be soon. Was he part of Sam's gang? Noah was curious about this piece of the puzzle.

He liked a neat, orderly world, with everything in its place. Trouble was, the world rarely cooperated. That's why he liked Rangering over anything else he'd tried. Pete moved the family to Texas when Noah was fifteen. It was right after the war, and Sam and Pete wanted to make some fast cash during Reconstruction. They'd tried to involve him again in a few of their shenanigans but Noah flatly refused.

He had to—because in spite of everything—the

glamour of what they did appealed to him on some level. He knew it was wrong. He still saw that girl holding her dead daddy and crying—but a tiny part of him wanted the excitement that came with the crime. He had a bad side that was itching to come out. He had to guard against it ever happening again. He had to protect Jenny from it, too.

He made good money as a ranch hand instead of joining his daddy and Sam. Noah hired out in the first cattle drives after the war. Texas had been cut off from the Confederate cattle markets during the conflict, so afterward the herds ballooned. With five million longhorns roaming the range and the postwar burst of railroad construction that would get those cattle to Chicago slaughterhouses from the plains, he'd been in the right place at the right time. It was honest work for honest money but he'd tired of it after several long drives. Abilene, Wichita, Dodge City. They all began to look the same after a time. He'd enjoyed his flings in the saloons and dance halls and gambling palaces and always proved popular with the ladies, but he wearied of that empty, unsatisfying life.

And the more Pete stole and the more famous he and Sam became, the more Noah was embarrassed by their exploits. It had attracted him to the lifestyle of the independent Rangers. He joined them at twenty-one and hadn't looked back. Until now. He'd been a crack shot and though his mama constantly worried about him he felt in some way Rangering helped atone for Pete and Sam's many sins.

The Rangers had become like family. When he was a boy, Pete would show up after months of being absent and they'd have to move, no questions asked. It made it hard to make friends, much less keep them. He never really had friends, other than his brother and sister, until he joined the Rangers. Many of them were loners as he was. They bonded with few words, their actions and pride in a job well done being the glue that cemented their friendships.

He owed it to his fellow Rangers to solve this case and bring closure to the life and times of the Robin Hood of the West.

Noah stood and dusted off his black wool pants. He had questions to ask and notes to take. And he promised himself he wouldn't think about Jenny McShanahan even once.

Well, maybe once. He hated to break a promise. Even if it was to himself.

CHAPTER 22

R iley Withers pitched forward in his seat as the train braked heavily and skidded to an unscheduled stop.

"Dammit." He cursed himself again for the hundredth time. Why had he been foolhardy enough to try to take a train?

He knew why. He was a shiftless son of a gun whose hip had been bothering him for a good year or more. He also had the sore shoulder, courtesy of Sam, as the reason to head to Prairie Dell in the most comfortable manner possible.

He hadn't especially liked the looks of the guide Jenny McShanahan settled on. The escort might have played easygoing to Sam's daughter but Riley saw the way the man moved. The way his eyes searched out things. Riley didn't want to tangle with him. The guide would be a hard man to shadow out in the open. He knew better than to take unnecessary chances. He liked his hide intact.

That caused him to take the lazy man's way out and travel by train as far as he could. That way he'd be fresher and it would take about the same amount of time as the overland route.

Excepting his trip up to Boston and back to Texas,

he had never spent much time on trains. While getting to Boston from Texas and back had been a piece of cake, he had no idea how western trains in remote spots ran. Until now. The fact was, they didn't. There had been delays, cancellations, roaming buffalo on the tracks, and two different robberies. Countless times he'd been ready to get off and find a horse. The one time he actually looked, nothing satisfied him. Riley had decided to tough it out.

His thoughts were interrupted by an all too familiar voice. He groaned inwardly but put a smile on his face.

"Lookee here, boys. If'n it ain't Riley Withers."

He couldn't believe the Purnell brothers had appeared. They were the last men he would choose to run into if given a thousand wishes. They were bumblers, dumb as dirt, and bad luck chased them wherever they went. Wherever the Purnell boys showed up, the law wouldn't be far behind. He did not want his wagon hitched to this sorry trio.

"Hey, boys."

Riley wanted to seem moderately friendly, seeing as how the Purnells were robbing his train, but at the same time he didn't want any passengers connecting him with them. He walked to the front of the car where they stood, the better to have a more private conversation.

"What the hell are you doing on a train bound to nowhere, Riley?"

"Had a little business to do, Jack. I'm sure you get my drift."

All three brothers chuckled as if on the inside of the joke. He doubted two of the three had a clue what he was talking about.

"Been like a slow train to Hell, though. Too many delays. Especially holdups. Why anybody rides on a train is beyond me."

They cackled loudly. "That's a good one," said Jake. "Holdups."

He smiled, his jaw clenched in a show of camaraderie. "Actually, it's true. I've already been through a couple robberies and a derailment. Damn buffalo. Had to switch trains after that happened," he said affably. "Now you boys show up and I'm gonna be further delayed."

He motioned and took Jim, the eldest of the trio, aside. "I have gotta get where I'm headed, Jimbo. Think you can let me off while you do your business here?"

Jim tilted his head and signaled for his brothers to come over. "Riley here needs to be gone, fellas. Either of you have an objection to letting him off while we go about our collecting?"

Jack snickered. "I'm collecting me rings and watches and maybe a purdy girl." He flashed a toothy grin at Riley. "Don't bother me none if'n he gets off."

Riley tipped his hat. "I'd be mighty obliged to you three." He walked to his seat and picked up his coat. "Good luck to you, now."

He returned to the back of the car, passing the white faces of frightened passengers. Hell, if there was at least one man with some gumption on this train, the Purnells wouldn't get anything. They were as yellow-bellied as they came. Anyone who stood up and said boo to them would have the brothers cowering in a corner in two seconds flat.

Reaching the rear of the train, he opened the heavy door. The cold air felt good after the stuffy confines of the railcar. Too many mewling kids and unwashed bodies to suit his frame of mind. He let go of the steel door and it slammed hard behind him. He looked around and spotted a young kid with a set of horses. Jumping to the ground, he made his way over.

"Hey, there," he said amiably. "You related to the

Purnells?" The freckled-faced stranger couldn't have been more than fourteen and was unarmed.

"Who're you?" the boy asked sullenly.

"Don't go sassin' me, son. I'm friends with those boys. We go way back. I've got some business to attend to and I didn't have time to shoot the breeze with the Purnells while they took their time holding up the train. There's too many passengers and my time's as precious as money."

The kid studied him. He could see the boy was as goofy as the group he'd left on the train. That would help.

He walked over and nuzzled a black and white horse. "Hello, Old Paint. Been a long time since I've seen you."

"You know Old Paint?"

"Sure I do. Used to be mine. Jack done won him off me in a card game." He stroked the horse fondly. "Jackie's gonna let me borrow him for a while, seeing as to how I need to get gone."

Riley swung into the saddle and tipped his hat to the lookout. "Nice meeting you. Hope to see you real soon."

With that, he kicked the horse and Old Paint took off at a full gallop. He'd chosen this particular mount because he knew despite the horse's looks, it had deceptive speed. Old Paint left Riley and his own horse in the dust over three years ago when he and the Purnells held up a stagecoach in Texas, down around San Antone. He'd always wanted a fast horse.

He'd finally gotten his wish.

He smiled to himself, wondering how far Jack Purnell would kick the kid when he found out the idiot let Riley Withers ride off on his prized horse.

One which Riley had never, ever owned.

❦

Jenny could not fall asleep. The day's events had been too earth-shattering. Physically tired at the end of such a long journey, she had been further depleted with the news about Sam's death. To think she would never see her beloved papa again. And he was beloved. Interspersed with all the bitterness and regrets was a deep love for him that would always abide within her. Sam might have been a notorious outlaw but he had done what he thought was best for her—even if it did lead to years of separation. Sam wanted more for her than he could have provided if they had stayed together. She needed to remember that.

As she lay in the darkness, Jenny thought of all those nights when he tucked her into bed. She could almost feel his large, warm hand as it stroked her hair, a soft ballad sung quietly in his rich baritone to lull her to sleep. Bits and pieces of the words he'd crooned began to come back to her, words she hadn't been able to recall in years.

She remembered *Red is the Rose* and *The Foggy Dew, Rocky Road to Dublin* and *The Cliffs of Doneen.* She thanked the Good Lord that He'd given her back this small piece of Sam, a father full of tenderness and love for his little girl.

The more the words returned to her, the more she knew they held the key to the map Sam had made. When morning came, she would make a list of all the song titles that she could think of and as many words as she could remember. Therein lay the key to finding Sam's haul.

Though Jenny knew he intended it for her and Mo, to offer them security for the rest of their lives, the idea of living off stolen money proved distasteful. If she could find where he stashed the loot, she could return it to the authorities. Maybe in some small way it would help clear a few of the black marks against her father's name. She didn't know if she would succeed but she had to try.

She slept fitfully. Images of the Sam from her childhood interspersed with those of Sam as a romantic Robin Hood figure, the king of larceny in the west. In her dreams Noah confronted Sam, a bright star blazing on his chest, demanding that Sam surrender. When he wouldn't, Noah shot him in cold blood, twirling his Colt through his finger, a smile on his handsome face.

"Damn waste of a man." Noah's eyes were like ice as he re-holstered his pistol.

Jenny sat up with a start, wide awake from her nightmare. Her eyes felt scratchy and tired from lack of sleep. Her head ached, too, and her limbs were sore from the weeks in the saddle on the road.

She looked down at Mo peacefully sleeping next to her on the floor. Mo insisted that Jenny take the lumpy cot.

"Wouldn't do for my guest to go sleepin' on the floor, especially as to how you're my kinfolk, too."

Jenny smiled at the thought. She had never known she had any relatives other than Sam. Her discovery of this one-eyed aunt helped to cushion the blow of Sam's untimely death. Mo might be gruff and a soiled dove but she had a kind heart. She had kept Jenny up until the wee hours of the morning, recounting stories of her and Sam's childhood in Ireland. Jenny vowed to go to Ireland one day and see her family's roots for herself. It might make her feel closer to her parents somehow.

She lay back against the soft, feathered pillow, new fragments of songs swirling in her head. The key to the map's mystery lay locked somewhere in her mind. She pictured the map, randomly littered with phrases. If only she could decipher what Sam meant by them.

She must have fallen asleep again, for the next thing she was conscious of was the savory smell of brewed coffee. Jenny sat up and pushed her tumbled curls from her eyes.

"Good mornin' to you," Mo called, nursing a skillet of sizzling eggs. "Hope you like yer coffee strong and yer eggs hard 'cause that's the only way I can make 'em."

She stood and stretched. "That sounds wonderful, Mo. Anything I can help with?"

"No, not now. After breakfast, though, you can go out and feed yer prissy horse. I put her in the coverin' out back last night with my Buffy. I don't know if those two fillies will take to being together. They both have mighty high ideas of how pretty they both are."

Jenny laughed. "Sassy will be glad for the company. She was very fond of Star."

She thought how fond she herself had been of Star —and his rider. She mentally shook off the thought and poured coffee for her and Mo.

After they ate, she fed both horses. She found herself humming *Maids When You're Young*. The words magically came back to her as she filled a bucket apiece for each horse so she sang the entire song to her audience of two. She was ready now to make a list of every song she could remember and compare them to the pieced-together map and its directions.

Mo had already cleared the table and rinsed their dishes by the time she returned. Her aunt bustled about, holding up first one dress, then inspecting another, until she seemed satisfied. She raised one high for Jenny's opinion.

"What do you think of this one?"

It was made of faded satin that had seen better days but it was clean and in decent shape.

"It's very nice, Mo."

"Good. Gotta get gussied up now. It's my weekly card game, love. Been doin' this every Thursday since I come to Prairie Dell years ago. It livens up the week a bit and it sure don't hurt my pocketbook." Mo smiled radiantly. "I win most every time and it's not because they let me, either. I'm good with cards. Don't even have to cheat to whip up on 'em, most times."

Mo combed her long, faded locks and twisted them up, pinning them artfully. She doused herself in rose water and then turned her back. Jenny saw she slipped off the black eye patch. She wondered what Mo was up to.

When her aunt turned around, she wore a patch of bright yellow, which picked up the piping in her dress. "Wanna look my best for the fellas," she said slyly.

"You look lovely, Mo," Jenny said with sincerity.

Mo kissed her cheek. "I do clean up nice, don't I?" She shuffled around until she found her reticule and stuffed a pack of playing cards into it. "I hate leavin' my favorite niece but I'll be gone most o' the day."

"Your only niece," she piped in.

"But you'd be my favorite anyway, dear." Mo smoothed her hair once more. "We'll have lots of time to visit but I do have to make the weekly game. Can't disappoint my boys."

Jenny smiled. "Go ahead, Mo. I've got plenty to keep me busy here."

"That's good." Mo kissed her cheek again. "Don't go anywhere since we don't know where that Riley Withers is. And if'n Noah drops by, tell him about the louse."

She snorted. "I doubt Mr. Webster will drop by. If he does, I don't plan to answer the door."

Mo guffawed. "If'n I know Noah, I don't think he'd let somethin' like that prevent him from coming in."

"Just go, will you?"

Mo arched her brows. "I will and hope to come home richer 'n when I left." She waved and headed out the door.

Jenny leaned back in her chair. She rubbed her eyes and yawned. "Better get another cup of coffee," she told herself, and poured the bitter brew into her mug. She spent the next two hours listing ballad titles in her journal and writing down as many lyrics as she could remember for each one.

She believed that she was on the verge of a breakthrough but her eyes blurred as she looked at the open map. She closed them and noticed for the first time how sore her neck and back were from hunching over the table for so long. It prompted her to decide to stretch her legs a bit and take in some fresh air.

Mo showed her earlier where a stash of sugar lumps were kept, strictly for Buffy's pleasure. Jenny decided to visit the horses and give them each a treat. She wouldn't be gone more than five minutes, only long enough to clear her head and start fresh as she tried to unravel Sam's cryptic chart.

She put on her cloak and slipped two lumps into her pocket before pulling open the door and stepping outside. Immediately, she pulled her cloak closer as she rounded the corner. It had gotten downright cold since yesterday. She would make this a very quick trip.

Both horses greeted her. As she pulled the sugar lumps from her pocket, Buffy knew exactly what Jenny held and nudged her fist playfully.

"All right, girl. Here's your treat."

Mo's horse delicately lifted her allotted lump from Jenny's palm. Sassy nosed in as close as she could, curious as to what her friend had.

"You're going to love this, sweet girl."

Jenny offered the lump to Sassy. She didn't know if the horse had ever been given sugar before or if she simply followed Buffy's example, but it was gone in a flash.

"My smart Sassy." She stroked the horse's neck for a moment and decided it was time to head back inside.

As she turned, Jenny saw a lone figure in the doorway. A form she knew only too well.

CHAPTER 23

Noah had been busy. Since he'd last seen Jenny the day before, he'd interviewed every person in Prairie Dell—all twelve of them—or at least the eight that could talk. One old geezer was mute and two babies were less than a year apiece. Another died in his sleep two days after Sam passed on but most residents still considered him a part of the town.

He also found out that Sam hadn't been buried yet. The town had his remains in a storage shed behind the general store. He would receive a proper Christian burial when the circuit preacher rode through. Fortunately, the winter was cold and Noah was able to recognize Sam's perfectly preserved body. He begged the old fellow that showed him the wasted corpse not to tell Jenny. He knew how badly she had wanted to see her daddy but this was not the last impression anyone would want of a loved one. It made him glad that he hadn't seen Pete's bullet-ridden body.

No one had seen hide nor hare about the money or the treasury bonds Sam had stolen in Texas. The outlaw had ridden in on a single horse, looking like death warmed over, from several descriptions. Noah suspected Sam had hidden his cache before he came to Prairie Dell. He also realized if Sam had known he was dying, he would darn sure give Jenny and Mo the directions to the loot.

That's why Noah had come to see them both. He watched Mo leave, yellow eye patch and all, and make her way to what amounted to the local saloon—Sherm's one-room shack. He remembered it was Thursday, the day of her weekly card game. Mo would demand Satan release her from Hell if it interfered with her Thursday poker game. Actually, her poker marathon. Mo wouldn't be back until the sun set if she followed her usual pattern of play.

Still, he hesitated. Noah wanted to see Jenny so badly. He needed to do his job. He stood there debating what to do and how to handle things until he was practically frozen to the spot. A raging swirl of conflicting emotions seemed to keep him inert. Then he watched as Jenny left Mo's place and headed to where the horses were. He followed her there.

Jenny glared at him now, her breath visible in the crisp air. He stood, legs apart, hands resting easily on his hips, his hat pushed back far on his head as he drank her in. Those moss green eyes of hers glittered in anger.

"Get out of my way, Mr. Webster."

Noah moved with a catlike grace, all speed and silence. Before she even blinked, he had her about the waist and pulled her to him. She threw her arms up in front for protection as he crushed her to his chest. As always, the contact between them ignited a spark of desire that heated his loins. He sensed her weakening as she responded to his fervent kiss.

But he still had a job to accomplish.

He broke the kiss and caught his breath. "I need to know where Sam hid the money, Jenny."

Her brows shot up. He sensed her anger returning, coiling within her as she spat out, "I don't know where he hid the money."

His gaze pierced hers. "I don't believe you."

"I said I don't know and if I did, you'd be the last person I'd tell, Noah Webster." She tried to pry his hands from her but his hold was unshakeable.

"Do you think you can force it from me? Sweet-talk me, maybe? Kiss me senseless? Well, I'm not the same innocent girl I used to be."

He winced at her words. Regret filled him to the brim.

"Your betrayal caused me to grow up fast. You're not man enough to own up and do the right thing."

"And if I did?" His hands tightened around her waist. "Would you marry me?"

Jenny didn't miss a beat. "Are you asking?"

Noah cocked his head and studied her, keeping his emotions in check. "Sure. Why not?"

And then wanted to kick himself for his flippant response.

He watched her eyes go wide before she glanced down at the ground, trying to compose herself. Why had he said such a thing? Instead of declaring his love for her, he'd diced her heart into tiny pieces with his careless words.

When she lifted her eyes and met his, he saw a steely resolve in them. "You'd be the last man I'd marry, Mr. Webster. You're a liar, just like every other man. That's one life lesson I've learned. Every man I know lets me down. You're like all the rest. You'd never live up to your promises."

Her words infuriated him. He tightened his grip on her, his thoughts jumbled up until he acted on instinct.

Noah kissed her. Hard. It was a searing kiss, full of power and heat. Full of his rage and frustration and desire. He propelled her back and they fell into the hay behind the horses. The sweet smell drifted up and enveloped them. He was aware of that scent, mingled with the lavender on her skin and in her hair. It drove everything from his mind.

She clung to his coat as one kiss became another and yet another. He lost count of where one ended and the next began as he rode the sensual waves of his mouth on hers, hot and lustful.

Noah realized he couldn't get enough of Jenny. He'd dreamed of her taste, lived for it without admitting it to himself. He refused to fool himself any longer. He had to have her—forever—no matter what consequences it would bring. He'd thrown an offer of marriage out to her in anger but now he meant it. Could he convince her?

"Jenny?" His voice was a hoarse whisper as he nuzzled her throat. When she didn't answer, he stopped.

Her eyes were unfocused, glazed in passion. "Honey?" He kissed the tip of her nose lightly. "I've been a first-class fool."

She went totally still in his arms. She looked up at him, all the pain she'd suffered written across her lovely features.

In that moment, he didn't only desire her physically. Noah yearned for Jenny with a sweetness that words couldn't express. He'd come to enjoy her company. Her intelligence. Her innocence. Her laughter. Her compassion. He hadn't realized women were more than their physical sum. He'd never taken the time to learn that before. Jenny showed him that the outside package only wrapped up something much more important on the inside.

He wanted to spend every waking moment with this woman. It didn't matter to him that her daddy had been a big, bad outlaw. He didn't even have to be a Ranger anymore if that's what she'd want from him. Rangers made poor husbands, always gone and getting shot at and taking awful chances.

That's when he knew he was deranged. Rangering had been his whole life. It proved that there was some good in him and that he could use that good to help others and make Texas a better, safer place. No one woman should make him give up on his chosen way of life.

Unless that woman was the one he held in his arms.

"I meant what I said before, honey. It just didn't come out right. Would you do me the honor? Would you marry me?"

He knew the very moment she gave her trust back to him. Her body melted into his like butter on a hot griddle cake, her palms flat against his chest, kneading like a cat's paws when it's pleased about something. Noah pulled away from her long enough to stand and scoop her into his arms and returned to her mouth, that sweet, sweet mouth. Oh, God, he'd missed that mouth more than he'd imagined.

He strode around the corner and opened the door to Mo's one room cabin. As he shut the door, he relaxed his hold and set her down, only to push her against the closed entry way. His hands caught hers and raised them high above her head, his fingers entwining with hers. He pressed his body into hers, his tongue greedily gaining entrance into her mouth. He wanted her, all of her. He couldn't stop himself.

Noah took the ribbon from her bonnet in his teeth and slowly untied the bow under her chin. He caught her wrists in one hand and used the other to pull the bonnet from her head. The pins holding her hair came out with it, and those golden tresses fell around her shoulders and down her back. He ran his free fingers through the waves, lost in their silky texture.

He unhooked her cloak and pushed it aside. The blue wool fell to the ground at their feet. He reached to touch her breast. He could feel the nipple already erect through her layers of clothing. He massaged it slowly, enjoying the feel of it under his hand as he bent to kiss her elegant throat.

Her sigh nearly undid him. His gentleness fled. He

wanted her. Now. Forever. He released her hands and they locked around his neck. She drew him to her for a wet, passionate kiss as he moved his hands behind her to curve around her bottom and pull her close against his hardness.

"I want you, Jenny McShanahan," he said hoarsely, his breathing ragged and uneven.

"I want you, too." Her voice was like warm honey and whisky sliding down a parched throat. He'd died and gone to heaven.

Somehow he backed her over to the cot and removed her clothes as quickly as the myriad of buttons allowed.

"My God," he said softly as he pulled her shift over her head. He sat back on his heels and stared at her. She blushed from her lovely, long toes to the roots of her honeyed hair.

"You're beautiful."

He had touched her beauty that night in the cave but the low lantern hadn't let him witness the wonders of seeing her body. Her milky white skin and womanly curves spoke of absolute perfection. He'd never been more moved by the sight of a woman.

"Noah." Jenny tried to sit up but he pushed her back down.

"Just let me drink you in a minute, honey." He reached out and touched a palm to her cheek. "You are flawless."

Suddenly, the heat and desire built again and he quickly doffed his clothes, leaving them in a heap near the cot. The cool cabin was forgotten as he climbed next to her, his torso covering her body. He touched her everywhere. He heard the gentle sighs and felt the ripples of pleasure as he skimmed her smooth skin.

"Are you nervous, sweetheart?"

"No."

Her luminous, green eyes were full of faith in him.

He kissed each lid gently. He was the nervous one. He'd never been with a virgin before. From what he gathered, nice girls had little idea about the actual act of love. Since her mama died so many years ago, Noah was pretty sure Jenny was as uninformed as a novice nun.

He cupped her face. "It always hurts a woman her first time. But not after that. I promise."

She nodded shyly. His fingers stroked the seam of her sex, finding her already slick and ready for him. He used his fingers to drive her into a frenzy, stroking her until her body shuddered and she cried out his name. Moving quickly, he slid into her before she realized it, his mouth over hers, and thrust once. She stiffened, her nails digging into his shoulders, and he remained still.

After a moment, he said, "Talk to me, honey."

Her eyes glistened with tears. "It . . . hurts. I wanted to push you away but I don't feel any pain now. But, oh my . . . something's happening."

He chuckled. "That's what you're doing to me. Being inside you, I want to fill you up. Relax, honey. There's more."

Noah buried himself in her neck, nipping and licking her satin skin. She lifted her hips to him. He pulled away from her slightly and then pushed back in again in one, delicious motion.

"How was that?" he whispered in her ear.

She nodded, her eyes still full of trust, a smile playing about her rosy, kiss-swollen lips. He repeated the movement. Each time she rose to meet him. He knew she didn't understand why she did it, only that she had to. He began an easy rhythm, slow and leisurely.

A little at a time, he increased his pace and her hips continued to rise and meet each thrust, now long and deep. She began to whimper and moan. Each little noise brought him a thrill of satisfaction. He wanted to pleasure her. He wanted her to enjoy their dance of love.

"Oh, Noah!" she cried out as he came inside her.

He seized her mouth with his and smothered her with heartfelt kisses. He turned on his side, still in her, his arms wrapped around her.

"That . . . it was . . ." Her words hung in the air.

"Good?" he asked playfully.

She grinned. "I'd say better than good."

He kissed her sweetly, savoring the moment like never before. He rubbed his cheek to her forehead. Sex had never been like this before.

Because it wasn't just sex.

For the first time, Noah knew he'd found love.

CHAPTER 24

They cuddled awhile until Jenny fell asleep in his arms, exhausted. Noah had noticed the circles under her eyes and guessed at her restless night, having spent his in much the same way.

He looked down at her, his emotions brimming near the surface, threatening to spill over. They were a combination of tenderness and love, fear and possessiveness. He wanted to love her and protect her, laugh with her, be with her. These feelings, so new and fragile, frightened him. He would do anything, go anywhere, give up everything.

For Jenny.

He must have dozed himself, for the next thing he knew were soft, tentative kisses tickling his jawline. He opened his eyes slowly.

"You are the best thing I've ever awakened to, Miss McShanahan." He grinned at her, a lop-sided, lazy grin, knowing it had a bit of mischief in it.

"You're being awfully formal, Mr. Webster," she replied.

"I wouldn't want to stand on formality." He brushed his lips against hers tenderly as he slid his fingers into her hair. She shivered.

"Cold?"

"No," she said softly and snuggled against him. "You're as warm as a campfire."

"Be careful, darlin'. You just might be playing with fire."

He brought his mouth down on hers in a possessive kiss. She opened to him and his tongue delved in, stroking hers until his pulse quickened. Her breasts began to swell as he kneaded them leisurely.

He trailed kisses down her throat to her breasts, then down even further, running his mouth down to her flat belly. He moved lower and she sat up abruptly.

"Noah!"

He splayed his fingers across her stomach. "Hush, sweetheart. Just lie back and enjoy. There are all kinds of ways I can make love to you. We're going to try every one of them. Even if it takes a lifetime."

She hesitated a moment. "I trust you know what you're doing, Noah," she said primly and eased back down.

He couldn't help but smile. His schoolmarm was back. "I know you're used to doing the instructing, Miss McShanahan. You just tell me if I pass muster."

He pushed her legs up and lowered himself between her thighs. As his tongue brushed against her, she gasped.

"Noah!"

He flicked it lightly. Twice. "Is that all right?"

"Yes," she whispered.

He cupped her bottom in his hands and pushed his tongue inside, caressing her.

"And what about that?"

"Oh . . ."

"How about this?" He began to make love to her with his mouth, slowly, sensually. She moaned softly.

He raised his head. "Should I stop?"

She shook her head. "No. Don't. Stop," she choked out.

He continued to touch her intimately. She began writhing beneath him, entangling her fingers int his hair and pulling him closer. He sensed the slow ripples of pleasure that washed over her. Her breathing became shallow and she shuddered with their intensity until she trembled from head to foot. She cried out his name again as the waves peaked.

When she grew still, Noah lifted his head and met her gaze. "So. Did I pass?"

She laughed weakly. "I'd say you are at the top of your class, Mr. Webster."

He frowned. "I'm not sure. I think I might need more practice." He winked at her. "A lot more practice."

She laughed heartily then, a deep, rich laugh that he had never heard. He kissed her soundly, thoroughly, and as his belly grumbled asked, "Do you think we can take a break? I'm starving."

❦

AFTER THEY HAD EATEN, JENNY PULLED OUT THE TWO folded pieces of Sam's homemade map. She opened them on the table and fit them together.

"Sam sent me the right half while I was still in Boston. I had no idea what it was when I received it. He gave me strict instructions to guard it so I knew it had to be important."

"And Mo had the other part?" Noah asked.

"Yes. We were able to tell the two halves belonged together. But the labels seemed so odd."

He took her hand in his. "We'll figure it out together, honey."

She squeezed his hand in appreciation. "I've made a good start so far." She pulled out the list she'd made only a few hours ago. "As I lay awake last night, I began to have lyrics run through my head. I recorded the name of every ballad I could think of that Sam ever sang to me and wrote down whatever words I could remember for each."

She handed him the list. "Let me study this a while." He sat back in his chair, deep in concentration.

As she viewed the map in front of them for the umpteenth time that day, a sudden clarity formed. The pieces began to swiftly fall into place. She didn't know if it was the way she'd grouped the ballads or the lyrics that kept playing over and over in her head but all at once her father's cryptic markings and directions began to make sense.

"Noah, I think I'm onto something."

He pulled his attention from the reams of sheets she'd handed him. "Take it slow, honey. Talk it through. If something doesn't fit, backtrack and try another route."

She nodded, taking a deep breath. "Look at the place names on the map. In the lower right corner Sam labeled it *TUAM*. Two inches away, he's marked the name *MULLIGAN,* and farther up to the left is *DUBLIN*."

Her cheeks flushed with excitement and she started singing *The Rocky Road to Dublin* to him. He shuffled through the pages until he came to the lyrics she'd written down and followed along as she sang.

"See!" she cried. "This was all about a man who left his family and the girls brokenhearted in Tuam. He went about his travels, resting in Mulligan, until he finally reached Dublin."

She studied the homemade map. "I'm sure *Tuam* was Texas, where Sam robbed this last bank and left the people there brokenhearted. He then moved on and waited for me in Apple Blossom." She pointed to *Mulligan.* "Finally, he reached *Dublin*—Prairie Dell!"

Her excitement grew. "He's marked this large square to the left of Dublin *VAN DIEMANS LAND.* See the "X"?

Noah leaned forward. "Yes, but why's *MOUNTAIN DEW* written next to it? And why did he put *THE BLACK VELVET BAND* beneath that?"

She laughed. *The Black Velvet Band* was a song I clamored for again and again when I was small. It's about an apprenticed young man who passes a fine colleen as he walks down Broadway. She pulls a watch from her pocket and slips it into his hand. The man is bewitched by her eyes that shine like diamonds and her long hair tied up with a black velvet band.

"Unfortunately, the young apprentice is taken to court the next day and given seven years transportation for possessing a stolen watch. He's sent to Van Diemans Land."

Jenny consulted the map again. "Sam marked an "X" here where he left the stolen goods. The *MOUNTAIN DEW* makes sense, too."

She began to sing –

> Let the grasses grow and the waters flow,
> In a free and easy way,
> But give me enough of that rare old stuff,
> That's made near Galway Bay.
> Come gougers all,
> From Donegal,
> Sligo and Leitrim too,
> And we'll give you the slip as we take
>   a sip,
> Of the rare old mountain dew.
> At the foot of the hill there's a neat little
>   still,
> Where the smoke curls up to the sky;
> By the whiff of the smell you can plainly
>   tell
> There's poitin boys nearby.
> For it fills the air, with a perfume rare
> That betwixt both me and you,

> And as on we roll, we'll drink a bowl,
> Or a bucketful of mountain dew.

"That finishes the verse. The rare old mountain dew has to be what Sam hid. It was supposedly the best in all of Ireland."

"And this last haul was Sam's best ever. That's the connection!" Noah kissed her enthusiastically. "You've linked the clues together."

She read the directions in the top right-hand corner of the map aloud. "Go to one million bags of the best Sligo rags. Left two million barrels of stone. Connaught way to the five hogs. You've arrived in Sally Gardens—so watch for the Galway Races."

Jenny scrunched her eyes shut, willing herself to hear the vague melody pulling at the back of her memory. As she concentrated, it began to form. She softly hummed along as it became clearer to her.

The Irish Rover!

She grabbed a pencil and slipped a new sheet of paper in front of her. She wrote out the words to the song dancing in her head. When she had finished, the last puzzle piece fell into place.

"Millions must be miles. If we go one mile Sligo way that's north, because Sligo is in the north. Left is west, and then *back north again for Connaught.*" She smiled triumphantly. "And Sally Gardens is where a couple in love met in a field down by a river. Maybe Sam marked it for me somehow."

She stood and started to pace the small cabin. "Sally Gardens is down by a river in the song. With what I've seen of Nevada so far, it would probably be some barely running stream that passes along where the money is buried."

She returned to point at the last words her father had written in the corner. "He mentions to *'watch for the*

Galway Races' here. That ballad has a line about *'when the bell was run for starting.'*"

"I'll bet he's attached a bell where he's hidden his treasure. You've made sense of everything here." He took her hand. "No one but you could have figured out all the nuances and names Sam used."

Noah pulled her into his lap and nuzzled her neck. "I can't get enough of your mouth or this swanlike neck." He smiled. "Mo won't be back for a bit. I think we need to celebrate how clever you are."

"How should we celebrate?" she mused, her eyes lighting with desire.

"We'll think of something." His mouth met hers.

CHAPTER 25

M o returned from her day of poker minutes before the sun set, reeking of cheap cigar smoke. She flew into the cabin, pushed along by a brisk wind, and leaned her hefty weight against the door to insure it closed tightly.

"Win big, Mo?"

Jenny watched her aunt turn and beam at Noah, then she switched her gaze to her niece. She could feel herself color under Mo's scrutiny. Suddenly, her aunt burst out in hearty laughter and crossed the room to sweep Jenny into a tight embrace. Mo kissed both of her cheeks and then performed the same ritual on Noah.

"I can tell somethin' must've gone right today besides me whippin' the pants off Sid and Sherm." Her eyes twinkled at the couple as she placed her reticule on the table. "Tell me all about it. And I do mean tell all." Her broad grin caused Jenny's face to flame.

"All you need to know, Mo, is that we are on close speaking terms again." Noah reached out and pulled Jenny to him, his arm about her waist. He kissed her temple. She figured she had turned permanently crimson at this point.

Mo gazed at them fondly. "Let's fix us some supper, you two, and I'll tell you all about my day."

Shortly afterward, they gathered around the dilapidated table. Noah solved the problem of only having two chairs by settling Jenny in his lap.

"You look like the cat that swallowed the canary whole," Mo told him.

He smiled at Jenny and gave her a squeeze. "And if I am, Mo, I'm the happiest cat this side of the Mississippi."

Her aunt shared how she had beaten her companions soundly, especially Sid. "Those boys'll never get the hang o' poker. They lose to me regularly and they still come back for more every week."

"Have you ever thought that they might lose to please you?" Jenny asked.

"Pshaw! Ain't nobody fool enough to toss good money away, gal. Exceptin' maybe your da."

"The map!" Jenny explained how they had gone about trying to figure out the meaning behind Sam's garbled directions.

"I'm sure we'll locate the money tomorrow, Mo."

"Wait a minute, Jenny." Noah gave her a stern look. "There's no *we* to this. It's not that far. I'll ride over tomorrow morning, check things out, and hopefully locate Sam's hidden treasure. If I do, I'll come back and let you know."

"You don't think you're going without me?" She scooted off his lap, her hands fisted on her waist. "You've got another thing coming, Noah Daniel Webster, if you believe I'll be content to stay behind."

He stood and placed his hands on her shoulders. "Now listen, Jen—"

"I am not going to listen to—"

"Will you both be quiet?" Mo demanded.

They turned and looked at her.

"First of all, no more arguin'. I don't take kindly to

fightin' o' any kind. Come back over and sit down and we'll discuss this calmly."

They glared at each other. Neither made a move.

"Jenny's going with you, Noah," Mo announced, "so sit down and let me tell you why."

She gave him a triumphant smile. He sat, pulling her back into his lap. She perched stiffly. She was very interested in what Mo had to say.

Her aunt was blunt. "Riley Withers killed your da for that money, Noah. He'll kill you, too, without blinkin' an eye."

Jenny saw the stunned look on Noah's face. "What? I knew Pete was shot dead in the bank robbery. I assumed a lawman took his life."

"When Sammy got here, he shared everythin' about that last job with me. Riley Withers prevented two of their gang from escapin' with them. He shot Pete in cold blood several miles outside of town. Sammy couldn't save Pete's life but he tried to take Riley's."

Noah sighed. "Sam was about the worst shot I've ever seen. If he were aiming at Withers, it's likely he shot his horse instead." His mouth grew hard. Jenny saw a new light burning in his eyes.

"It was business before. Now? It's personal. I will find the money, Jenny. I promise you that. And I will search this earth until I find the lowlife that killed Pete."

"That's why you have to take her with you, Noah." Mo shook her head. "If'n Withers follows you here— and it seems he's been after Jenny since Boston—I don't want him to find her alone and unprotected. If he shows up tomorrow, I can say I haven't seen either of you yet. With Sammy dead, he won't know what to do. The man never did have a lick o' sense."

He seemed reluctant. "What about you, Mo? Withers could hurt you, trying to see if Sam passed along any information to you about where the treasury bonds are located."

Mo frowned. "Hadn't thought of that. 'Course I'm ten times the shot Sammy was. I suppose I could take him out," she mused. At Jenny's gasp, she amended her tone. "I think I'll just stay with Sid. He may not be a grand poker player, but he's a helluva mean cuss. Even Riley Withers would think twice 'fore he messed with someone like Sid."

"Then it's settled?" Jenny asked.

Noah wrapped his hand around her nape and brought her lips close to his. "I guess so." He kissed her tenderly. Her pulse leaped at the contact.

"Oh, Lordy," she heard Mo say.

❦

NOAH SLEPT IN FRONT OF THE DOOR THAT NIGHT. HE intended to keep Riley Withers out, no matter when the man showed up. He hoped he had enough restraint to subdue the outlaw and not shoot him at first sight when the time came. He would need to return both the bank's holdings and Riley Withers intact.

Then he could begin a future with Jenny.

He looked at her now, still asleep, the dying firelight catching the highlights in her hair. The cabin was cold but he contented himself to gaze at her a few more minutes, a sense of possessiveness stirring within him.

Finally he rose, his legs stiff, his neck sore from the position he'd slept in. He tiptoed over and knelt beside her to press a soft kiss on her lush mouth. She awoke with a start and then smiled when she saw him. That smile nearly did him in. Her arms wound around his neck.

"You're lucky Mo's here," Noah whispered.

"Am I?" she murmured. "I thought I was lucky you were here." Mischief lit her eyes.

He kissed her in reply, a deep, soulful kiss that left him weak in the knees.

"Will you two behave?"

He turned his head to look at Mo. "You're just jealous."

She sat up. "Maybe I am and maybe I ain't. I do know I'm hungry. Let's get this day started with some flapjacks."

Jenny put on the coffee and they discussed what they would need to take with them.

"According to the map, we're not more than two, maybe three hours from Sally Gardens," he estimated. "Still, it may be harder to locate than we think—and even harder to find where to dig."

"Remember the Galway Races. I'm sure we'll find a bell nearby as a marker."

Jenny's positive tone caused Noah's optimism to grow. "Once we find Sam's haul, it may be too late to start back."

"I don't mind. I think I got used to life out on the range. Mr. Mulholland—"

"Don't go there, Jenny," he warned. "I can't stand to hear another pearl of wisdom from Milton Mulholland. Promise me you won't mention his name again."

Her green eyes sparked impishly. "I'll think about it."

He tried not to sound so disagreeable. "I'll need to get a pick and shovel. Some flour and beans. We've got enough coffee for a short trip."

"What will you do when we find the money, Noah?"

"Bring it back here for now. Normally, I'd head straight to the nearest Wells Fargo office so it would be in good hands." He raked a hand through his hair. "With an unknown variable like Riley Withers wandering around, though, I figure I need to be here to greet him personally. The money can serve as bait. I can kill two birds with one stone and bring both in at the same time."

She shivered. "What if he doesn't show up anytime soon? What if we're wrong about him?"

Mo snorted. "Ol' Riley Boy will be here. Mark my words. He's a slippery eel but he'll be drawn to all that free money. He killed more than one man for it. Withers isn't the type to give up."

Noah rose from the table. "I think I'll feed the horses and head over for supplies." He glanced at Jenny. "Want to help shovel feed down that prissy-footed horse of yours?"

"Sassy is a lady, Noah," Jenny said with mock haughtiness. "She doesn't want you to forget it."

He shrugged into his coat and then held her cloak out. He wrapped it around her shoulders and she tied it, pulling the hood up for extra protection.

He opened the door, glad to see yesterday's strong wind had died down. A light dusting of snow covered the ground but no wind would make for a more pleasant ride. He grabbed Jenny's hand and hurried her around the corner to where the horses were stabled. Once they reached the protection of the open shed, he pulled her into his arms for a searing kiss.

"Mmm." She pressed her head against his shoulder. "I didn't know how entertaining feeding horses could be."

Noah kissed her again. "I bet even Mr. Mulholland hasn't discovered that secret."

"I thought you said—"

"—that *you* weren't supposed to mention the all-knowing Mulholland. I didn't say anything about me."

"Then I'm glad I made no promises about dime novels."

He groaned. "I only know one way to get Milton Mulholland out of your head." He dropped to one knee, his hands wrapped around hers. "Miss McShanahan, I know that Mr. Mulholland holds a special place in your heart but do you have it in you to push those tender feelings for him aside—with good reason?"

Jenny smiled down at him. "I am rather fond of Mr. Mulholland. However, if the reason were important enough, I might consider nudging him aside."

"Is spending the rest of your life with me sufficient?"

She bit her lip. "Are you asking?"

He grinned. "I am, indeed. Jenny McShanahan, would you do me the honor of becoming my wife?"

"Didn't you ask me this same question yesterday?"

"Yes, I did." He brushed his lips against her gloved fingers. "But as I recall, you never gave me an answer. We got caught up in . . . other things." He smiled at the memory of their lovemaking.

Tears glistened in her eyes. "Yes, Noah Daniel Webster. Yes, yes, yes! I will marry you."

He rose and cradled her face in his hands. "I love you." He kissed her carefully, as if she might break.

Laughter bubbled up from her. He loved the sound of it. Almost as much as her sweet mouth and generous nature and quick mind. And he'd done the right thing by asking her to marry him again. The first time he'd been flippant. He wanted this to be the proposal she remembered.

"I love you, Noah Daniel Webster, former consumptive guide and current Texas Ranger."

He grew serious. "I'll be giving up Rangering, Jenny. I'm not sure what I'll do or where we'll even settle."

She frowned. "Why? Being a Ranger is something you love."

"I've found something I love more," he answered. He wrapped her in a tight embrace, his lips brushing her hair. "A Ranger leads a nomadic life, honey. There's danger aplenty. I don't plan on making you a young widow."

She studied him a long moment. "You're really willing to give it all up? For me?"

He nodded, not trusting himself to speak. He held her close for a few minutes. The feel of her in his arms let him know he had made the right decision. Rangering paled when compared to Jenny.

Noah finally broke the contact between them. "Come on, woman. Let's get this chore done."

When they'd finished, he said, "I'm going over to the general store now. I'll be a half-hour or more."

She gave each horse a love pat on the nose. "Why so long? You don't have that much to purchase."

He shrugged. "There's a particular way things are done in Prairie Dell. You don't walk in and right back out. Talk—and gossip—is the lifeline of a small town. Put that in the guidebook."

"I understand. I'll be sure I'm ready to leave when you return."

Noah escorted her back to Mo's door. "Be good." He kissed the tip of her nose and she went inside.

As Jenny turned from closing the door, fear invaded every pore of her being. Riley Withers sat in a chair by the table, his ankles casually crossed in front of him.

"What the hell took you so long?"

CHAPTER 26

Jenny quickly took in the scene. Her aunt sat tied to the other chair. Her eye was huge but her mouth was set in stone. She could see swelling already on one side of Mo's face. The monster must have hit her hard.

Riley Withers twirled his Colt in one hand. She could see he made an effort to guard his temper because he took a cleansing breath and addressed her in a more pleasant tone.

"Let's start again, shall we? Greetings, Miss Mc-Shanahan. Or may I call you Jenny? We have been introduced before."

He looked over at Mo. "And of course, I know your lovely aunt. I was a guest here long ago."

Her heart hammered so loudly, she was afraid it would leap from her body and scurry out the door. Though his tone was civil, the malevolent smile betrayed his true character. This was a man who enjoyed inflicting terror upon others.

Withers placed the gun on the table, on top of the folded map. "Mo tells me that Sam's dead and didn't bother to tell her where the bonds are. I tend to believe her after our little talk."

He stared at her a long moment. Jenny willed herself

not to look away. She'd never been one prone to fainting. She was determined not to start now.

"You, on the other hand, know. I'd stake my last dollar on that. Sam was always sweet on his little girl."

He stood and began pacing the small room. "Mo here tells me that a Texas Ranger, a fellow named Webster, is the man who escorted you to Prairie Dell."

He shot a look at her. She refused to react to his words. He continued moving about the small space. Though Jenny longed to fling open the door and flee, she couldn't leave Mo alone with this outlaw.

"Pity. Those Rangers are such straight arrows. I bet Mr. Webster will try to turn that loot over to the authorities and waive the finder's fee. So much for Sam's desires."

He moved toward her and she stepped away until her back pressed against the door. He bent close enough that she could feel his hot breath on her cheek. "I don't think I much care for this Ranger. Do you, Jenny?"

He laughed softly and answered his own question. "I think you do. I saw you leave with him fifteen minutes ago. That's an awful long time to feed a few horses. And you've come back with rosy cheeks and swollen lips. The kind that shows you've been up to no good."

He brushed the back of his rough hand against her cheek. She flinched at his touch. He threw back his head and laughed aloud. "You and I are going after the money. I haven't come all this way not to claim it. I want it all. Every dime. From what Mo tells me, this Ranger doesn't have a clue where to look. But I know you do. I can see it on your face."

Withers walked back and holstered his gun. He slid the two pieces of the map from the table and into his pocket. "Let's go." He walked toward her.

"I wouldn't go anywhere with a murdering thief like you." She spit in his face.

Withers backhanded her. The blow knocked her to the ground. Jenny wiped away the trickle of blood that oozed from the corner of her mouth and stared up at him with hate-filled eyes.

"Oh, I think you'll go with me."

From the corner of her eye, she saw Mo rise, the chair still tied around her ample frame. Before she could warn her away, Mo rushed the outlaw, slamming into him. Both fell to the ground, Mo on top of the thief. Withers pushed her off him and then righted the chair in a quick show of his superior strength.

"You dirty whore." He lifted the chair by its rickety arms and flung it backward. Mo struck the wall. The chair tilted and then toppled over. Mo lay still.

Jenny leaped to her feet to rush to her aunt, panicked that Mo had struck her head and might already be dead. Withers had other ideas, though. He grabbed Jenny's waist and yanked her back.

"Leave the bitch," he muttered. "She's a worthless piece."

Jenny struggled against him, tearing at the hands that encircled her. He spun her to face him and she clawed at his face. He punched her then, a swift jab that caught her left eye. Stars whirled through the air. She grew faint.

"No, you don't, you little fool. Don't go passing out on me."

Withers shook her and threw her down on the worn cot. The stars began to fade as blackness raced up to meet her. Suddenly, cold water hit her in the face. She sputtered and sat up, her eye throbbing.

The outlaw wrapped his large hand around her nape and brought her close to his face. It was mottled a bright red. Wrath pulsated from him. She knew he might kill her with one blow.

But he needed her still. That was her one ace in the hole.

"Take me to Sam's loot. Now. No more games."

He slapped her once again for emphasis, not as hard as before, but enough to stun her while he wrapped a piece of cut rope around her wrists several times. He yanked it tightly.

She winced at the pain. Her hands would go numb within minutes. She had to do something. She opened her mouth to shout for help but he was one step ahead of her and thrust a wadded handkerchief into her mouth. Before she could spit it out, he placed another handkerchief over her mouth and tied it behind her head. Her scream came out a muffled whimper.

He put on his long, dark coat and dragged her to her feet, not bothering to shut the door as they left. Her heart cried out for someone to see them and find Noah, to stop Withers—or at least to find Mo and take care of her. With the temperature falling so low, Mo could freeze to death with that open door if she remained unconscious for long.

Her captor's horse was tied behind a shack two doors down. Withers swung into the saddle and reached down for her, placing her in front of him. One hand went about her waist and pulled her against him. She almost gagged at the intimate contact between them.

He seemed to read her thoughts and chuckled. In a low tone, he said in her ear, "I have all kinds of plans for you, Jenny McShanahan. We're gonna have us some real fun as soon as the money's found."

Her insides heaved. She would retch if she didn't get away. She threw herself from the saddle, taking her kidnapper with her. They landed on the hard ground, the blanket of snow too thin to cushion their fall.

He grunted as she staggered to her feet. He latched onto her ankle and pulled hard, causing her to fall face down. He rolled her over and said with a snarl, "Quit delaying us. If you think that Ranger'll catch up to us, you're wrong. And if he does, I'll shoot him between those sky blue eyes of his."

His threat hung in the air as he lifted her to her feet. He ripped her cloak from her and tossed her into the saddle. This time he wrapped a length of rope around her waist and tied it to the saddle horn. Between the taut rope and freezing weather, she was miserable. She also struggled to breathe with the gag in her mouth and the handkerchief threatening to cover her nostrils.

"Try it again and I'll let you drag along a mile or two. Even your pretty little face might not appeal to me much after the hide's been torn off it."

Jenny went cold inside. She had to conquer her fears. Even if she led him to Sally Gardens, Noah knew where to find her. Texas Rangers were legendary. Everything she had heard or read—especially in Mr. Mulholland's guidebook—said they could outshoot, outride, and outsmart anyone on the planet. She put her trust in the man she loved. Noah would know how to handle Riley Withers.

They rode away hard and fast from Prairie Dell for a few minutes when Withers brought his horse to a stop in the middle of nowhere. He untied the handkerchief that held her gag in place and ripped the other one from her mouth. She greedily sucked in quick breaths of air.

Cold steel touched her jaw. She heard the click of a gun. "You need to give me some instructions, Jenny. If you're lucky, I'll take the money in trade for your life." He nudged the pistol into her flesh. "So, where do we begin?"

NOAH LEFT THE GENERAL STORE, HIS STRIDE A LITTLE longer than usual. He was in a hurry to get back and start out. He'd spent longer at the store than he wanted to, visiting and even sampling some of the eggs and bacon the owner's wife had made. With two breakfasts now sticking to his ribs, he was sluggish.

The twitter in his neck stopped him dead in his tracks. That kind of tingle always meant trouble—big trouble—especially as fast as it came on. He drew his revolver. Thoughts of Pete's killer danced before his eyes.

He wanted to break out in a full run down the little strip of a street but if Withers were already here, Noah would need the element of surprise. His neck was almost stinging now, leaving his entire body on edge.

He approached the shack carefully. His first surprise was seeing the door wide open. No sensible person would leave a door open in this kind of cold. Instinct told him Withers had already come and gone.

The second surprise greeted him when he saw a motionless Mo lying on the floor, tied to the remains of a shattered chair, her breathing shallow. He quickly undid the bonds and eased her onto her back. He moved his fingers through her hair and found a lump the size of a goose egg.

Her eyes fluttered open and tried to focus. "Noah?" Her voice was raspy.

"I'm here, Mo. You all right?"

She nodded, only to wince. She brought a hand to her scalp and rubbed it gingerly. "Jenny!" she cried out and pushed herself to a sitting position.

"Withers?"

"Yes," she moaned softly.

Noah swallowed his rage. He needed a clear head. Anger wouldn't do him any good. He had to put aside the fact that Withers had killed Noah's own daddy and now held the woman he loved.

"Tell me what you can."

Mo took a deep breath. "Showed up right after you

left. Roughed me up some. Waited until Jenny came in." She paused and took another breath. "Took her 'n the map. Said the money was all his. They left . . ." Her voice faded out. "I don't know how long ago." She began to weep. "You gotta find her, Noah. She's all I got left."

"I'll find her. I promise." He lifted Mo to her feet and walked her to the cot, where she collapsed. "I'll get someone to help you."

He grabbed his Winchester and raced out the door, hurrying back to the general store. He didn't have time for long explanations.

"Mo's hurt. I'm going after the man that did it."

He knew that would be enough. The residents of Prairie Dell would pull together and help one of their own. He quickly saddled Star. As he rode out, a prayer formed on his lips.

"Please, God. Let me find her. Let Jenny be all right."

CHAPTER 27

Jenny tried to fight the tremors that ran through her body. The day held no breeze and a moderate amount of sunshine but it was so cold. It seeped into her pores and tickled her bones. She didn't want Withers to have the pleasure of knowing how her body ached within her woolen dress.

Her hands, too, had absolutely no feeling in them. The cord around her wrists cut off all circulation. The rope around her waist rubbed and chafed at her skin. For once, she wished she had the protection of her thick, heavy corset.

She pointed them in the general direction of what Sam called Sally Gardens. She had a good idea of where to go but she wanted to slow them down as much as possible in order to give Noah time to catch up. He would remember the details of the map even if it wasn't in front of him.

She refused to allow her teeth to chatter so she'd clenched her jaw for miles now. She had to forcibly relax it in order to speak.

"We need to stop. I've got to look at the map."

Withers grunted but slowed the speedy horse. He removed the pieces of map from his pocket and opened them both. He placed them against the saddle horn, his hands resting on her thighs to keep it in place. She fought the wave of revulsion.

She studied the map several minutes without speaking, trying to buy as much time as she could, but she sensed his impatience.

"I will do the best I can but Sam's instructions are in some kind of code. I might have figured it out but I won't be sure until we get to where I believe it's leading us."

He cursed under his breath.

"Look for yourself. It's very unusual. I'm filling in the blanks the best I can."

More than anything, Jenny wanted to protect the knowledge that Noah would know exactly where they headed.

"We need to continue north. I'll tell you when to change direction."

He seemed satisfied for the moment and refolded the map. After he tucked it back into his pocket, he pulled her closer.

One hand had the reins. The other slipped from her waist back down against her thigh. She froze in fear.

His rough stubble grazed her ear. "We will have us some fun, Jenny McShanahan." He nibbled on her lobe. "You're not a pretty sight now but there's still plenty of you to use up before I sell you to a brothel."

Her eyes filled with tears but she refused to let them spill. She wouldn't give this brute the pleasure of seeing that.

He laughed softly. "Wouldn't old Mo get a kick out of it—sluts running in the family and all."

Her thoughts strayed back to Mo. Jenny desperately wanted her aunt to be alive. She wanted Noah to find her. For this nightmare to end.

Withers spurred the horse and she fell back against him. If she'd had a gun at that moment, Jenny knew she could have shot Riley Withers through his black heart and never looked back.

They rode on in silence. Her mind wandered a bit. The dime novels she'd read had never been this realistic. They told stories of outlaws and robberies, gunfights and heroes, but none of that prepared her for Riley Withers.

Or Noah Webster.

Despite everything, a glow ran through her as the thought of him—his laugh, his touch, his burning kisses. A dime novel could never describe the feelings Noah stirred within her.

They pulled up fast. She returned to the reality around her.

"Damnation and hellfire." The words were a whisper.

She looked out to see three riders coming their way. Their own horse turned in the direction of the approaching men and would have taken off if Withers hadn't held it back.

He jerked her against him. "Don't say a word, especially about where we're headed. These boys are trouble, through and through, and stupider than a prairie chicken. Just keep your trap shut. I've got some fast talking to do."

He held up a hand in greeting as they approached. Jenny counted three dirty riders. All wore an angry look upon their unshaven faces. It was obvious they weren't happy to see Riley Withers.

"Helluva place to run into you boys."

One man in his early twenties jumped from his horse and marched straight to them. "Why in the hell did you take Old Paint?" The man glared up at Withers for an eternity before breaking his gaze. He turned it to the horse instead.

"How's my girl?" he cooed.

Withers laughed. "What are you talking about, Jack?

Some kid gave me Paint when I left the train. You said I could take a horse. Remember?"

The one named Jack scratched his head. "I did?" He frowned as if trying to recall what had been said.

"Sure, you did. And I was much obliged to you fellas for letting me get about my work." He shifted slightly. "Hey, how did your train robbery turn out?"

An older man still in the saddle replied. "Not a bad day's work, Riley. Wish you coulda stayed around and celebrated with us." His eyes sparkled with meanness.

"Thanks for the offer, Jake. I'll have to take you up on it sometime."

"Never did find me that purdy girl, though." The one named Jack eyed her hungrily. Jenny's stomach contracted in fear.

Withers chuckled. "This one appeal to you?"

Jack nodded. "I could take a fancy to her. That I could." He licked his lips as he stared at her.

"Well, I'd planned on selling her when I finished up with her. If you're really interested, I'm sure we can work out a deal."

Before Jack could reply, the oldest of the three men said, "You're not calling the shots anymore, Riley. I want you to give Jack his horse back. Now."

Jenny sensed the anger that rippled through Withers. "C'mon, Jim. Your kid made a mistake. I'm sorry he gave me the wrong horse. No harm done, is there?"

Jim's eyes remained wintry. "We'll take the horse. The girl, too." He stared at Withers. "And I want to know what's up. We want in on whatever deal you're up to. You owe us."

She thought fast. If she could cause enough problems between these men, it would be another delay. Noah would have more time to catch up to them.

"I'm Jenny McShan," she blurted out. "Sam's girl."

The trio eyed her curiously. "Famous Sam had a daughter?"

"Yes." She tried to sound eager and feminine. "We're on our way to see if we can figure out where Sam buried his last haul. Maybe you gentlemen could help us out?" She batted her lashes coyly, though it was difficult with her swollen eye. Apparently, it worked.

"Get off, Riley. I want my horse. Sam's girl, too."

Withers held out his hands and shrugged. "Suits me, Jack. She's a little spitfire anyway. Good luck in controlling her." He tossed a leg over to dismount and loosened his saddlebag, then stepped away from the horse.

As he did, she felt him deliberately—but subtly—jostle her. He moved back and she slid off the horse, caught by the rope that was tied to the saddle horn.

"Seems you weren't joshing, Riley," Jack exclaimed as he came closer to her.

"Do you think you could untie my hands, sir? I've lost all feeling in them."

Jack grinned. "I betcha I can rub some feeling back in them, little lady." He whipped out a knife and bent over her hands.

She looked over his shoulder. What happened next was a blur. Withers threw his saddle bag at the man named Jake. It hit him square in the face and he fell from his horse. Withers quickly pulled his pistol and shot first Jim, the only one still in the saddle, and then Jack, the one about to slice through her ropes. Jack gave her a startled look before sinking to the ground, pulling her down with him.

Withers turned and shot Jake in the gut. She thought his cry sounded worse than a wounded animal —high, piercing, and then mournful. No sound came from the other two.

Withers kicked Jack away from her and lifted her back onto Old Paint. He inspected the cord that bound her wrists. Satisfied that it was intact, he rifled through each man's pockets, placing the money he found into

his own. He then searched their saddle bags and removed the more valuable items.

Jenny watched in dull fear. She had known Withers
to be a thief and murderer but she hadn't realized how
dangerous he could be. He had shot three men in cold
blood without a blink of an eye and now methodically
robbed their corpses, as well.

He re-packed what he wanted to take with them
and loaded it onto one of the dead men's horses, which
he then tied to his own. He caught her horrified gaze
upon him and flashed what could only be termed an evil
grin.

"Maybe you finally realize just how serious I am."

CHAPTER 28

Noah arrived at what had to be Sam's version of Sally Gardens. He'd made good time by angling across country instead of following the map's instructions to the letter. A pitiful excuse for a stream did run nearby, or at least it had till it froze over, probably within the last week. He'd hoped to catch up to Jenny and Withers but had no idea he would actually beat him here.

This puzzled him. They'd had a good half hour start on him, maybe more. He didn't think they were lost. He prayed they hadn't run into any trouble. Even as desolate as this part of Nevada was, the west could be an unpredictable place. Instead, he figured that Jenny had done everything in her power to slow them down, giving Noah time to catch up.

He tried to quell the fear that raced through his veins. Jenny meant the world to him. He couldn't imagine a life without her. He thought back to the condition Withers left Mo in. At least he knew the outlaw needed Jenny alive to help in his search for Sam's loot. She had to be all right. *She had to be.* He wouldn't let his thoughts go elsewhere.

Noah skimmed his eyes across the ground. The snow had started coming down hard almost twenty minutes before, obscuring the earlier sunshine. It would hide a man's footsteps within two minutes. He wondered if it concealed the bell Jenny was so sure would be here. He got down from Star and led the horse behind him, searching for it.

A glint of something caught his eye. He hurried toward it and found the bell mounted on a thick stake about the size of a ruler, slightly tarnished, but a welcomed sight. The Galway Races started here. He was certain when they dug they would find the money and bonds. All he needed now was to have Jenny safe while he did so.

He scanned the surrounding land for an element of surprise and decided on a rock formation about twenty yards to the south. He could place Star around the corner and out of sight of approaching visitors. He tied the horse to a scraggly bush next to an overhang of rocks. Star had always been good about staying in place, never even shying around gunfire. Ever since he'd been traveling along with that prissy filly, though, Noah didn't think he could trust his mount anymore. Sassy had put some strange notions into old Star's head.

He gave the horse a fond pat. "We'll be with our women soon, boy. That should make you happy."

Star's ears pricked up—but not because of the words Noah spoke. The little wind had died down in the last half hour, which made it possible to hear a galloping rider approach from a half-mile or more. More than one horse, from the sound of it.

Removing his Winchester, Noah cocked it as he slipped up the backside of the gathered rocks to their top. A small, flat surface greeted him. He slid on his belly to the edge.

He had a perfect view of the travelers that drew near.

As two horses came closer, he saw one was tied to the other. He sucked in his breath when he spotted

Jenny sitting in front of Withers on the lead horse. They rode up and stopped. Both surveyed the area, heads turning slowly as they searched. The outlaw pointed to the bell first and cackled with glee as he dismounted.

"Looks like there's some digging to do." His voice carried through the desert air. Noah clenched his rifle.

Withers pulled Jenny roughly from the horse and she stumbled. She hung about six inches above the ground. He could see the rope around her waist and wrists, which was attached to the saddle horn. His blood boiled at the sight.

Withers jerked her up and as she faced Noah's direction, he could see her split lip and swollen eye. He took aim but Withers shifted so that Jenny now had her back to Noah. He didn't have a clean shot.

The outlaw untied the rope from the horn and her feet touched the ground. Withers pulled out a pocketknife and cut through her bonds. Noah saw her flinch as the ropes fell. She began to rub her wrists, her shoulders hunched in pain.

Her kidnapper reached to the saddle and took out a shovel, which he thrust into her hands. "Now dig, darlin', and maybe I won't be so rough on you the first time we go around."

It was hard to tell what hit Riley Withers first—the bullet from Noah's rifle or the shovel Jenny swung. Both the bullet and the farm tool made contact and the bandit fell to the ground in a heap.

Jenny whirled and brought the shovel back up as protection while she scanned the area for the shooter. Noah swallowed the lump in his throat and stood, hands in the air, to show her she'd come to no harm.

She dropped the shovel as he put down the Winchester and ran across the space between them.

Then she was in his arms. He held her tightly, aware of how close he'd come to losing her. She was frozen to his touch, and he realized she didn't have on her cloak. He rubbed his hands up and down her arms to warm her. Tears flowed freely as her teeth chattered noisily.

She tried to speak but no words came out, which caused her tears to fall even harder. Noah released her and took off his coat. He wrapped it around her and enveloped her in his arms once more, pulling her as close as he could. Her heart beat rapidly against his chest. He kissed her temple gently and touched his hand to her eye, nearly swollen shut now. She shied away and ducked her head.

"It's all right, honey. He won't hurt you ever again."

She looked down at Withers, still unconscious from the blow she'd struck. "I hope one of us killed him. He's pure evil, Noah."

"I know, baby." He continued to smooth her hair and rub her back. He needed to touch her as much as she needed to be held.

She suddenly jerked up her head. "Mo?"

He returned her head to his chest. "She'll be fine. She was hurt but she'll be right as rain."

She began crying again softly. He knew to let her cry it out. She'd been in a life-threatening situation and come through it alive but the shock had set in. He kept his arms around her until he heard Withers moan. Slowly, he released her. She clung to him.

"I need to take care of him, Jenny. You'll be safe."

She nodded and dropped her arms. She took one look at Withers and hustled away from the fallen outlaw to retrieve Noah's Winchester.

He knew Withers only suffered a shoulder wound. His mind screamed out to kill the bastard for even touching Jenny, much less hurting her, but it was against his code of honor. A Ranger never killed unless the situation called for it. He put his feelings aside. The law would deal with this sorry excuse of a human being.

Withers sported a large lump on his forehead from

Jenny's accurate hit. Noah quickly handcuffed the criminal with his hands in front of him. It would be too much strain on his shoulder wound to do so from behind.

The man slowly opened his eyes. They were cold, flat, and deadly.

"You'll live, Withers. Let me take a look at your shoulder."

The outlaw oozed contempt as he said, "No. Just leave me to die. If 'n I can't be rich, I'd rather not live at all."

Noah shook his head. "You won't live long anyway. You're going back to Texas to stand trial for robbery and murder." His eyes glinted hard as steel as he looked the bastard in the eye. "For murdering my daddy."

He saw the confused look on Wither's face.

"My daddy was Pete Webber. You might remember him. You killed him for something you'll never have."

The wounded man groaned. "I was born with all the bad luck in the world. Worse 'n the Purnells."

Noah turned to Jenny. "I've got to dress his wound and then dig for Sam's loot. Will you be all right?"

She took a step forward. "Let me take care of his injury. I've had practice with that at the clinic. You can start to dig."

He went to her and took her elbow, leading her away from Withers. "You don't have to do that, Jenny. In fact, I don't want you near the son of a bitch."

She shook her head resolutely. "No. I have to prove to myself that I'm not afraid of him." She smiled weakly. "Besides, he's handcuffed. And you'll be right here."

He swiftly brought his mouth down on hers for a quick kiss. "You are an amazing woman, Jenny McShanahan. That must be why I love you."

NOAH LEANED AGAINST THE SHOVEL AND STARED AT the bonds on the opened oilcloth in front of him. It was incredible that the paper before him translated into all that money. Some cash, mostly large bills, were also included but it was the treasury bonds that made up the bulk of the fortune Sam stole.

Sam hadn't buried the package very deeply. There'd been no need. That crazy map of clues from Irish ballads would never have led anyone but Jenny here to the middle of nowhere.

She came to stand beside him. She seemed unimpressed by what lay before them. "What do we do now?"

He wrapped the oilcloth back around the loot and tied it tightly. "I'll take you back to Prairie Dell first. The bank's goods will go to the nearest Wells Fargo office. Then I'll escort Withers back to Texas to stand trial."

"Alone?" Concern blanketed her features.

"One Texas Ranger for one prisoner? That's nothing, sweetheart. I've taken in eight or nine at one time in the past."

He loved how her eyes grew wide at that. "Let's go."

Noah placed the oilcloth in a saddlebag. He'd already secured Withers on his painted horse, which Noah tied to Star. The extra horse he hitched to the one Withers rode upon. Noah pulled out a blanket to wrap around him since Jenny still wore his coat. He hadn't been cold while digging but it definitely pierced him now. He figured it to be around twenty-eight degrees and he was never far off in his estimates.

"Where's your cloak?"

"He took it. He said . . . never mind what he said." She bit her lip and winced.

He wanted to thrash Withers all over again. He didn't know if he'd ever get over his anger in how the man mistreated Jenny and Mo.

"Noah?" She called his name softly. "Why don't you take your coat back? It would easier for me to wrap myself in the blanket." Her sore mouth attempted a smile. "And I will have you to keep me warm, won't I?"

He grinned at her. They traded garments and he mounted Star. He lifted Jenny up in his lap and settled her against him. Her curves seemed made for his body as they dissolved into him. He snaked both arms around her waist and breathed in her sweet scent.

It would definitely be a more enjoyable ride back.

They made it to Prairie Dell about an hour before sunset. Sid and Sherm greeted them as they rode down the short strip. Both men knew instantly that Riley Withers was the man who had harmed their Mo.

"We'll sit up with him all night, Noah. No sense for Mo to have to be stuck with looking at the sumbitch before you leave."

He thanked them and they took away the handcuffed Withers. Both men had pistols aimed at the outlaw, looking for any excuse to shoot.

Noah brought the horses to Mo's shed. Sassy nickered a friendly greeting and Star looked frisky at the sight of the filly. He dismounted and reached up for Jenny. She placed her hands on his shoulders. He lifted her down but kept his hands around her waist.

"I can't seem to let go of you." His voice was raw with emotion.

"Then don't—but you do need to kiss me."

He lower his mouth to hers. He was aware of how sore she was so he gently brushed his lips against hers.

"I'm not broken, Noah," she murmured against his mouth.

It was all the invitation he needed. He kissed her until they were both breathless.

Finally, he dragged his mouth from hers. "We need to go inside and check on Mo. I'll come deal with all these horses in a minute."

She nodded. He took her hand and led her to the door. They entered the welcomed warmth of the cabin.

"Jenny, my gal!"

She ran the few steps to her aunt and flung her arms about the stout woman. "Oh, Mo. I was so worried about you." She buried her face in Mo's shoulder. "I'm so glad you're alive."

"Damn straight I'm alive. Wouldn't want that pond scum to get the best of a McShanahan."

She reached to touch Mo's head and located the huge lump. Mo pulled away from Jenny's probing fingers.

"Now don't go messing with that. It hurts bad enough without you touching it."

"But Mo—"

"No buts, child. Let's round up some supper and we'll all have ourselves a good chat. You come home with raw wrists and a swollen face, dragging this Webster boy behind you. I've got to hear all about it."

"It's not a pretty story, Mo."

She brushed a lock from Jenny's cheek. "And you're not a pretty sight either, hon."

Both women looked at each other and began to laugh. Noah wondered if he would ever understand women.

As they ate, Jenny explained how she had dragged her feet in reaching the spot on Sam's map where they hoped the treasure was buried. He saw the anxiety on her face as she told about running into the Purnell brothers. He recognized them from the descriptions she gave.

"It was frightening how fast Withers killed all three men. I knew then that nothing would stop him. At least until Noah arrived."

He covered her hand with his. "That's just three more charges of murder to add to his slate." He gave her a reassuring look. "He will pay, honey. Texas will hang him from the highest noose."

They bedded down for the night. All too soon, the morning light signaled his departure. Noah made sure everything was loaded and packed for the long trip to Texas.

Mo went out to get a good look at Riley, leaving them a private moment in which to say goodbyes. Already, Noah missed Jenny, a dull ache in his heart.

"You'll stay here with Mo until I return."

She nodded, her green eyes glimmering with unshed tears.

"It'll give you time to get to know one another. I'll be back for you as soon as I can. You know that?"

Jenny stared at his chest. "I know."

He lifted her chin until their eyes met. "Don't worry, honey. I'm a Ranger. The best there is."

He kissed her, tenderly at first, not wanting to hurt her, but her mouth sparked feelings of fierce possessiveness within him. He wanted to leave her with something to remember him by.

Noah deepened the kiss, his tongue branding her, letting her know in no uncertain terms that she was his, for all time. He ran his hands up and down her arms, finally cupping them around her face.

"I'll be back, sweetheart. I promise."

With that, Noah left Prairie Dell with his prisoner in tow.

Jenny couldn't shake the sudden chill that ran through her as Riley Withers smiled back at her.

CHAPTER 29

Jenny missed Noah but she was grateful to have the time to get to know Mo. Her aunt was witty, irreverent, intelligent, and simply fun to be around. In the week that had passed, Jenny had grown very fond of Mo, as well as the people of Prairie Dell.

She had never had a group welcome her with such open arms as did the denizens of this tiny town. All her life she wanted to be accepted for who she was. The town did just that and she was quickly caught up in its daily affairs.

Mo was a voracious reader who collected newspapers from everyone who'd ever come in contact with Prairie Dell. Traders, travelers, customers—all shared their newspapers with her aunt. She had fun going back through the stacks, seeing America through the eyes of reporters twenty years ago.

At night, the two women carried on long conversations. She told Mo all about life at The Thompson School and working at the clinic for Dr. Randolph. In return, Mo regaled her with tales about life in County Cork and the various scams she and Sam pulled throughout the west in their heyday. Some of the stories were incredibly outlandish but Mo swore they were all true.

As they sat in front of the fire after dinner one night, Jenny expressed her longings.

"I feel I'm just beginning to know my father through your eyes."

Mo smiled. "And he was a fine one indeed, love. Full of vim and vigor, with his sweet baritone and love for life. A scoundrel? Perhaps. But a happy one, nonetheless."

Suddenly, her aunt flashed a smile—a brilliant smile that gave Jenny a glimpse into the young woman Mo once had been before age and a hard life painted the deep wrinkles about her mouth and brow.

"I have a delicious idea, Niece." She took Jenny's hands in hers. "I know the best way of all for you to know yer da." Mo squeezed her hands in delight. "His letters!"

Mo released Jenny's hands and went to her storage chest. She rooted around in it until she came up with a thick bundle of letters tied with a faded ribbon. She held them up triumphantly.

"Sammy done wrote these to me over the years. I know he wouldn't mind me sharin' them with his daughter."

Mo offered her the thick packet of letters. Jenny reached out tentatively and took them. She placed them in her lap and stared at them, wondering if she should read them.

"Go ahead. You'll see yer da in a way few children can."

Probably forty or fifty letters total stared back at her. She carefully opened the first one. Soon, she was engrossed in her father's life.

The first few were written after Sam had gone back east. He'd met Suzannah almost immediately after he arrived in New York. They fell hopelessly in love. When Suzannah's father denied his only daughter marriage with a penniless stranger, the couple defied him and eloped. Later, they married in the Catholic Church but Suzannah's parents were unforgiving souls.

Sam's love for his wife poured off each page he had written and was only surpassed when he wrote his sister of his daughter's birth.

Mo –

You won't believe Jenny's beauty. I've never seen anything so tiny and so incredibly wonderful. She has Suzannah's looks, the bright green eyes, and she already has a head full of hair. The sweetest disposition of any babe born on earth.

She is a McShanahan, though, mark my words. She is long for a babe—at least that's what they tell me—so I know she'll have our family's height. Her fingers and toes are long and elegant. I could go on about her for days. I don't know how we'll manage, but you've got to meet her someday.

Sam went on to write about how ill Suzannah became. How each breath was a labored one. At her death, his emptiness made Jenny's heart ache. Not one letter went by after that where her father did not mention his beloved wife and all she meant to him.

Sam's pride in his only child took up the majority of the letters that came afterward. He wrote verbatim what her teachers reported to him, how fast her progress was, what a good student she'd become. He rarely told Mo where he was or what he'd been up to but every letter raved about Jenny and her accomplishments at The Thompson School.

The candle burned low by the time Jenny finished. She knew she would re-read the bundle of letters again before she left Prairie Dell. When she did leave, however, she would take a piece of her father in her heart. It still hurt that Sam had left her but she'd been truly blessed to have a parent who cared so deeply for her. It was bittersweet, though, knowing she'd never be able to place her arms about his neck and tell him in person—just once—how much she loved him.

Mo was already fast asleep, snoring lightly, when she blew out the candle and went to bed. Jenny said a quick prayer for Noah's safe return and drifted off into a dreamless sleep.

AT BREAKFAST THE NEXT DAY, JENNY THANKED MO for sharing the letters with her.

"I learned things I would never have been able to, thanks to you." She placed her hand over her aunt's and gave it a quick squeeze. "It was like traveling back in time. I could picture Sam at different places in his life. That was a special gift you gave me, Mo." She brushed a quick kiss on her aunt's cheek.

Mo sighed. "I take them out every now and then and read them myself. It does take a person back." She brightened. "I read Noah's letters, too."

"Noah wrote to you?"

"Oh, many times. Maybe you'd like to read those, too?"

She hesitated. "I'm not sure. It's not like with Papa's." She thought on it. "I do wish I knew him better."

Mo slapped her hand on the table. "Then that settles it." She returned to her chest and shifted items around. This time she brought up two separate packets.

"Noah was a much steadier writer than your da." She smiled fondly at the stacks. "Before you read them . . . I just want you to realize what a special boy he was. He was growin' up as he wrote these letters, Jenny. He's matured into a wonderful man. I'm sure you'll agree with me."

She beamed at her aunt. "I can attest to that."

"Well, I'm needin' to get ready for my poker game.

Why don't you help fix me up? You'll have the place all to yourself then."

She helped Mo choose a gown, along with a matching bonnet and eye patch. It amused her how Mo wore a serviceable black patch on a daily basis. On poker day, however, she needed to be outfitted in one that matched her attire.

After Mo left, Jenny settled in with another cup of coffee, stealing one of Buffy's sugar lumps to sweeten the strong, steaming liquid. She opened the first of well over a hundred letters Noah had written to Mo over the years. The neat, schoolboy hand had given in to a heavy scrawl over time but she heard his voice in her head as she read. She knew from the previous night that Mo had all the notes in chronological order and she was careful to keep Noah's letter arranged the same way.

Much of his correspondence made her hurt. He was a lonely boy, guilt-ridden because he couldn't change his father from being a career criminal and his mother from being bitter over her marriage to such a man. Mrs. Webber had lost her family with her hasty elopement— just as Suzannah had—and it was something Sarah Webster never got over.

She drove Noah hard. Maybe because he was the oldest but he shared a heavy burden as the man of the house at a tender age. Noah never seemed to blame his mother for her feelings but she subconsciously instilled in him notions of worthlessness, simply because his father was Pistol Pete Webber.

Mrs. Webster also drove her son to pursue education as much as possible. They never were in a place long enough for him to attend school for any length of time but she was a well-educated woman in her own right and passed along her learning to her eldest child.

It was apparent how close he was with his brother and sister but it seemed he'd never made any friends. He wanted so much to help support his family—to keep them in one place—that he was willing to do anything to achieve that, even if it meant giving up his own stability by pushing cattle to market.

He wrote from the cattle drives, late at night, around the dying campfire. While the other cowboys slept, Noah wrote to Mo and dreamed of another life, one that would curb his wanderlust and prove that he could be a decent man.

Then the tone of the letters changed. An excitement filled them. He'd met a Texas Ranger.

Mo –

I can't really explain it yet. The words haven't even formed in my own mind, else I could get them down better on paper for you. But this Ranger seemed a giant of a man, though he's not much taller than I am, yet he commanded a respect beyond measure. I wish I could pursue something like that. To be on the right side of law. To do good for others. I know I would be a better man for it.

FINALLY, THE LETTER CAME THAT TOLD MO NOAH had signed on as a Ranger.

I AM CONVINCED THAT I'VE FOUND MY LIFE'S WORK, MO. They weren't just impressed by my shooting skills or my book knowledge (which I have to thank Mama for), but by me! I have finally found something I excel at. Something that makes me feel alive. Something I can take pride in. I promise you that nothing—nothing—will ever take me away from this life of Rangering. I'd be miserable otherwise.

THIS THOUGHT ECHOED TIME AND AGAIN IN THE letters Noah sent after joining up with the Texas

Rangers. He wrote of cases he handled. Of men he'd brought to justice. Of the happiness he experienced as he helped others. No vanity or conceit was involved, just a deep, abiding respect for his office and what he accomplished every day.

And he was giving it all up. Because of her.

Her throat was thick with unshed tears when Mo returned, earlier than usual, a dusting of snowflakes in her hair. Jenny had re-bundled the letters and placed them back in Mo's trunk.

"What's wrong, gal?"

"What do you think being a Ranger means to Noah?"

Mo grew thoughtful. "I'd say it means more to him that anything on this earth. He's made for it. It's a hard life but the one for him." She paused. "He's always thought he needed to prove something to the world because he sprang from Pete's bad blood. Rangering lets him lend people a hand. Gives him self-respect. Brings outlaws to justice. I can't see him doing anything else."

Jenny pondered on Mo's words the remainder of the day. She continued to turn it over in her mind long after they bedded down and her aunt's snores began. She wrestled all night with the quick decision Noah had made by choosing her over being a Texas Ranger. She understood why he believed he must give it up. Rangers dealt with dangerous criminals and savage Indian tribes as they tried to protect the citizens of their state. If he remained a Ranger, he would be gone more often than he was at home and in peril at every turn. By sacrificing his career, he thought he was doing what was right for their relationship.

She couldn't live with that. She couldn't ask him to give up what gave him purpose.

Jenny made the only choice she could as the sun rose. She refused to take Noah away from the only life he loved, one that gave him value and worth in his eyes.

She wouldn't selfishly keep him from doing what made him happy. If they married, he would never forgive her for having to abandon what he was meant to do. He would repeatedly tell her it didn't matter but she knew his love for her would turn bitter as the years passed. He would long to return to what he loved best—serving the law—despite being shackled to her side. And she wanted the best for him.

So much that she would give him up.

A sudden rap at the door startled Jenny. Her emotions raw at the moment, she tossed off her blanket and walked reluctantly to the door. She had just made the biggest decision of her life, one that already brought a twisting agony to her insides. She wasn't exactly in the mood for entertaining company before breakfast.

Opening the door, she was hit with an arctic blast of cold. A stranger stood there—clean-shaven, wavy blond hair, his hat in his hand.

"Miss McShanahan?"

She was taken aback that he knew her name, then realized he might be referring to Mo.

"Yes, I'm one of them. Please come in."

She stood aside and let the man enter and quickly shut the door to block out the frigid temperature. The fire flickered slightly from the sudden draft.

"I have a check for Miss Jenny McShanahan." The man reached into his inside pocket and extracted an envelope. She saw the bold handwriting and instantly recognized it as Noah's.

"Ma'am, this is from—"

"I know who it is from, sir."

She took it from his outstretched hand and held it

in front of her. She was curious that Noah would write so soon. Only a week had passed. He would have had to write the missive almost immediately after departing Prairie Dell. She wondered, too, about the hand delivery, afraid to open it.

"Won't you come warm yerself by the fire, young man?" Mo motioned him over. "I bet a good cuppa coffee would hit the spot."

He smiled eagerly. "Yes, ma'am, it would. I'm Ted. Ted Simmons."

"Well, pull on up, Ted Simmons, and give us the latest gossip. Word doesn't always reach Prairie Dell in a timely manner." Her aunt gazed at the newcomer greedily. "You wouldn't happen to have a newspaper on you?"

Ted nodded. "In my saddle bags, ma'am. Mr. Webster warned me to come prepared. Let me fetch it while you get that coffee." He pulled his coat about him and left to retrieve the newspaper.

Jenny went over to the cot for a little privacy and sat as Mo prepared the coffee. Her hand moved over the envelope in her lap. It was so like all the ones she had read yesterday. Before she could embarrass herself by bursting into tears, she tore open the envelope and removed the contents inside.

She pulled out a check, the finder's fee for the return of the money and bonds that Sam had stolen. Made out to her. She was surprised at the amount. Even when split equally between her and Mo, it was a generous sum.

Noah had enclosed a brief note to her.

JENNY —

Wanted you and Mo to have this reward money as soon as possible. I know it's not exactly what Sam planned for either of you but at least the money's honestly gained. Can't say how long

I'll be. Withers is a pain in the rear. Nothing I can't handle, though.

I plan to stay for his trial. I think I owe that much to Pete. As soon as it's finished, I'll make my way back to Prairie Dell.

I miss you, Jenny. You're in my every waking thought.

With all my love,

Noah

❧

JENNY KEPT TO HERSELF WHILE MO CONVERSED WITH their visitor. Ted finally begged off having breakfast with them and left three fairly recent newspapers in Mo's proud possession. She flipped through them excitedly as they ate, pointing out first one item and then another.

When Mo realized Jenny's responses were half-hearted at best, she bellowed, "Shake it off, gal. You knew you weren't goin' to see Noah for weeks. I don't know why yer mopin' around so. Quit pickin' at your food like a love-struck fool."

"I'm leaving tomorrow, Mo."

Her aunt snorted. "What the blazes are you talking about? Noah told you to stay put and stay put is what you'll do."

"I've decided not to wait for Noah."

Mo was dumbstruck. "I don't understand."

Jenny shrugged. "I'm not quite sure I do either but it's something I have to do."

Calmly, she explained how Noah told her he would give up being a Ranger for her. Mo's jaw fell open, the shock plain on her face.

"See what I mean? I've only known Noah a short while. You've known him half his life. You recognize what being a Texas Ranger means to him. I do, too— now that I've read his letters."

"But he loves you, Jenny."

"Yes, I think in his way he does. But he loves Rangering more. Those letters made it clear to me."

Mo frowned. "I should never have suggested you read them."

She placed a hand on Mo's arm. "No. I'm glad you did. You saved us both time and heartache. Noah would've grown tired of a stagnant life. I see that now. He would have withdrawn from me and I would never have known the reason he was dying inside a little bit every day."

She wiped away a tear. "I'll always love him, Mo, but I can't see that love destroy the only thing he's meant to do. It's *because* I love him that I have to let him go. Can you understand that?"

Mo put down her fork and slid her chair next to Jenny, drawing her into a warm embrace. "Go ahead. Cry it out."

Jenny buried her face against Mo's shoulder. The tears flowed for a long time.

Finally, she got hold of herself. "I want you to come with me, Mo. We have the reward money the bank sent us. We can start a new life."

Mo's look of alarm almost caused her to laugh. "I ain't goin' back east, Jenny. It's not for me. Give me the wide open spaces of the west. I'm like Sammy in that respect."

"I don't want to return to Boston."

Mo looked surprised. "But that's the only life you've ever known. Where do you think you'll live?"

"I want to go to San Francisco." She paused. "I've also fallen in love with the west, Mo. The spirit of the people. The room for opportunity. There's nothing left for me back in Boston. I'd like to make my life here. From everything I've read, San Francisco's the place to be."

Mo patted her hand. "I'll come visit you but I intend to live in Prairie Dell until my dying day."

They discussed it for a while but Jenny knew how entrenched her aunt was in this cabin. In the long run, she convinced Mo to promise to make a yearly visit to see her.

"What'll you do there? In Frisco."

Jenny shrugged. "I have a few ideas. It's the largest city west of the Rockies so there's bound to be room for a McShanahan. What's the fastest way to travel there?"

"If yer heart's really set on leavin', I guess you could go up to Carson City. Get a train or stage from there." Mo thought a moment. "Sid'll take you. He gets itchy feet every now and then and likes to take off. If'n you leave after our regular Saturday night date, he can get you there and be back in time without missing out on any action."

She grinned. "Ever the businesswoman, Mo?"

Mo returned her grin sheepishly. "Wouldn't stay in business otherwise, dear." She hugged Jenny tightly. "Oh, how I will miss you, Niece."

☙❦❧

NOAH GAZED AT THE LANDSCAPE THAT RUSHED BY THE window. He closed his eyes. They were tired and gritty from lack of sleep. He rubbed at them and turned his head away, pushing it into the cushioned upholstery.

"Bah-stahn. Next stop in ten minutes."

The conductor passed by Noah as he sat forward and placed his head in his hands. What had happened to his well-ordered world? The one where he was in charge. The one where he knew who he was and where he was going and why he did what he did.

Jenny McShanahan had happened. That's what. Her image danced before him. He had turned his life upside down for her. He'd quit his job as a Texas Ranger after Withers had been found guilty, not even staying to see the slimy outlaw hang. He rode like hell back to Prairie Dell, only to find Jenny gone.

The scene with Mo had been an ugly one. He ranted and raved but Mo wouldn't budge an inch. She'd only say that Jenny had decided they shouldn't marry. No, she didn't know exactly where she'd gone, only that once she settled in, Jenny promised to write.

He knew of only once place she'd go. Back to Boston. So, he'd hopped on an eastbound train to a place he didn't want to go to seek out the one thing he couldn't live without.

Jenny.

He ached at the thought of her but he'd realized he couldn't live without her. He needed her like birds needed to fly and fish had to swim. He needed her because when the sun came up in the morning, he didn't feel he could live through another day without her. Noah would find her and convince her he loved her. He had to. He couldn't stand the pain anymore. He'd live anywhere she wanted and do whatever she wanted him to do.

But they had to be together.

The train rolled to a halt. Noah gathered his lone bag and disembarked. The best way to trace her would be through the person who had meant the most to her —Dr. Randolph. The only way he knew how to find the man was at The Thompson School.

Three-quarters of an hour later he stood at its gates. The stone edifice rose four stories high. He wondered how it had looked to a young Jenny when Sam first brought her here all those years ago. She'd probably been scared to death.

Noah walked through the gate and up the stairs to knock at a massive oak door. A gray-haired servant in a starched white pinafore answered.

"May I help you, sir?"

"Yes, ma'am. I'm needing to get in touch with Dr.

Randolph. My name is Noah Webster." He watched her brows raise in typical fashion as he introduced himself in his western drawl. "I'm an old friend of his family and in town for a day or two. I would really like to call on the Randolphs and let my mama know how they are," he finished politely.

"This way, sir." The retainer motioned him into the imposing foyer and closed the heavy door. "Wait here, please."

She indicated a seat, which he took, and placed his bag next to it. He watched her ascend the main staircase and then looked around at his surroundings. He stood to look more closely at a sketch on the wall, which looked like a Winslow Homer. A voice interrupted his inspection.

"May I help you?"

Turning, Noah saw a dour woman behind him, glasses perched on the edge of her rather prominent nose. Her white hair was caught in a severe bun and emphasized her homely face. In that face, though, lay a great strength and cruelty.

As she sized him up he said, "Miss Thompson, I presume?" She was everything he'd imagined the old dragon to be.

The headmistress looked startled. "Why, yes. And you would be?"

"Noah Daniel Webster, ma'am." He enunciated each name slowly and for once took delight in the reaction it caused.

"Mr. Webster?"

He turned to see a man in his mid-forties descending the stairs at a rapid pace. He was impeccably turned out in a gray pinstriped suit and starched white shirt that looked as if it could stand on its own.

"I believe you've met Miss Thompson, Mr. Webster." The physician nodded curtly at his employer.

"I see you are taken care of, Mr. Webster." The

woman's frosty stare lingered on him a moment before she turned and retreated behind a nearby door.

Noah held out his hand. "Thank you for seeing me, Dr. Randolph." He judged a man by his handshake, and the doctor lived up to what Jenny had shared about him.

The older man looked him in the eye. "What's this about, us being old friends?"

"A small untruth that I hoped would guarantee me an audience with you, sir. I need to speak to you about Jenny."

Dr. Randolph's eyebrows raised a notch. "Hmmm. Why don't we adjourn into the parlor?"

He led Noah to a sitting room off the main hallway and indicated a seat. The physician sat opposite him.

"So, where is she, young man? I know you were her trail guide at one point."

He blanched. "You mean . . . she isn't here in Boston with you and your family?"

"No. Frankly, I'm puzzled by the whole business. I had word from her as she traveled to Nevada to meet up with her father." A withering glance crossed his face. "I certainly didn't approve of her taking off across the open countryside with a stranger as her guide."

"She can be mighty headstrong, sir."

Randolph grunted. "I see your point, son." He frowned. "She wrote me again weeks later from Carson City regarding her father's sudden death from illness. Pity, her going all that way. Said she'd write me in more detail when she was settled but that's been a while." He looked into Noah's eyes. "Are you telling me you don't know where she is either?"

A sick feeling churned in his gut. "No, sir. I left her with her aunt in Prairie Dell. When I returned for her, she was gone."

He looked pleadingly at Randolph. "Her aunt

wouldn't tell me where she'd gone. I've got to find her, sir. It's very important."

The physician studied him carefully. "From her brief correspondence earlier, I gathered Jenny was having the time of her life out west. Said she felt like she'd come home." He squinted as if trying to remember something. "She said, *'The confines of the east no longer hold any appeal to me.'* That's the phrase she used."

He sighed and resumed his inspection of Noah. "You came an awfully long way to track her down, Mr. Webster, for purely a social call."

"Yes, sir, I did. When I find her—if I don't strangle her first—I'll tell her I love her and that I want to marry her. I thought she'd understood that before I left."

Randolph burst out laughing. "Got under your skin, did she?" He slapped Noah on the back. "Might as well come home with me for supper, Mr. Webster. You can catch a train first thing in the morning. I bet we can entertain you with some stories about Jenny in the meantime."

CHAPTER 31

Noah rode into Prairie Dell, ready to have it out with Mo. Carson City had been a huge bust. Dr. Randolph said that was where his last communication with Jenny came from so he headed there first.

He'd been able to track down the last place she was seen, a bank where she deposited the finder's fee check. Without his Ranger credentials, though, he was hard pressed to find out much else. He'd taken a pretty little clerk to lunch and flattered her until the cows came home but all he got from her was that Jenny had set up two accounts, one for herself and one for Mo. The gal wouldn't divulge anything else to him. She was afraid she would lose her job and he couldn't blame her.

It might take half his lifetime to scour every town in the west. He didn't want to find Jenny after twenty years, only to show her his gray hair and wrinkles. He had a lot of living to do—and he intended to do all of it with only one woman.

That's why he was back in Prairie Dell. Surely, Jenny had contacted Mo by now. He believed Mo when his friend said she didn't know where Jenny was that first time. He also knew Mo had a stubborn streak a mile wide. This was going to take more than sweet talk.

Noah must convince Mo McShanahan that he was the right man—the only man—for her niece.

He stopped Star in front of Mo's cabin. Before he could dismount, Sid and Sherm came sauntering down the street to meet him.

"Hello, boys."

"'lo, Noah. Come to see Mo?" Sherm gave him a huge grin.

"As a matter of fact, I did."

Sid snorted. "Ain't there. She's off in Frisco, visiting that sweet niece of hers."

His heart skipped a beat. "When's she due back?"

Sid laughed. "I'm going up to Carson City tomorrow to get her. Made her promise she'd be back in time for our regular Saturday night date."

"Mind some company on your way up there, Sid?"

"Better 'n talking to myself." Sid smiled at him. "You must really need to see Mo pretty bad."

He didn't reply.

Sid shifted from foot to foot. "Can you leave 'bout seven?"

Noah tipped his hat back from his face. "I'll be there."

⚜

THE TWO MEN WAITED IN THE NOISY STATION FOR the train to pull in from San Francisco. Sid did his best to pump Noah for information but this was a private matter. All he asked for was a few minutes alone with Mo before Sid escorted her back to Prairie Dell. Sid agreed only too readily. He realized that Mo would share the entire story with Sid on their journey home.

Noah hoped this one would have a happy ending.

Mo descended the stairs, looking around for Sid. She saw him and waved, a wide smile on her face. He caught a glimpse of Jenny's smile in her aunt's and his heart fluttered. Sid greeted her and took her bag and then conferenced with her briefly.

When he finished speaking, Mo looked up. She spotted Noah and nodded. She said something to Sid and then made her way over through the teeming crowd on the platform.

"Mo."

"Noah."

They stared at each other for a moment, neither one knowing how to begin.

He finally broke the ice. "I've gone out of my mind, Mo," he said bluntly. "I've already been to Boston and back. You've got to tell me where she is."

She hesitated. He placed his hand on her shoulders. "Mo, you know that I love her. That I'll go crazy without her. Please." His last word was a whispered plea that he echoed again. "Please."

He saw the minute she decided to open up. Her face lost its stubborn determination and seemed to melt with relief.

"I never wanted her to leave, Noah. I want to make that clear." She sighed. "It's all my fault that Jenny took off in the first place."

He listened patiently as she told him about encouraging Jenny to first read Sam's letters to Mo and then the ones Noah had written to her. She explained how Jenny got the notion in her head that Noah was making a dreadful mistake by giving up the Rangers for her.

"She thought you'd eventually come to resent her, Noah. She said she loved you enough to let you go and allow you to keep following your heart's desire. She learned from your letters how important being a Ranger was to you. Jenny didn't think you'd ever be happy if you had to settle down."

He shook his head in disbelief. He couldn't begin to understand that kind of sacrifice. It made him love Jenny all the more.

"I would give up the earth and go live on the moon as long as I could do it with her."

Mo winked her one good eye at him. "Then you need to tell her that, son. It's a good thing you are."

⁂

Noah arrived on Jenny's doorstep a little after nine at night after a busy day catching up with his brother, Mark, and making plans for the future. He was surprised not to find her home. It wasn't safe for a woman to be out alone on a cold, dark night in a big city like Frisco.

He waited one hour, then another, and then several more. Mo had told her Jenny was working as a seamstress and midwife, thanks to her experience at Dr. Randolph's clinic. He couldn't imagine where she might be. He planted himself on her doorstep and dozed fitfully, waking every few minutes full of worry.

Dawn was breaking as he saw her come up over the rise. She looked tired. Even in the dim light, he could see the dark circles under her eyes. As she neared him, he could hear her humming in the quiet, cool morning. It was her childhood favorite, *The Black Velvet Band*.

Noah began singing the words of the last verse as she approached.

Oh all you brave young fellows,
> *A warning now take you from me,*
> *Beware of pretty young damsels,*
> *You might meet around in Tralee.*
> *They'll treat you to whiskey and porter.*
> *Until you're unable to stand,*
> *And before you have time to leave them,*
> *You'll be sent down to Van Diemans Land.*

JENNY STARED AT NOAH AS IF SHE WERE SEEING A ghost.

"You exiled me to Van Diemans Land, you know. I've been miserable without you."

His low voice, raw with emotion, caused her throat to tighten. She tried her best to sound matter-of-fact. "You look tired, Noah. I'll get you some breakfast and then I have a lot to do. That all-night delivery of twins has thrown me behind on my dress orders."

She pushed past him and inserted her key in the lock, quickly opening the door and setting down her basket.

He followed her silently inside and closed the door. He grabbed her and spun her around. "You're not too busy for this."

She was pulled into his arms as his mouth descended on hers. She would not give in. Not this time. She had to be the strong one. She had to do what was best for him.

Even if it meant her heart would break.

Jenny put her hands on his chest to push him away but he wasn't going anywhere. She fought his kiss, fought with everything she had, but it was deep, fierce, possessive. Then it turned utterly tender. She couldn't help but respond to it.

Her hands crept up around his neck, her fingers pushed into his wavy hair. She kissed him with all the longing and love that had been bottled up inside her, all the loneliness and heartache she'd experienced since they'd been apart.

She finally broke the kiss and gazed up at him. His sky blue eyes were still full of passion and desire. She tried to pull away from him but his arms held her fast.

"You want me, Jenny. You can't hide that."

Her face puckered. She willed herself not to cry. "That's not good enough, Noah."

He gazed at her tenderly. "Yes. It is. I've always wanted you. I think I loved you from the moment you marched into that whorehouse, bursting into doors and rattling nerves. You were the sweetest angel with an iron will. I wanted you from that moment on. I'll always want you, Jenny. Always."

"Oh, Noah." She dropped her head to his chest. He stroked her hair as she began to cry.

"Don't cry, sweetheart. Everything will be fine."

She raised her tear-stained face. "No, it won't. I can't let you give up being a Ranger, Noah. I can't sit by and watch you grow unhappy. I won't—"

"I don't *want* to be a Ranger anymore, honey. I've found something I love much, much more." Her brought his hand to her cheek and grazed his knuckles across it. "Being a Ranger was good. But being with you is even better." He brightened. "And I landed a job today. I start tomorrow alongside my brother at the *Examiner*. As a reporter. Same thing my grandfather did for a living, on my mama's side. I guess reporting runs in our blood. It's the start of something new. As *we* finally begin our lives together."

The tender look he gave her caused her to shiver.

"But it doesn't really matter how I earn a living, as long as I have you by my side, honey. I want to wake up beside the woman I love for the next fifty years."

Her heart overflowed with love. She could tell by his face that he'd thought everything through. Jenny knew then and there that they could build a life together, a good one, full of love and laughter.

"Would you settle for seventy-five instead?"

The bright smile that lit his face melted her soul.

"Sold! And we'll make babies. None of them will ever even think about robbing any banks." He grinned at her. "How many do you want? Three? Four? Five?"

"How about one to start?"

She opened her cloak and guided his hand to her belly. The bulge was small but still obvious.

Noah's eyes gleamed with surprise. He kissed her again, a kiss that bonded them together for all time.

"Jenny. My ballad beauty." His voice was rough yet tender. "You've given me a second chance at life. Now, for the third time—will you marry me?"

In reply, she brought his mouth down to hers.

NOVELLAS:

Diana

Derek

Thea

The Lyon's Lady Love